**Praise for the Novels
of Michele Bardsley**

Over My Dead Body

"Bardsley's romantic vampire series is a roller-coaster ride filled with humor and action, and sure to entertain."
—*Booklist*

"Combining humor with romance and a serial-killer mystery . . . a fun, lighthearted tale."   —The Best Reviews

"I either laugh or cry with each and every character, but I always come back for more! I can't wait for the next one!"   —Fresh Fiction

Wait Till Your Vampire Gets Home

"Has action aplenty and a free-spirited, wittily sarcastic heroine who will delight fans."   —*Booklist*

"Witty. If you like your vampires with a dose of humor, I highly recommend Bardsley's Broken Heart series."
—Romance Novel TV

"Bardsley has one of the most entertaining series on the market. The humor and wackiness keep hitting the sweet spot. Add Bardsley to your autobuy list!"
—*Romantic Times* (top pick)

"Michele Bardsley's latest installment in the Broken Heart series is just as hard to put down as the ones before."
—Bitten by Books

"Michele Bardsley gives us another amazing addition to the Broken Heart series."   —Night Owl Romance

"An enjoyable mix of humor and romance . . . fast-paced, steamy, and all-around entertaining." —Darque Reviews

continued . . .

"Fun and lighthearted. . . . This book will appeal to fans of MaryJanice Davidson, Katie MacAlister, and Kathy Love since it has the same mix of fun comedy, paranormal fantasy, and romance." —LoveVampires

Because Your Vampire Said So

"Lively, sexy, out of this world—as well as in it—fun! Michele Bardsley's vampire stories rock!"
—*New York Times* bestselling author Carly Phillip

"If I could, I'd give this story a higher rating. Five ribbons just doesn't seem to be enough for this wonderful story!"
—Romance Junkies

"Another Broken Heart denizen is here in this newest, hysterically funny first-person romp. The combination of sexy humor, sarcastic wit, and paranormal trauma is unmistakably Bardsley. Grab the popcorn and settle in for a seriously good time!" —*Romantic Times*

"Vampire romance readers will enjoy the return to Broken Heart, Oklahoma. . . . Michele Bardsley provides a fun paranormal romance with an interesting undead pairing." —The Best Reviews

Don't Talk Back to Your Vampire

"Cutting-edge humor and a raw, seductive hero make *Don't Talk Back to Your Vampire* a yummylicious treat!"
—Dakota Cassidy, author of *The Accidental Werewolf*

"A fabulous combination of vampire lore, parental angst, romance, and mystery. I loved this book!"
—Jackie Kessler, author of *The Road to Hell*

"All I can say is *wow*! I was totally immersed in this story, to the point that I tuned everything and everybody out the . . . entire evening. Now, that's what I call a good book. Michele can't write the next one fast enough for me!"
—The Best Reviews

Come Hell or High Water

Michele Bardsley

A SIGNET ECLIPSE BOOK

SIGNET ECLIPSE
Published by New American Library, a division of
Penguin Group (USA) Inc., 375 Hudson Street,
New York, New York 10014, USA
Penguin Group (Canada), 90 Eglinton Avenue East, Suite 700, Toronto,
Ontario M4P 2Y3, Canada (a division of Pearson Penguin Canada Inc.)
Penguin Books Ltd., 80 Strand, London WC2R 0RL, England
Penguin Ireland, 25 St. Stephen's Green, Dublin 2,
Ireland (a division of Penguin Books Ltd.)
Penguin Group (Australia), 250 Camberwell Road, Camberwell, Victoria 3124,
Australia (a division of Pearson Australia Group Pty. Ltd.)
Penguin Books India Pvt. Ltd., 11 Community Centre, Panchsheel Park,
New Delhi - 110 017, India
Penguin Group (NZ), 67 Apollo Drive, Rosedale, North Shore 0632,
New Zealand (a division of Pearson New Zealand Ltd.)
Penguin Books (South Africa) (Pty.) Ltd., 24 Sturdee Avenue,
Rosebank, Johannesburg 2196, South Africa

Penguin Books Ltd., Registered Offices:
80 Strand, London WC2R 0RL, England

First published by Signet Eclipse, an imprint of New American Library,
a division of Penguin Group (USA) Inc.

First Printing, January 2010
10 9 8 7 6 5 4 3 2 1

To Dakota Cassidy
Thanks for coming to the rescue.

To Eleanor Cartwright
Ditto.

ACKNOWLEDGMENTS

As always, I owe my BFFs, Renee, Dakota, and Terri, the world. They are my family. I mean it. Friends are the family you choose, and I am so grateful to have these three women as my soul sisters.

My agent, Stephanie Kip Rostan, and her assistant, Monika Verma, kick freaking ass! You both always go above and beyond. Thanks for all that you do.

Big heapin' cheese-covered thanks to Kara Cesare for keeping me on track and helping me create better books. I so love this writing gig!

I owe *mucho* gratitude to everyone at NAL, from cover artists to line editors, from marketing gurus to the dude (or dudette) who gets the coffee, and to the ever-patient production team, for contributing to the success of the Broken Heart series.

As always, I lurve my Yahoo! Group (http://groups.yahoo.com/group/MicheleBardsley/

join). Thanks so much for your support. I appreciate it more than you'll ever know.

I'm very grateful to be a member of the League of Reluctant Adults (http://www.leagueofreluc-tantadults.com). Here's a shout-out to my fellow members: Mario Acevedo, Dakota Cassidy, Molly Harper, Mark Henry, Stacia Kane, Jackie Kessler, Caitlin Kittredge, J. F. Lewis, Richelle Mead, Kelly Meding, Nicole Peeler, Cherie Priest, Jennifer Rardin, Michelle Rowan, Diana Rowland, Jeanne C. Stein, Anton Strout, and Jaye Wells.

The awesome information about hoodoo I found at http://www.luckymojo.com. Any errors made (or liberties taken) are mine. Please don't goofer me.

To the makers of *Rock Band* and *Guitar Hero*: Bet you didn't figure that women in their forties would love your games, did you? We do. A lot. We *insist* you do a version with songs from the 1980s, because we want to relive our youth. Plus, some of the songs on the current games kinda suck. If you need help deciding which tunes should be included in the "Older Women Rock: 1980s Edition," just e-mail me at michelebardsley@yahoo.com.

"We are each our own devil, and we make this world our hell."   —Oscar Wilde

"Somehow our devils are never quite what we expect when we meet them face-to-face." —Nelson DeMille

"What do you want me to do, Sam, huh? Sit around all day writing sad poems about how I'm going to die? You know what? I've got one. Let's see, what rhymes with 'Shut up, Sam'?"
  —Dean Winchester, *Supernatural*, "Fresh Blood"

Chapter 1

"Off to the ol' coffin, Phoebe?" asked Connor Ballard. He'd finished his shift at the Old Sass Café a few minutes early and had helped me finish mine. We'd wiped down tables together, and flirted all the while. He was Scottish, so every one of his words sounded like melted sugar.

"Ha. Ha." I'd been a vampire for nearly four years now. A few weeks after my son, Danny, was born, I was killed. I woke up undead, sporting a shiny new set of fangs and no heartbeat.

Oh, it gets better. Not only had I become a vampire, but I had the ability to control demonkind. Y'see, every bloodsucker gets the basic package: glamour, strength, speed, the inability to tan. Then each of the seven vampire Families has a different superpower.

I'm from the Family Durga. I can summon demons, send them back to the Pit, make them clean my house. They really hate scrubbing toilets. (Who doesn't, right?) I'm joking. I wouldn't let a demon in my house on purpose. Woe to the Pit dweller who even tried.

Thanks to the Consortium, we lived in a safe paranormal community protected by an invisible force field. Technology and magic at their finest. Ever since the Invisi-shield went operational, we've enjoyed some peace and quiet. The town's prospered. Vampires, dragons, witches, *sidhe*, lycanthropes, and even a few ailuranthropes, or were-cats, had settled down here.

Connor and I leaned against my car, which was parked in front of the café, and flicked glances at each other. It was a few minutes past four a.m., which was closing time for most of Broken Heart. Nearly all the lights on Main Street were off, including the neon sign for the café. Broken Heart businesses usually closed about three hours before dawn; that way we could get our kids and ourselves tucked in in plenty of time.

According to Connor, he was Ghillie Dhu, a Scottish fairy. Once, they lived in birch trees and used their powers to protect the forests. But the Ghillie Dhu numbered too few these days. So he'd moved here and I'd hired him as a short-order cook. It seemed to me he should've been a gardener, or maybe even joined the security team. God knows he was built like a warrior.

Even though I managed the place now, I'd been waitressing at the café since I was sixteen. I didn't figure death should stand between me and a paycheck. Besides, the café was like a second home to me.

I went by my maiden name, Phoebe Allen, though I'd been Phoebe Tate for all of two minutes. A quickie marriage to the guy who'd knocked me up turned out to be a big-ass mistake. Don't get me wrong: Jackson Tate was nice enough, and definitely a good daddy. But we sucked as a couple and called it quits before our kid was born. We shared custody of Danny, and since it was the summer, my son was with his father. Jackson had taken him to Florida yesterday, the start of a two-week vacation at Disney World. I was in that mommy limbo of feeling relief (four-year-old's absence equals sleep and quiet and tidiness) and the ache of missing my kid, shaded by irrational panic that something might happen to him if I wasn't there to protect him.

"Am I borin' you, lass?"

"No," I said, laughing. "I'm just thinking 'bout stuff."

"You miss your boy."

I was surprised he'd guessed my thoughts. Connor had never struck me as the familial type. I looked at him beneath my lashes. His face was slashes and angles. Hard-edged. Even the look in his eyes was all knives. The only softness I detected was the lushness of his mouth, the bottom lip slightly fuller than the top, lips that showcased perfect white teeth. And there was the dimple, of course. He had chocolate brown hair that he wore long; the ends brushed his shoulders. His eyes were the color of Crown Royal, rich amber, filled with secrets.

Wickedly handsome.

He exuded a caged strength I'd wanted so badly to see unleashed in bed.

Whew.

It was unusual for me to waste time flirting. Or hoping for, you know, a little nooky. Well, not all-the-way nooky. Since sucking blood was such a sensual act, the original seven vampires magicked up the binding. If you had intercourse, you were bound to your lover for a hundred years. Needless to say, most of us were careful about mealtimes.

Mm-mmm. Connor sure knew how to get a girl riled. A secretive look, a quiet compliment, an unexpected touch . . . Yeah, he'd employed them all over the last month.

I liked him. More than I should, really.

"Sunrise is only a couple hours away," I said, patting the hood of my beat-up 1965 Mustang. She needed a paint job and some interior work, but her innards were top-notch. I'd taken my baby to our local mechanic, Simone Sweet, and she'd made the car purr like a baby tiger. "Think I'll take Sally for one last run before bedtime."

Connor's lips quirked. "Mustang Sally?"

"Well, she was brand-new in 1965," I said, grinning.

He laughed. Oh, Lord. He was sexy. I turned toward him, inched closer.

"Well, then," he said, his gaze on my mouth, "I suppose I should kiss the pretty girl good night."

I rolled my eyes and punched his shoulder. "Lame."

He put his hand over his heart as if I'd wounded him there.

"You have that fancy brogue," I teased, "and you can't give me a better line than that one?"

He cupped my face and kissed me.

His lips were firm and warm. He tasted like cinnamon and coffee. His fingers threaded through my hair, and my hands flattened against his muscled chest. His tongue slipped past the seam of my lips, beckoning me, daring me.

I met his passion with my own.

Heat poured through me, every nerve ending pinging with need, every molecule within me *wanting*. We parted briefly, he gulped in a breath, and then he recaptured my mouth, deepening the kiss, his tongue dueling with mine, his heart thundering under my palms.

Anything I'd ever had before was nothing compared to this maelstrom. I wanted to breathe in Connor, absorb him, take him into me and become whole.

"Lass." He pulled free, leaning his forehead against mine. He inhaled greedily, shuddering. Inhaling wasn't really an option for me, but quivering? That I could do.

My mouth felt swollen and tingly.

I looked down. My white Nikes and his black

boots touched, our knees rubbing against each other, and I thought: *We could be naked*.

"Come home with me, Connor."

He drew me in close and tipped my chin so that I was staring into his eyes. An old word floated to the surface of my mind: *aurum*. Latin for "gold." His eyes were tarnished with the kind of sorrow I'd seen only in my mother's troubled gaze, usually when she was thinking of my father, who'd died when I was fourteen. I wondered about the tragedy that had dulled the shine of Connor's gaze.

"When you look at me like that," he said, running his fingers down my throat, "it's like you can see into my soul."

"No." I stilled his roving hand and took it to kiss his fingertips. "I just see you."

He sucked in a breath, and I was surprised my words had affected him so. Was this the game people played when they felt as if their hearts had met before the world began?

No, Pheebs. Animal attraction is not love.

"You wish to spend the night with me?" he asked. "And you make this choice of your own free will?"

His formal language threw me, but I went with it. *Impulsiveness, thy name is Phoebe Allen.* "Yes," I murmured. "I choose you, Connor."

He kissed me until my knees felt wobbly, and I knew, right then, that I was in for one hell of a night.

Connor slid into the passenger seat as if he belonged there, Clyde to my Bonnie. I glanced at him and saw him staring out the window, his eyes lifted to the full moon. For a moment, he seemed as though he might be praying.

Then he looked at me, and his eyes were not those of a penitent man.

The house was dark, quiet. We both got out of the car, the muggy heat an insult after the cold of air-conditioning.

I hesitated, my gaze traveling the cracked sidewalk, studying the dandelions that poked through. Devil's Shoestring grew in thick brown clumps all around the house. After Daddy passed, Momma's schizophrenia had gotten worse, and so, too, had her strange habits. She insisted we plant the Devil's Shoestring. "Purpose bound," she had said when we were finished. "Promise made."

Guilt flickered like a dying candle's temperamental flame. *Oh, Momma.*

My mother had committed suicide.

I was eighteen. I just wanted to take Sally and travel around, get out into the bright, beautiful world. I'd saved nearly all my waitressing money. Aunt Alice had agreed to take Momma in for a while, and had driven from Louisiana to get her. On an overnight stop, Momma went into the hotel bathroom and took razor blades to her wrists. She didn't mess around, either. The lines went from wrist to elbow, and were so deep that the paramedics glimpsed bone.

I'd failed her.

I'd wanted a life all my own. It was almost as if her illness had been killing me. I'd just wanted to breathe again.

And now? I didn't breathe at all.

Momma hadn't left a note, so there was an autopsy and a police investigation. While we waited for bureaucracy to crawl toward the obvious conclusion, Aunt Alice and I cleaned out the house. It was hell going through Momma's bedroom, organizing her clothes, inventorying the items she'd considered precious, tossing the stuff she wouldn't need anymore. You ever clutch a half-used tube of toothpaste and just lose your shit?

I did.

I had held on to that stupid tube of Colgate, sat on the toilet, and wept. It didn't do a damned bit of good. Momma was gone. I didn't feel relieved, either. I just felt like my chest had been clawed open. That kind of emptiness was never filled.

You just got used to living with it.

Digging through the boxes in her closet, I found the journals. And that was how I'd discovered Momma practiced hoodoo. Weird things we'd done—mostly to keep Momma's mind settled, like weekly floor washings and planting the Devil's Shoestring—were hoodoo rituals.

Momma had been trying to keep out the bad spirits, the ones only she could see (when she wasn't medicated). Believe me, ever since I got undead and found out demons were real, I'd wondered whether Momma had been able to look into the beyond. I'd been so intent on hanging on to reality, I couldn't consider the possibility that she'd been right.

Y'see, I didn't want to be crazy. I made sure my world stayed in order, that it made complete sense all the time, no matter what I had to do. In a way, that was its own kind of crazy.

The week of Momma's death was when I crawled into Jackson Tate's embrace and we made a baby together. All that yearning to leave Broken Heart and all that money I'd saved went toward fixing up the house and preparing for Daniel Allen Tate.

"Phoebe?"

I realized I'd been staring at the Devil's Shoestring for a little too long. I didn't want to get lost in those memories. I didn't want to feel that same sense of vulnerability and fear that had me scrambling for a human connection.

Well, I guess I didn't need to worry about the human part, now, did I?

Connor's hand pressed lightly on the small of my back and I looked up, realizing how tall and broad he was, how much of a man he seemed when I still felt like a girl.

"Changin' your mind?" he asked softly.

"Nope." I strode down the walkway, digging my house keys out of my purse. I had the door unlocked and opened when I realized Connor hadn't followed me onto the small porch.

"Invite me, lass," he said, his gaze filled with wicked promises.

"Come in," I said, smiling.

I felt the air move, an odd breeze disturbing the damp night, and then he smiled, too.

He sauntered up to the house and followed me inside.

Chapter 2

I lit candles and arranged them on the hard-wood floor of my bedroom. Connor's eyes were on me, hungry. As if I were a buffet, and he a starving man.

I was nervous.

My experience was limited: small-town boys who fumbled and shook and found their own pleasure too quickly. Jackson had been a good lover, but even with him, I'd never felt this kind of anticipation. My body vibrated with expectation, as if what would unfold tonight would ruin me for all other experiences.

Connor wrapped his arms around me and kissed me, and the world tilted.

The heat of him snaked from his flesh to mine. His fingers skimmed and his tongue flicked, and then I was naked, but for the locket.

He touched the gold heart that hid within it a picture of Momma and one of Danny, and I told him the story: how the locket was a family heir-loom, how the first daughter received it on her eighteenth birthday. I told him how important it was, how I loved that it was mine.

"Leave it on," he said, his eyes like fine Scotch. "That, and nothing else."

Oh, Lord. What was I doing? I wanted Connor so badly. It made no sense. I'd known him a month, a stranger who came to town. He never talked about himself, never had visitors. Still, I couldn't help the foolish thought that my soul recognized his. That it had been whispering, "He's the one," ever since I laid eyes on him.

It was stupid.

It was impulsive.

It was true.

I wanted Connor. Not like I had wanted others. Those boys had elicited only slivers of desire; their crude fumbling mocked real yearning. My feelings for Connor were complex, confusing. I wanted to protect him, and have wild sex with him, and make breakfast with him, and fall asleep to the sound of his heartbeat.

"Let me undress you," I murmured. I could give him tenderness, show him affection. Whatever lies we might later tell ourselves, I wanted what was unfolding now to be the truth. Our truth.

He lay down on the bed and I tugged off his boots and socks. My fingers wandered around his feet; I tickled his ankles.

"Lass," he said, choked with laughter.

I grinned.

He released the buttons on his jeans. I leaned over and helped him pull off the denims.

"Boxers?" I said. I studied the material. "Red devils? Really?"

"It was these or Scooby Doo," he said, straight-faced, and it was my turn to laugh.

I was hesitant to draw down his underwear. I wanted to see what those little red devils hid, but all the same, I suddenly felt shy and unsure.

Connor took off his shirt. Then he sat up, drew me onto his lap, and kissed me.

He kissed me until I felt as though my muscles were gonna slide off my bones. That oh-my-God-what-am-I-doing panic melted under the hot assault of his mouth.

"Sweet," murmured Connor as he dragged his lips down my throat. "You taste so sweet."

I attacked his mouth, desperate to lose myself in physical need. Because I would not listen to the ghost beat of my heart, the tiny voice whispering, *This is shiny like new love*, and then, *No, no, no. Not now. Not him. Not this.*

"Connor," I said. "I can't . . . you know. Not all the way."

"That silly binding curse? Ach. That has no effect on the Ghillie Dhu."

I stared at him, shocked. "What? The Consortium told us—"

"You believe everything they say?" he asked. "You think the Consortium doesn't have its secrets?"

His words were tinged with bitterness. Doubt started to chill my ardor. What did I really know about Connor? Why had he come to Broken Heart? And why did he so obviously despise the Consortium?

"Someone would've figured out the binding spells didn't work on you guys."

"Who's to say they didn't?" He shrugged. "Doesn't matter now. Not many of us around. Besides, the Ghillie Dhu sexual exemption is the least of the Consortium's problems."

"Connor . . ."

"I've worried you." He smiled, his eyes edged in sorrow, always sorrow. "It's all right, *m'aingeal*. Do you want me to go?"

I got the odd impression he was hoping I would say yes, even though evidence to the contrary was lancing the sweet spot between my thighs. My body was screaming with oh-my-God-it's-been-four-years-please-don't-ruin-this lust, while my mind whispered, *Caution, caution, caution*. It made no sense for Connor to lie to me. After all, he'd be stuck with me as his mate for the next century. He didn't want insta-marriage any more than I did.

"Stay," I said.

Connor cupped my breasts, his thumbs sweeping across my nipples. Electric sensations pulsed. Lightning on flesh. Passion buried into muscle, wormed into bone. I felt overtaken by it, possessed.

He licked around my areola with short, hot strokes until he finally pulled the peak into his mouth and sucked. Hard.

I grabbed his shoulders, digging my nails into his flesh as he split his attention between my breasts.

He tormented me until I wrenched free of his wicked mouth and pushed him down.

I quaked.

Need was a living creature, hungry, greedy, unfulfilled.

I tugged his boxers, and he helped me wiggle them off.

Whoa. I stared at his cock. Hel-lo, would that thing even fit?

"I'll fill you up," he promised. "I'll make you come."

Embarrassment swept over me, and he chuckled as he cupped my burning face, kissing me as he twitched his cock on purpose. That was the most impressive muscle I'd seen yet. And Connor, beautiful Connor, had a lot of muscles.

I pulled away, my mouth swollen, my body throbbing in frenetic rhythm. Yet I took my time looking at him. He was gorgeous. I trailed my fingers over his ridged stomach. There was a long, white scar on the left side of his rib cage. I traced it. "What's this?"

"Old scar. Bad memory."

His flesh wore other scars, the badges of a warrior. I was romanticizing because the truth was probably less thrilling. I couldn't help but touch them all. After my fingers paid homage, I leaned down and kissed every old wound.

I felt his belly tense under my lips. The knowledge that I affected him the way he did me was powerful. I continued my exploration, tempering my own urges to conquer and to take. I somehow knew he'd had little enough of kindness.

Connor watched me through hooded eyes. Amber desire glinted in his gaze, and I felt his patience slipping. He wanted me in such a desperate way I was stunned.

I walked my fingers up to his pectorals.

I traced the quarter-sized brown circles and flicked his tiny nipples until they hardened.

I touched him everywhere, memorizing his contours, worshiping every imperfection. I knelt between his legs, and as I swept my hands down to his cock, he sucked in a sharp breath. I cupped his balls.

Wow. He was big.

I kissed his cock, my hair falling in a curtain. Connor fisted his hands, his breath erratic, his body tight, wound like a spring, ready to let go, to fly.

His penis was warm, silky, and oh-baby hard. As the length slid between my lips, pleasure trembled in my belly.

His taste filled my mouth, made my whole body burn. I moaned; the sound vibrated on his cock, made him gasp.

He grabbed my shoulders and dragged me over his body.

He was much stronger than I was, and I wasn't afraid. I was emboldened.

His cock nestled against me, pressing hotly against my clit.

"You're so wet." His hands were filled with my breasts. His thumbs flicked the peaks. They hardened, aching. He rose up and suckled the sensitive nubs. Pleasure rocked every nerve ending.

I moved over his cock, slick and swollen. My core welled with that unique bliss. I reached for it, moving in tandem with Connor's rapid heartbeat. I didn't want relief from the ache, from the need. I wanted more of it. I wanted more of him.

"Phoebe," he murmured. "Kiss me."

He captured my lips, plunged his tongue inside, and mimicked our bodies' motions. He attacked my mouth, sucking my tongue, biting my lips.

Our mouths mated, and I held on to him because I felt myself falling away into lust so great, I realized it would never be satisfied. I would always want him like this, and it scared me. I'd never felt like merging with someone else, as though I would always be incomplete because I had known this—I had known him.

He kneaded my breasts and pulled on my nipples. Lightning struck at my core, and the shock of it was wondrous.

He was heat; he was need; he was mine.

So I took him.

Passion was fangs tearing, claws ripping away the tenderness I'd fostered. The ancient beat of drums, the rise of primal music in my breast, in my heart, in the very center of my being.

"Bite me," he said. "Please."

I sank my fangs into his neck, drinking the nectar of his blood. I was already in overload, but the pleasure of tasting him, of taking him, was too much.

Connor cried out, his fingers digging into my hips as he came, his thick cock shoving deeply, pulsing hard as his seed filled me.

I went over the edge.

Into the music we'd created.

I awoke the next night with the bedcovers pulled up to my chin. I drew back the quilt; the musk of our lovemaking still scented the sheets.

I had a taste in my mouth, too. Something metallic. It wasn't bad, almost like I'd accidentally bitten the wrapper along with a dark chocolate candy bar.

Okay, time to brush my fangs.

The room was pitch-black, thanks to the lack of windows and the über-sunlight-protection paint that coated the whole room. Any extremely bright light could fry a vampire, so extra precautions were necessary. I didn't expect sunlight to seep through regular walls, but the Consortium—

appointed protectors of all Broken Heart Turn-bloods—insisted on it.

I flipped on the bedside lamp. Its glow didn't do much to diminish the darkness. It was after nine p.m. Seems weird, right? All the kids—well, *all* the townfolks—were on a nocturnal schedule. The only people moseying around town during the day were the town's security teams and the occasional zombie. I'd slept much later than I usually did. Sleeping in with a four-year-old was not an option, for one thing. Shoot. It was past ten o'clock in Florida. I bet Danny had spent the whole day at Disney World and was already tucked into bed. All the same, I picked up my cell phone from the nightstand and dialed Jackson. He said that Danny had been conked out for a while. The rest of our conversation was short, and I promised to call by eight the next evening. I was disappointed that I hadn't woken in time to connect with my son, but I was glad he was having a good time. I'd never be able to take him to Disney World; it made me glad Danny had a human father, one who could give him all the things I couldn't. Being a demon-hunting vampire wasn't exactly conducive to parenthood.

Thanks to my undead senses, as foggy as they often were upon awaking, I smelled cooking bacon. Due to an accidental fairy wish, we resident bloodsuckers could eat human food, but only as long as we stayed inside the borders of Broken

Heart. And, ooh-wee, I still loved me some fried pig.

I heard the scrape of a pan across the electric burner. Then water gushed. Rinsing the cookware, too? My Ghillie Dhu was a keeper.

I scurried out of bed and went into the master bathroom. I scrubbed my teeth, and then I took a quick shower. After throwing on a T-shirt and some shorts, I brushed my hair and considered my complexion. I'd died at nineteen, even though by human years I'd be almost twenty-four. Something about vampirism made skin bright and beautiful. The pregnancy stretch marks on my belly and hips had disappeared. My eyes were brown, my features on the narrow side. I had high cheekbones, a thin swoop of a nose, and a mouth with too much pout.

I pulled my hair into a ponytail and decided makeup would be a waste of time.

I couldn't wait for a cup of coffee, which didn't do much for me other than taste really good. It's icky to admit, but that first warm gulp of blood was way better than an extra shot of espresso.

I stopped in the living room, my toes wiggling into the threadbare carpet, and listened to the domestic sounds coming from the kitchen. I felt a little giddy. Lucky me, I'd found the only being in existence not affected by the vampires' hundred-year marriage curse.

I walked to the swinging doors that led to the kitchen. I looked over the top and watched him plate up breakfast. Fluffy pancakes, crisp bacon, scrambled eggs, and orange juice awaited us. My gaze traveled along his backside. He wore only his black jeans. He was fi-ine. I got an attack of lust all over again.

"Like what you see, lass?" Amusement ghosted his tone as he turned to look at me.

"Hell to the yeah," I said as I entered the kitchen.

"Where's your locket?"

I automatically reached for the gold heart, surprised to find it missing. "It must've come off. The clasp is twitchy. I'll go—"

I paused, getting a distinct whiff of rotten eggs. What the—

Sulfur.

The base of my spine tingled, which was the equivalent of my spidey senses indicating trouble. Specifically: demon trouble.

"Shit." I stared at Connor, and his eyes went wide.

"I thought I had more time," he said. "Damn it!"

The plate of food in his hand crashed to the floor and he reached for me. I shook my head, and his hand dropped.

The house was protected from demons; Momma's hoodoo and my own protection spells had made sure of that. Or so I thought.

In crackles of black energy, three men appeared in a semicircle around us, all wielding weapons and grim expressions.

I whirled to stand in front of Connor, fists cocked. I had no doubt he could protect himself, but I was the one with demon-ass-kicking skills. Connor stood behind me, tension radiating off him. I knew he was just waiting for the fight to begin. I didn't have my knives or my Glock, but I had trained with the best warriors in Broken Heart. Between those skills and my magic, I could vanquish these three assholes.

The man to the left of me was a couple inches shorter than his companions, who were both well over six feet, given that they were as tall as Connor. He wore his red hair shorn on the sides and long on top, which was pulled back and braided. Snake tattoos slithered up his neck. He dressed like a Hell's Angel, all black leather and badass. He looked me over, sneering.

The blond in front of me held scimitars. With his light hair and narrow features, he looked like the warrior elf Legolas—or rather the character played by Orlando Bloom in the film. He wore tight black pants with an odd blue vest that tied at the waist. His eyes were light blue, the color of a glacier, and just as cold. *Sheesh.* He looked like he'd fallen out of a fantasy novel.

The last dude, the one on the left, was huge—as tall and wide as a freaking oak tree. He was dressed in a worn black concert T-shirt that touted the KISS 1983 "Lick It Up" tour, a pair of faded jeans, and black cowboy boots. His face was built like a boxer's: flat and square, with a nose that looked as if it had been broken a few times. He had eyes the color of dark chocolate and wore his black hair short and spiky. He held two gleaming silver SIG Sauer P226 pistols, both pointed at the floor. I had no doubt he could aim and fire in nanoseconds, especially being supernatural.

As we all assessed one another, the room felt as though it were getting smaller and smaller. I didn't speak and I didn't press closer to Connor, either. We both needed room if we were going to bring on some whoop-ass.

"Well, well, well. What have we got here, boys?" The redhead spoke in a guttural English accent. "Looks fresh as a peach, she does. Too bad she's Connor's whore."

I hit him first.

Chapter 3

The second my fist connected with that mouthy bastard's face, I realized he wasn't a demon.

He was a vampire.

"Bloody hell," he roared as his head snapped back. If he'd been human, that blow would've felled him. He pointed his left forefinger, and a long beam of red light unfurled from his sharp, black talon. The light-whip snapped as he raised his arm, and I knew he was gonna try to slice me in half.

Connor grabbed my shoulder and hauled me backward. Even though I was certain the English dude was a vampire, the stink of sulfur permeated the room. Surely that meant the other two were demons? Why the hell had a vampire taken up with Pit dwellers?

"Berith! Hold!" yelled the blond.

Berith's whip instantly disappeared. His expression was seven kinds of pissed off; I could've cooked eggs with the fury boiling in his gaze.

Blondie pointed to me. "Can you not see her aura, *mon frère*?"

So, the Legolas wannabe was French. I couldn't get a bead on him, but he didn't seem like a demon, either. That left the really big dude. Awesome.

I wasn't sure what was happening now. None of them seemed to want to fight, though they were prepared for it. They were examining me as though they'd never seen a girl before. Maybe I should've put on a bra. Oops.

Connor moved so that he was by my side. I glanced at him, but his gaze was locked onto Blondie. Frustration emanated from Connor, and, if I wasn't too far off the mark, panic, too. Realization hit me hard: He knew them.

"My name is Nicor. And you? You are with the Family Durga, *oui*?" he asked pleasantly. He nodded toward Connor. "You have slept with him."

"You know what, Dr. Phil? I'm not in the mood to answer questions about my personal life. So I'm giving you two seconds for you and your demon buddy over there to take a freaking hike."

Nicor's eyebrows flew upward, his gaze slanting toward Big Dude. "You are mistak—"

I gathered my magic, slathered it with some brimstone, and tossed the fireball at Nicor. The orb hit him full in the chest and flung him backward. He slammed into the small table wedged into the tiny nook. Breakfast items went flying, including the syrup, which burst open (fireballs are hot, you know) and splattered him.

Bonus.

"Phoebe!" I heard the shock in Connor's voice, but he didn't hesitate. He punched Berith in the face, and the redhead yelled as he hit back. At least he didn't unleash the crazy whip again.

I created another fireball and launched it at Big Dude. He went through the kitchen wall, debris flying, and slid across the foyer. He managed to hold on to the guns, though, and he raised them toward me.

"No, Pith!" yelled Nicor as he picked himself up. Syrup dripped from his flaxen locks. *Ha.*

Pith grimaced as he sheathed his guns, shaking drywall out of his spiky hair as he climbed to his feet.

Nicor stomped toward me, his fists clenched and his face a mask of fury. Smoke rose from his fancy vest, which hung in tatters. His pale stomach was red and blistered. Black blood dripped down his left cheek. Terrific. My suspicions were confirmed; he was Family Durga, too. No other vampire Family fared as well with demonfire. Part of being able to wrangle demons was the ability to draw upon the same magic as demons. I know. Powers derived from hell seem kinda . . . creepy. I didn't get to choose my Family, but hey, I had to take the cards fate dealt.

"You should not have done that!" he yelled.

"You started it." I gathered my magic again. I formed another fireball and shot it at Nicor.

He caught it as if it were a freaking beach ball lobbed across the pool, and poof, it disappeared.

"Stop!" he demanded.

Berith and Connor ignored him. The meaty slap of fists connecting and low grunts permeated the kitchen. Nicor turned toward me. "You do not understand what you are doing."

Emotions rioted through me, with fury in the forefront waving its torch. "I know that I'm gonna kick your ass, elf boy."

Nicor glanced at Pith and shook his head. The giant stopped creeping toward me and stayed in the foyer, staring at me through the massive hole, which, FYI, was right next to the swinging doors. If I'd aimed better, I could've knocked 'im through there instead.

Nicor looked as though he were contemplating crossing the distance between us. If he did, I'd shoot two fireballs at him.

"Berith! *Enough.*"

Connor had broken Berith's nose, and I took a perverse satisfaction in seeing the blood dribbling down his face. Connor backed away, his gaze on Berith as he joined me. I grabbed his wrist and we continued going backward until we hit the counter.

I jumped up to sit on the countertop and reached for the canister I kept near the sink. It wasn't easy to do with my hands flailing behind my back, but I knew its location, and better yet, what was in it.

Connor glanced at me, frowning. Then he looked at Nicor. "You're too late," he said.

"You still need the other half of the talisman," said Nicor. He laughed harshly. "You are a fool if you think Lilith will let her live."

"Why do you care?" asked Connor softly. "I warned you all, and you did nothing. The blood of those who've died is on your hands."

"You speak to me of blood!" Nicor's eyes flashed with fury, and Connor tensed.

I was feeling a little bit rattled by this turn of events. Because, hel-lo, Connor knew these guys, and in a bad way. And I was somehow part of it now.

I sidled a glance at Pith. The demon hadn't moved from his position in the foyer, though his gaze was trying to drill holes through me.

Connor brushed against me, offering strength as well as trying to better cover my movements.

Two against the world, that was us.

"Sorry, *chérie*," said Nicor. "This is necessary."

He extended a hand toward me.

Connor shouted, "No!"

A red beam shot out from Nicor's palm. I threw my arms up, an automatic gesture of protection. The whole world went red. I squeezed my eyes shut, heard a sizzle-pop, then nothing.

"Did you see that?" asked Nicor, his voice filled with awe.

I cracked one eye open. Whatever Nicor had aimed my way was an epic fail.

Nicor and Berith both looked stunned. Connor's gaze was on me; his eyes glittered with a mixture of pride and astonishment.

"What?" I asked.

"Have I told you how amazin' you are, lass?" He grinned, and I grinned back. Then I grabbed the canister of rock salt, flung off the lid, and scooped out a handful.

I threw some at Berith, at Nicor, and at Pith. With my vampire speed it was quick—a second, maybe—and then I said, "You sons of a bitches, don't come back here."

One by one, they popped out of my house. I jumped off the counter and flung more salt around the room, then some by the front door and at the back door.

"What just happened?" Connor asked.

"Hoodoo," I said. "My mother was kinda into it. I learned a few things from her journals."

I put the canister down. Connor pulled me into his embrace and kissed me so tenderly my heart ached.

"I wish I deserved you," he said.

I laughed, even though foreboding squiggled across my stomach. "What does that mean?"

"I dinnae want to tell you."

His voice held secrets and regret, and I felt unnerved by what lay unspoken between us.

"They came here for you. Why?"

He let me go and then knelt to the floor to start picking up the broken dishes. Unsettled by his words and the sudden coolness of his manner, I got out the broom and swept up the congealing food.

"What would've happened if Nicor had zapped me?" I asked.

"Think of bein' trapped inside glass."

"Yeesh. Doesn't sound fun."

"It isn't." The tone of his voice suggested he'd had experience with Nicor's prisons.

"C'mon, Connor. What's going on? I mean, have you been hiding out here or what?" I emptied the dustpan. Then I dropped it on the floor and rubbed the base of my spine. It was still tingling like a mo-fo. Why hadn't the smell of sulfur dissipated yet? I sniffed, gazing around the kitchen to see if there was an alternate source. When was the last time I cleaned out the fridge?

"I'm surprised I was able to hide it for as long as I did," Connor murmured, defeat in his tone. "Nera asks a high price, but at least she guarantees her work."

"Nera?"

"A month," he said. "That's all I had." He was explaining things to me, things I didn't understand, but I had a very bad feeling I would. "I sent the hunters on a wild-goose chase. I was out of time even then, but I couldn't just . . . take you. And then . . . Well, it doesn't matter anymore. It's done."

"You're scaring me, Connor. What the hell is going on?" I turned and saw his gaze. Pure black. No iris, no whites, just . . . demon. *Oh, fuck.* The broom slid out of my limp fingers and clattered to the floor, crunching against the rock salt scattered on the linoleum.

My undead heart offered phantom beats of panic as I stared at Connor. "You're not Ghillie Dhu, are you?"

"Oh, but I am," said Connor. He blinked, and the inky black faded until he had human eyes once again. His smile held no warmth. "My mother was Ghillie Dhu. And my father was a demon."

I swallowed the knot crimping my throat.

"You're half demon?" I asked in disbelief.

Most demons were born in the Pit, which was another plane of existence, one that had many layers. "Born" was a kinder term than the reality of their creation. It wasn't a pleasant place or a nice life. Demons didn't have souls, but, as the goddess Brigid explained to me once, they had purpose.

It just wasn't a very nice one.

I'd been told demons weren't all that fertile, and if they did manage to breed, it was with a magical being. Still, finding a willing lover wasn't easy, much less one thrilled to carry around demon spawn. Demons seduced humans all the time, but couldn't procreate with them.

"I'm an anomaly," he said, as though I'd spoken my thoughts aloud. "My mother was a nymph. And my father was a demon lord who liked to come and play on the earthly plane. 'Twas her nature to be sensual. 'Twas his to be deceitful."

"Looks like the apple doesn't fall far from the tree," I said bitterly. I gathered my magic and snapped out a binding coil. I dropped it over him, tightening it quickly.

He quirked one eyebrow, and then he wrapped his hands around the glowing rope of magic and yanked on it. I flew across the kitchen and into his arms.

My magic snapped and dissipated.

"Trained properly, you would've been able to hold me," he said. "Might've even trapped me."

Just how much did I not know about my powers? And why the hell hadn't anyone told me or taught me?

His palms cupped my hips, his grip just loose enough to give me hope that I could escape. Except that I couldn't and we both knew it.

I hadn't had my pint, and I could smell Connor's blood pulsing like sugared poison in his veins.

"You want to sink your fangs into me, lass?" He grinned flirtatiously, as if he hadn't betrayed me. As if we were still lovers. I felt shattered, and I wanted to cut him with the pieces of me that were left.

"You're a bastard."

"I know." For a moment, he dropped the cynical-asshole act and let me see his pain. Despite all he'd done, I knew that pain, whatever its source, was real.

I wanted to believe that the man I'd known for

the last month, the man who'd loved me so well last night, was the true Connor.

But demons were liars. They were also charming beyond belief—until they got what they wanted. I'd fallen for his act, as easily duped as an innocent human instead of a demon-hunting vampire. I was so ashamed.

"We're bound!" I couldn't even wrap my brain around the concept. I'd mated. With. A. Demon.

The true horror of my situation hit me. Bile rose in my throat. *Danny.* How could I raise my kid married to a demon? Even a half demon was bad. Connor's lie—and, let's be honest, my stupid, impulsive nature and rusty goddamned libido—had stripped me of motherhood privileges.

"I'm going to kill you."

"You can't. And if you could, would you really rob Danny of his mother?"

"You already did!"

His cool expression slid away as regret filled up his gaze. "For that, I'm sorry."

"Right. I'm sure it's tearing you up inside." Rage burned through me. Whatever happened to Connor happened to me now, too. The vampire marriage curse was absolute. We were mates, bound for the next century, and there was nothing I could do.

Despair wound through me.

"Why, Connor?" I whispered. "Why did you do it?"

Chapter 4

"To protect you," Connor said quietly. Wow. He was good. I almost believed him.

"Yeah. 'Cause you're such a nice guy." I yanked out of his embrace and he let me. I stumbled back, feeling so vulnerable, so overwhelmed.

What have you done, silly little girl?

It was my mother's voice, so gently chiding, and she was unable to keep the sparkle of humor from her eyes when trying to berate me. Even now she was the small, still voice in my head. *Oh, Momma. This isn't shoplifting a candy bar at the Thrifty Sip.*

"I don't know what's going on, but I know this is about you. So our mating wasn't some altruistic scheme to protect poor ol' me. You're protecting yourself. *You're* the bad guy here." And I'd probably ousted the good guys. Nicor had certainly danced around the subject enough. If he'd said, "Hey, you just boffed a demon . . ." I heaved an internal sigh. No. I wouldn't have believed him.

I wondered if I could get back to my phone and call Damian. He was in charge of security. And I was in charge of demons. I just couldn't get my hands on this one.

Oh, you know what I mean.

Connor glared at me, but he had no right to be offended. If he didn't like the sarcasm, then too damned bad—it wasn't the worst he was gonna get from me. I pressed my hands against my cheeks. I felt hot even though I didn't have the capacity for heat to flush my skin. Usually after imbibing a pint, I could mimic responses. I felt nearly human. For a short while.

I scrubbed away the feeling. Maybe it was the flames of hell licking at me for binding myself to a demon.

What really sucked was that mates couldn't live apart—not for long. We didn't have to be in each other's presence every second of the day. However, the longer the amount of time mates were apart, the weaker they got.

"We need to go," he said.

"Um, no. You need to go." Only I knew he wouldn't. He couldn't.

I needed to get away from him for a minute, to think. To plan. In the history of vampire bindings, there had been only one known breaking—and it had taken a very rare fairy wish. The world had been losing its magical beings—just look at how giants and pixies had disappeared. It still blew my mind that humans and paranormals used to know of each other, used to live together, if not in harmony, then at least with the certain knowledge that the world belonged to more than just one dominant species.

I circled back to my original thought: How could I get a fairy wish? And what else might break a binding?

I might as well try to find Atlantis.

"The demon hunters will return." His gaze flicked away. "And others will find us. Nicor gave away our location."

"Oh, boo-hoo," I said. Then, because I couldn't help it, "You've hidden your demon-ness from them for a month. Why'd they figure out it now?"

"Don't you know?" he asked, knowing full friggin' well I didn't. He shook his head. "Family Durga vampires are trained since their Turning to fight demons. But not you, Phoebe. Why is that, I wonder?"

There was something knowing in the tone of his words, and underneath that thin veil of arrogance I sensed he knew things about me, about my undead life, that I didn't. Other than a few terse lessons from the Family founder, Durga, who betrayed Broken Heart a couple years ago and ended up banned with her cohort, the Ancient Koschei, I hadn't had any contact with other Family Durga members. I was the only one who lived in town. And though we'd gotten plenty of new residents, we hadn't gotten any new vampires from my Family line. I'd learned how to fight, though, and how to access my magic. Until this moment, it had been enough. I was angry that he was right, and curious about what else I should know. Damn it. If I'd known those secret things Connor hinted at, I would've pegged him for a demon before I'd slept with him.

"How'd he find you?" I asked again.

His lips thinned. "The transmogrification spell ended. They know my magical signature. Most demons have a unique pattern. If you know what you're doing, you can use it to track them."

I was surprised he'd actually told me, and I wasn't sure how to handle the dichotomy of truth wrapped in lies. Or lies wrapped in truth.

"What do the demon hunters want?" I asked. "Better yet, what do you want?"

He studied me, and then shook his head, as if he'd found me unworthy of the truth. "Get dressed."

"I'm not going anywhere with you."

"You are," he said in a hard voice. "Willin' or not."

My belly squeezed and it took every ounce of willpower I had not to take a step back.

"You threatening me?" I asked, trying to keep a bold tone. I wouldn't turn away from his gaze, which glittered like gemstones.

"Why wouldn't I?" he asked coldly. "I already lied to you." He crossed the room in the blink of an eye and clamped one of my wrists. "I already fucked you."

I slapped him, which made my hand sting and his cheek go red. *He* had blood pressure, and a heartbeat. Still, the smack had been a reaction born from shock, and there'd been no real power behind it. Certainly no vampire strength: I could've knocked his head off his shoulders.

Satisfaction glowed in his eyes, and there, too, was the shadow of that unimpeachable sorrow of his. I'd made the bastard feel better, less guilty, because he'd far prefer to deal with my anger than with my wretchedness.

"Get your clothes, lass. Or you'll go as you are."

"Where?" I said, frustrated. "Where are you taking me?"

Connor didn't get a chance to answer the question.

The entire room shook—and I thought, *Earthquakes in Oklahoma?*—and a roaring sound like thunder blasted through. I covered my ears, but it didn't help much. Jesus. That was some noise right there.

The roar turned into a loud *crack*, and light flickered like a crazed disco ball.

The silence was sudden.

In front of us stood a woman and a demon. The demon had marbled skin, which made it look as though an emo kindergartner had painted it from horns to claws. It was seven feet tall, maybe taller, and had creepy yellow eyes. Granted, all demons in their true forms had creepy eyes. Actually, they had creepy everything. This thing had wings, too, not leathery like bats', but like an angel's—huge and filled with soft black feathers.

The woman was another story.

She looked sixteen, all fresh-faced and inno-cent—an impression furthered by her outfit: a red T-shirt with HOT scrawled in gold across her pert breasts, a pair of faded denims, and red Converse sneakers. Her silky black hair was pulled into a sassy ponytail. She wore no makeup, but with her looks, she didn't need any. Her bone structure was pure supermodel. Only her eyes, which glowed red, gave any indication she was demon.

"Who are you?" I asked.

"I'm Lilith, sweet cheeks. Aw. You the new bride?" She smiled indulgently, but her gaze was filled with knives. She turned her cutting gaze to Connor. "Think you're clever, don't you?"

She raised her hands and two binding coils shot out and wrapped around us like crazed pythons. Mine tightened painfully, cinching my arms to my sides.

Oh, for fuck's sake! I was sick of people just popping into my house whenever they felt like it. And these were demons. Had the Devil's Shoe-string stopped working? No. More than likely these two were more powerful than a crazy wom-an's hoodoo.

"You can't hurt her," said Connor. His voice

sounded pinched, and I realized his bonds had tightened even more than mine. I also realized that Connor had been right about others coming for us. For him. It wasn't my fault he'd dragged me into this mess. Still, if I'd been a little less stubborn, I might not be making the acquaintance of more demons.

"You really think your mating with her will offer her protection?" sneered Lilith.

"You know it does."

She shrugged. "You really should stop listening to Astria Vedere. She's crazy."

"She's a prophet."

"Yeah. Like I haven't seen one of those before. Real party killers, those people." She stared at Connor. "Give me the talisman, and I'll let wifey go."

"I am the son of Asmodeus, and my mate falls under the protection of the demon lord." He sucked in a strained breath. "You can't kill Phoebe."

"*I* can't," she agreed.

Oh, crap. I did not like the sound of that, and neither did Connor. He looked warily at the demon waiting patiently behind Lilith. Its yellow eyes were on me. Its beaklike mouth clicked and a split tongue wiggled out, flicking at me.

Yech.

Had Connor really tricked me into mating to protect me from this really scary lady? Right now, I hoped so.

Connor said nothing, but his expression was pure hatred. He didn't like this woman. I'd known her for only a minute, and I didn't like her, either. He watched her carefully, the prey gauging how soon the predator would attack. Fear skittered through me.

"Didn't we have this conversation before, pumpkin?" Lilith sauntered (in jeans, but she totally pulled it off) to Connor and walked her fingers up his chest. "You. Can't. Win." She tapped his nose. I glanced at him and saw the distaste he didn't bother to hide.

"Brimstone's hell on the complexion," he drawled. "You might want stock up on some aloe. How long you got before the portal closes?"

The only indication that Connor's words bothered her was a slight downturn of her lips. "I really don't know what Asmodeus saw in your slut of a mother."

"An' you never will," he said. "Because you don't have a heart."

"It wasn't her heart he was interested in," she snapped. She sucked in a breath, her nostrils flaring. Then she smiled. "You know what they say about marriage. Partners should be equal in all things."

"Lilith," Connor said, his voice sharp, "leave Phoebe alone."

"Shut up." She slapped him hard, and the shock of the swift violence made me go cold. Especially since I had done the same thing to him minutes ago, and I did not want anything in common with this bitch. "Don't you dare act like you give a shit about her. She's a means to an end. Like father, like son. Use, use, *use*."

Connor said nothing.

"Give me the talisman that you stole from the hunters," she said, "and I'll leave."

"You'll leave anyway once the portal closes."

"Stubborn," she said on a long sigh, "so very stubborn."

She snapped her fingers.

The demon materialized in front of me. Reached out with sharp claws to grab my shoulders. Hauled me so close I flattened my palms against its clammy, blackened flesh.

Its fetid breath made me gag.

I cast a binding spell, but the red sparks drifted onto the demon and melted like snowflakes. Big surprise. I hadn't had my pint, and I'd already expended too much energy fighting the hunters. And Lilith's coil was sapping me, too.

I felt sick.

Lilith giggled. "She is adorable."

The demon shook me until my head rattled like a bobble-head doll. Then he squeezed me so hard, I felt my ribs buckle. Agony jabbed me like thin, savage blades.

"Phoebe!"

I looked at Connor and saw Lilith lift her hand. Her nails grew long and sharp; then she raked his cheek. "Say her name again and he'll rip off her legs."

My vision went gray, but I kept my eyes open, eyes that couldn't give in to the hot ache of tears.

The demon sank its big, black teeth into my shoulder. Pain ripped through me as my flesh was savaged. The evil bastard reared back and grinned. My blood dribbled down its chin and my skin hung grotesquely from its mouth.

Oh, no, you did not.

Being pissed off made my magic surge.

Light erupted from my hands.

The twin blows propelled the demon backward. Its claws raked at my flesh as it scrambled to hold on. Pain spiked my shoulders.

Without the demon holding me, I didn't have the wherewithal to stand. I fell to my knees, swaying, watching as it staggered into the table.

It growled and stalked toward me, but Lilith held up her hand. The demon instantly halted; its hate-filled yellow stare ravaged me.

"She's a little spitfire, isn't she?" She patted Connor's wounded cheek. "You know what just happened, don't you? Just so we're clear, she'll be dead in a day, maybe two, and not by my hand." She sent a fond look to her demon pet.

"You bitch," said Connor, his voice ragged. "I willna let her die."

Agony shuddered up my spine. I couldn't work up the energy to scream. The pain was excruciating.

"I'll give you the antitoxin if you give me the talisman."

"I only have half!"

"But you'll find the other half, won't you? I bet you even know where it is."

"I willna give you the means to escape your hell-bond!"

I felt a shift in the atmosphere, and then a cold wind blew into the kitchen. Lilith's face contorted and she stamped her foot. "No! I'm not ready!"

There was a sucking sound, and she and the demon disappeared.

My bindings dissipated. I dropped forward to my hands, trying to stay on all fours. I couldn't find the energy to stand or to move. Pain throbbed in every nerve ending. Blood burbled in my throat. My vision went fuzzy.

"Phoebe," muttered Connor as he knelt beside me. "Phoebe."

I tilted to the side and fell into the strong arms of my demon husband.

Then I passed out.

Chapter 5

"Phoebe?" The ragged voice dragged me down, down, down, into a terrible, exhausting heaviness. "Please, *m'aingeal*. Open your eyes."

"Can't." I felt weighed down, like a pallet of bricks pressed on me. Pain radiated from the back of my skull, down my spine, to every nerve ending. My lungs felt wet. I coughed, and rust-colored liquid dribbled from my mouth. Blood.

A wet cloth pressed against my lips and the ick was wiped away.

"Did I fall under a wheat thresher?" I asked. Gah. Even my throat hurt.

"Worse," he said. "You'll be okay, lass."

"Liar." I tried to work up a good bout of righteous anger, but I was too tired. I should be thoroughly pissed at Connor. He was the reason I was married to a demon. And the reason Lilith's pet beat the crap outta me.

"I hate you," I said without much venom. "A lot."

"I know, and I deserve every ounce of it." He stroked my hair.

My eyes fluttered open. I was lying on a very comfortable bed, my head cushioned by the fluffiest pillows ever. The covers were whisper-soft, and felt good on my sensitized skin. I felt like I'd been dipped in acid and thrown into a wood chipper. Connor sat on the edge of the mattress and hovered over me, looking so relieved I wondered just how badly I was hurt.

"Where am I?"

"Somewhere safe."

I didn't have much choice except to believe him. We were mated, after all, and aside from the obvious reason to keep me alive, I was an important pawn in whatever game he was playing with Lilith.

"Why do I still feel like shit?" What happened to my super-duper healing mojo? Every part of me throbbed in pain, from my toes to my eyeballs. I felt as if I were gonna throw up.

"The demon bit you."

I focused on Connor's concerned gaze. Concerned, my ass. He was a faker. "I was there, remember?"

"When you're well, lass, I'll teach you to fight."

A demon teaching a demon hunter? Riiiight.

"I can kick your butt." I lifted my hand to poke

him in the chest, but I missed. My vision blurred. I felt woozy—like I'd been doing tequila shooters all night. "I was the only Family Durga vampire in Broken Heart. But . . . but . . . *but* I got trained all over the place. And, you know, Durga showed me a few things before she went all superevil and got banned."

"She dinnae show you enough. Fightin' demons is a far greater challenge than stavin' off other kinds of enemies."

"I got moves." I put up my fists and rolled them. Then I giggled. "Dude. I feel weird."

He grimaced.

"I need blood," I said. "If I take a pint, maybe two, I'll heal faster."

Connor shook his head. "It won't stay in your stomach long enough to be absorbed."

His words burrowed through my queasy, fuzzy sickness. "So, I can't eat? How am I supposed to heal? I can't just . . . loll around."

Connor looked away. When he returned his gaze to mine, his expression was blank. "There are things you dinnae know, lass."

"Tell me about it." I frowned. "Lilith said I would be dead in a day or two." Panic wobbled. Or maybe it was nausea. "What's wrong with me?"

"The Taint," he said.

I went utterly still as cold horror swept through me. "No. No!"

"Do you know why the Taint is the only disease

that affects vampires? The first infection started when a demon bit a vampire. And the vampire passed it along to others, and, as diseases do, it mutated. It became something else. Something terrible."

"I really am going to die."

"No. You won't." He stroked my shoulder as though the motion could also wipe away my fear. "I want you to rest," he said. "Let me take care of you."

Oh, he sounded so sincere. Like he wanted to help because he had actual feelings for me. It galled me that he'd seduced me so easily, that I fell for him. Even through my fury beat the soft pulse of knowledge that I wanted him. If he hadn't betrayed me, I would still be his.

I had the Taint.

Lilith's freaking demon had given me the disease.

My body felt shivery and achy, and my head throbbed as if it were about ready to explode.

The Taint. I couldn't wrap my brain around it. Was it true? Would Connor lie to me? I was obviously sick; why tell me it was the worst thing ever for a vampire?

"Why didn't the Consortium know? Why did royal lycan blood offer a cure?"

"I dinnae know. Ah, lass. Knowledge is lost," said Connor. "And sometimes it's found again." He sighed. "You an' your friends live in a bubble. All you ken about the paranormal world is what you're told. Have any of you traveled elsewhere since your Turnings?"

Honestly I couldn't think of one Turn-blood who'd ever permanently left Broken Heart after the Consortium took over. I drove my son to Tulsa for his visits with his daddy, but it was straight there and straight back.

"It's hard to protect the supernatural secret," said Connor. "Especially with those new to our world. It's why humans have so many myths and legends. Humans are verra creative, but if they met a real werewolf or demon, they'd shit their pants. We survive because the humans dinnae believe we're real."

"You think the Consortium keeps us caged because they're afraid we'll spill the beans?" I snorted a laugh. Pain lanced me. *Ouch.* "That's stupid."

"Believe what you like, lass."

Agony rolled over me, as sudden and awful as tripping and falling on a land mine. My body seized. Then I leaned over the side of the mattress and puked. Blood and black sludge splattered the pretty floral carpeting.

Connor held my hair away from my face and made soothing noises. He took a wet cloth and wiped my face. I let him do it because I didn't have the energy to tell him to fuck off.

I felt like I'd gotten onto a crazy merry-go-round. Everything was spinning, and it was getting unbearably hot. Uh-oh. Passing out was imminent.

"You willna die."

It was a promise I hoped he kept.

I faded in and out. I felt like my insides had turned into ice even though sweat beaded my upper lip. My entire body quaked, caught in an endless cycle of hot and cold. My teeth clattered together. I felt like mean little elves were marching under my skin and tearing at me with tiny, sharp claws. God. I bet somewhere in parakind there were psycho elves who did that kind of shit. What bastards.

At one point, a few minutes or years later, I swam through the murk of unconsciousness and opened my eyes. They felt tight and crusty.

Hovering above me was a scaly green creature with black eyes. It wore a tattered gray robe with a hood drawn over its head.

A yellowed claw traced my forehead.

I yelped.

"Ssshhh," said Connor. He popped into view on the other side of the lizard thing. "Nera is here to help."

"My saliva produces an antitoxin," rasped a feminine voice. "Without it, you will not survive the night."

"You want me to drink your spit?" I coughed. My gaze went to Connor. "Why not some Freon or battery acid?"

I didn't know who the lizard lady was, or why Connor could find her, but not someone in Broken Heart, or how I could possibly trust him. I guessed if he wanted to, he could just let me die. Then again, keeping me alive meant keeping himself alive. However, demons were true immortals. How could the vampire binding curse affect him?

Ow. My head really hurt.

Connor stroked my face with trembling fingers. "Stay strong, lass."

"I'm dying?"

The look in his eyes was pure fear. My useless heart dropped into my stomach and convulsed. "Okay," I whispered. "I'll do it."

Nera cocked her head at Connor. "You agree to the bargain?"

"What bargain?" I asked. My throat felt swollen and hot. Darkness crimped the edges of my vision, and I knew I was gonna pass out. Again. Stupid demon's poison.

Nera's lipless mouth stretched into a mocking grin. "No demon helps another without a bargain. You know this, hunter."

"You called a demon?" I accused Connor. "And you bartered?"

"'Tis the only way to save you, lass." He looked at Nera. "I agree."

She picked up a chipped ceramic bowl. Connor held out his forearm and she slashed his flesh with her talon. He didn't even flinch. Black blood poured into the bowl. When it was half-full, she nodded, and Connor grabbed a cloth and pressed it against his wound.

Nera made a disgusting hacking sound and a

noxious liquid spewed from her mouth into the bowl. She mixed it all up with the same claw she'd used to hack Connor's arm.

When she lifted the bowl to my lips, I managed to drink.

I craved the blood so much that getting the concoction down wasn't as difficult as I thought it would be. The texture was like that of egg drop soup.

"Excellent," said Nera. Her gaze flicked to Connor. "I will give you time to get her settled. Then you must come to me and fulfill the bargain."

"Aye," said Connor.

Nera rose and turned, gliding into the darkness.

"C-c-cold." The chill leaked from my pores. It drove away the heat—all of it, until I felt like a Phoebe Popsicle.

Connor crawled onto the bed with me. I should've protested, bein' a girl of principles an' all.

But I was too cold, too tired to work up the protest.

Connor's heat soaked me as he gathered me close. I pressed against him, and his strength and his warmth and his kindness weaved around me.

I'd be furious with Connor tomorrow.

With my check pressed against his chest, and the reassuring sound of his heartbeat in my ear, I fell asleep.

Chapter 6

It's raining.

I'm standing on the back porch, watching the silvery water pummel the backyard. People are in the house drinking iced tea and speaking in low tones about death. About my mother. These people went to Momma's memorial service, came to the wake to eat casseroles and Jell-O and pies, and want to tell me how sorry they are.

Aunt Alice joins me. She's thin and pale, her graying hair pulled into a bun. Her black dress is wrinkled, as though she slept in it. Mine is black, too, and I know I will never wear it again.

I don't want anything around that invokes the memory of this day.

My aunt says nothing. We watch the water sluice down the sloping hill with its patchy grass. The fence clangs as the wind pushes through its rusted links. *It's so empty,* I think. *There should be flowers. And a swing.*

"You should take her. The urn with . . . her ashes," I say. "She was on her way home. She should"—I swallow the knot in my throat— "finish the journey."

"Her home was with you, Phoebe."

"Take her." I meet my aunt's sad gaze and lean down to kiss her papery cheek. "Please."

She nods, then slips back inside, and the murmurs recede, then strengthen, like waves lapping a deserted beach.

The door opens again and it's Jackson. We went to high school together, and I remember the way he used to flirt with me.

He puts his arm around me. "I'm sorry, Phoebe."

I turn my face into his shoulder and weep.

It's raining.

I'm staring out the kitchen window, my hands in the sink water idle against the plate I'm washing. It's midafternoon but it's overcast, thick gray clouds belching out torrents of water and cracking the sky with sound and with light.

It feels like midnight. Out there, and in my own heart.

I have realized something important.

And it will affect the life growing inside me. I use a tea towel to dry my hands and then put them, cold and trembling, on my rounded belly. Nearly five months along.

"Another Oklahoma storm," says Jackson as he

walks into the kitchen. He has grease smeared on his cheek and his hands are black with dirt.

My heart is thudding. *Say the words,* I think. *Be strong.* "Any luck?" I ask.

God, I'm such a coward.

"I need another part. I'll get logs for the fire-place," he says. "It'll keep us warm enough until I can get the heater fixed."

I look at him, and I see a good man. He is hand-some and strong and kind, but he's not mine. I am not his.

I suck in a breath, and on the exhale I say, "I don't love you."

His eyes widen and he opens his mouth to pro-test, but no words come out.

"Go on. Say you love me," I say softly.

His lips compress in a thin line. "I care about you. I care about our baby."

"It's not enough. You know it's not."

"Phoebe." His voice is an ache, the same ache that echoes all the way down to my soul. "Our son."

"Will be happy if his parents are happy," I say. "I don't want to hate you."

There is acquiescence in his gaze, and grief. "Okay," he says, "okay."

I am alone.

I'm standing in the middle of Main Street. If I look right, I see the old dance studio. It's boarded up. It seems vampires and werewolves aren't interested the art of dance, because no one has bothered to start it up again. I think about the lessons I took there as a little girl and I remember the gleaming mirrors, the polished ballet bars, the sleek pink leotards. It always smelled like lemon polish in there.

If I look left, I see the darkened windows of the Old Sass Café. I think about my work there, how much I enjoy talking to people and bringing them old-fashioned meals. The place is pretty in its own way, with the glass case showing off our freshly made pies, the red vinyl seats and the gold-flecked Formica tables, and the jukebox in the corner with its old songs. It still plays "Love Me Tender," and "That'll Be the Day," and "Oh, Pretty Woman."

I feel sad, and I don't know why.

It's dark, long past sunset, and there is only me, standing in the middle of the street.

Then I feel the ground tremble and I hear a terrible roar, and the glass blows out and the buildings explode with fire, crashing inward. I fall to my knees and cover my head. I'm screaming, but it blends with other screams.

When everything stops, I'm shaking so much I can barely lift my head. There is no more fire. Just crumbled buildings, and the smell of brimstone.

And there are bodies.

Where did they come from?

Scattered all around me, they are bloodied and still, with eyes staring up into the night. So many. So many.

"You did this." A thousand voices from nowhere, from everywhere.

"No," I cry. "Not me."

But the recrimination is too sharp and cuts
through me. I bleed guilt, and I look up, up into
the storm-laden sky.

It's thundering now, and lightning streaks
through roiling clouds.

Not me, I think as I look around. My friends, my
town, my life. *I would never do this.* How could I?

Broken Heart is gone.

Everyone is dead.

The voices scream their pain and vow their re-
venge, and I'm lost, so lost in the maelstrom of
their accusations. And then . . .

It's raining.

Chapter 7

"M'aingeal."

My eyes opened. I was shaking, my fingers twisted in Connor's T-shirt. My heart did not move, nor my breath, nor my tears.

But I felt them all. Phantoms of physical suffering I could no longer feel.

Oh, but I ached. I was swept away by the power of the emotions still echoing from that . . . dream or whatever, and I couldn't calm down.

"You were havin' a nightmare," he said softly.

"I don't dream," I said. My voice sounded hoarse; it felt like I'd been screaming. Maybe I had. "Vampires aren't supposed to dream."

He stroked my cheek with one calloused forefinger. "What troubles you, Phoebe?"

I couldn't tell him. I was embarrassed to be clinging to this man. He held me securely, and he felt so good. I didn't want him to feel good. Shouldn't I be repelled? He'd lied to me in the worst way.

Mated. Bonded. *Married.* It wasn't a drunken Las Vegas mistake. It was a hundred years together. What would happen to us? What would happen to my son? My thoughts circled back to the odd dream . . . vision . . . memory.

"Connor, why did you mate with me? And what does it have to with this talisman?" Each word sounded cracked and rusted, like an old gate that's lost its swing.

"How are you feelin'?"

Ah. The ol' change of subject. "I feel like shit. But I'm alive. Undead. Whatever."

"Ye'll be fine now." His breath ruffled my hair. "'Tis almost dawn," he said. "When you awaken, we'll talk."

"Promise?"

He chuckled. "You know demons never make promises."

"Well, I'm not gonna bargain with you."

"Good call," he said.

I'd slept the entire night, and I was still exhausted. And I still hurt.

"I didn't check in," I whispered. "I was supposed to call Danny at seven p.m. Jackson will worry. He knows I would never miss a call."

"You dinnae think the Consortium will cover for you? They wouldna want a worried human nosin' around."

He was right. If Jackson couldn't reach me, he'd call the backup numbers and get someone at the Consortium. I bet they'd already talked to him.

Yeah. They'd come up with a good reason why I didn't call, or they'd glamour him into thinking I had. Vampires from the Family Koschei had über-glamour—they could mind-whip just about any-body, even over the phone.

Honestly, I hadn't paid much attention to the Consortium or Broken Heart's paranormal gov-ernment. The Consortium didn't officially run the town. They were more like a think tank that spent money on research in technology and medicine. They had moved their headquarters to town, and their experiment gone wrong, poor Lorcan, had been directly responsible for eleven deaths. They took a particular interest in the Broken Heart Turn-bloods, and we had their protection forever.

I worked; I raised my son; I did all the things single moms do. I'd thought it was a simple life. A good life. But it bothered me that things were going on in Broken Heart, and out in the para-normal world, that I didn't know about. Who knew what was unfolding that would affect all of us? I thought of that horrible vision of Broken Heart being destroyed and everyone being killed. I hoped it wasn't a portent, because . . . God, I couldn't even fathom it.

I was so tired. Every so often, a lightning bolt of pain would shoot up my spine and radiate into my limbs. "I don't feel good," I muttered. If dawn was close, I would be asleep again in no time. Vampires were biologically designed to shut down during the day. I wouldn't have a choice.

"Just rest," said Connor. His lips brushed across my brow. "You'll be fine."

"Shouldn't be so nice," I said sleepily, my words slurring. "You're supposed to be mean, 'member?"

"I'm a demon," he said softly. "How could I have an ounce of kindness or conscience?"

"Damn straight."

"Close your eyes, Phoebe." He stroked my hair. "You can hate me tomorrow."

I woke up starving.

I pushed off the covers and swung my legs over the edge of the mattress. The bed was so huge and high up that my feet hovered about half a foot off the floral carpet. Wow. I never figured Connor for a flowers kind of guy.

Dizziness assailed me, so I clutched the bedspread until everything stopped spinning.

I looked down at myself and grimaced.

Total ickfest. My shorts and shirt were wrinkled and smelled like old sweat. My hair felt stiff, and my mouth tasted like ashes.

Nice.

Connor was gone.

I didn't have my cell phone or my knives or my Glock. I didn't even have shoes. I wanted to shower and brush my teeth and kick someone's ass.

Thoughts tumbled through my mind. It galled me that Connor had: a) disappeared. Just left me in his bedroom without a damn note or anything, and b) taken me someplace I couldn't begin to escape from, and c) saved my undead butt (unless you counted the fact that he was the reason I'd been beaten and given the Taint). He'd bartered with another demon for the antidote. Then again, it just required some of his blood. So not much of a sacrifice there.

God, I was hungry.

I stood up, delighted my legs didn't fold. I felt weak, but not sick. Nera's spit-blood soup (ew) worked miracles.

"Connor?" I called out.

"Are you okay?" asked a little girl's voice. The child, maybe seven or eight, skipped across the room and stopped about a foot away. Her blond hair was up in pigtails, her blue eyes fringed with long lashes. She wore a frilly dress the shade of pink cotton candy, little lace-rimmed socks, and black patent-leather shoes.

"Yeah," I said. Okay. I was so not expecting a kid. "Where am I?"

"It's my home." She looked around, her bow-shaped lips puckered into a frown.

"It's not Connor's?"

She giggled. "No. Why would he live here?"

"Yeah. That's just . . . silly." I studied her more closely. My demon senses started to tingle, and I realized taking things at face value was unwise. "What are you?"

"You're smart." She twirled and lights sparked

all around her. When the spinning sparkles faded, a teenage boy dressed like punk-band reject stood in her place. "And pretty. I can . . . you know . . . see why Connor digs you."

His voice was low and sullen, his dark eyes filled with doubt about my intelligence.

"What just happened here?" I asked. Look at me. Not freaking out. Go, Phoebe. I was probably still in shock. Yay, shock. "Seriously. That's freaky."

"If . . . you know . . . you saw my true form, you'd go insane." He slowly twirled a finger near his temple.

I absorbed this information. The sparkles appeared again, briefly enveloping the boy with wiggling, shiny beams. A woman dressed in a red cocktail dress and stilettos appeared. She looked like she'd fallen out of the pages of *Glamour*.

"Insane?" I asked. "Really?"

"Happens every time," she said in a whiskey voice. "It's difficult to have a conversation with someone babbling and weeping and tearing out their hair."

"I imagine so."

She nodded. "It's *really* annoying."

"And you know Connor how?"

She tilted her head, considering me. "I'm his sister. Well, his half sister. My name's Jennifer."

I blinked. "Jennifer?"

"The name my father gave me was long and terrible. Demonic names are so . . . melodramatic," she said in a bored tone. "Connor said I could call myself whatever I wanted. He was the first one to pay me any attention. I mean, other than those who were screaming and losing their minds. Do you know that during one conversation a man's eyes just melted right out of his head?"

I stared at her, horrified.

"TMI?" she asked.

"Yeah," I said. "Way TMI."

"Sorry. Connor says I need to learn"—she crooked her fingers into air quotes—"boundaries."

Another light show erupted and then I was looking at a man in his fifties wearing an Armani suit and a corporate sneer. I tried to comprehend calling this guy Jennifer. Was this being . . . well, okay demon . . . female or male or both? Or neither?

"The others are waiting," he said.

"Others?"

"Hmmm. Perhaps Connor would prefer you to stay here until he returns."

"From where?"

His gaze shuttered. "From . . . downstairs. He must really like you to barter again with Nera."

"The creepy lizard lady?"

She—er, he—nodded.

I remembered that Connor had mentioned Nera before, when all hell (hah) broke loose with Lilith.

"Maybe someone should go get him."

Corporate Dude, aka Demon Jennifer, looked at

me askance. "I don't think he'd like that. I mean, he's gotta stay there about a day or so to heal."

"Heal?" I shot off the bed. "Heal what?"

Had he gotten the Taint, too? You'd think if demons started the damned disease, they'd suffer from it as well, but maybe . . . maybe . . . I sat down heavily. Why was I so worried about him? I was supposed to be angry.

But I was having a hard time working up my fury.

"Oh, don't worry. It's just his eyes." Jennifer sat next to me. "Sure, it hurts when they're scooped out. But Nera's careful. Not to be nice, mind you. She doesn't want them to liquefy."

I stared at him. Her. Whatever! "What are you talking about?"

A panicked look crossed his features. "Oh. Was I not supposed to say?" His brows slammed down. "Connor doesn't usually ask me to keep secrets, 'cause he knows I'm not good at it."

"Nera took his eyes," I said carefully. "Why?"

"Payment. For curing you." He patted me on the shoulder. "He's immortal. So they'll grow back. In a day or two."

Connor agreed to give up his eyes. To go blind while they regenerated to make sure I survived the Taint. The least I could do was repay his kindness. "Jennifer, I want you to take me to Connor."

He slanted me a look. "You sure? The first level isn't bad. But my place is much nicer. I have mastered making chocolatinis. Ever had one?"

"No," I said. I didn't point out that as a vampire, I couldn't drink anything but blood. Unless I was in Broken Heart, of course. "I'm . . . um, Connor's wife. And I should be where he is."

He considered this piece of logic for a much longer time than I thought necessary.

"Weeeeeeell." His hand clamped over my shoulder. "Okay!"

Then the world went dark and twisty.

Chapter 8

I arrived in a cave.

Above me, the ceiling writhed with hundreds of shifting red shapes. Okay. What the hell was that stuff? I shivered at the idea of snakes or worms. The vermilion glow did little to illuminate the gloom of the cavern. Not even my vampire eyes could penetrate the thick darkness. The whole place smelled vaguely of rotten eggs. Or was that me?

I heard the *plink-plink* of dripping water. I realized that not only did I have the clothes I'd casually thrown on yesterday (was it only yesterday? I couldn't remember); I had no shoes (and no bra, sigh), but also I had no weapons.

One day, I'd really like to be prepared for a situation rather than just jumping into it. I guess I could always hope for a personality transplant.

"Connor?"

It was almost as if the sound of my voice were

swallowed by the darkness. I examined the ceiling. The red squirmy things pulsed and wriggled. Red light drifted down enough for me to make out the craggy rock wall behind me, the gritty floor, and about five feet of the cavern in front of me.

Then I heard: *Tiptiptiptip.*

What was that?

The sounds got louder.

Tiptiptiptiptiptip.

"Connor?" I screeched.

The noise stopped, then started again. Louder. It was coming in my direction. Gawd. Connor? Demons? Elves? What was it?

I could sorta make out a small form coming toward me. It was on four legs. I backed against the wall, knowing my demon powers and vampire skills were weak. I could still throw a punch and kick, but my strength wouldn't keep up through an extended fight.

I was so screwed.

The tiny figure finally emerged from the thick shadows and came right up to the pallet. It sat down, cocked its head, and stared at me.

"A Chihuahua?" I blinked down at it, unable to comprehend something so mundane. It was a mixture of white, black, and brown. He had big brown eyes, a tiny snout, and stick legs. He weighed maybe all of three pounds. "You're a dog."

His ears twitched, and he cocked his head the other way.

I couldn't be sure he really was a Chihuahua.

A wave of rotten-egg stench rolled over me. "Are you a demon or is that just gas? Ugh! Dude, you're disgusting."

The dog straightened, looking offended. Then he got to all fours, whirled around, and started barking.

He was fierce, but those little yips weren't scarin' nobody. However, the creature slithering out of the darkness was another matter.

It sorta looked like a fat python with legs. It was black and scaly, and much, much bigger than the Chihuahua. It slithered and slithered, coiling its seemingly endless body until it rose a good three feet into the air. Its front legs kicked, and it hissed at the dog.

"Hey!" I yelled. "Dude! C'mere!"

If my heart could beat, it would be hammering out of my chest. Unnerved by the demon, I clutched at the wall, my fingernails scraping against pocked stone.

The damned mutt kept barking.

The demon opened its maw, showing sharp, slimy teeth, and, with its red gaze on the Chihuahua, it struck.

The Chihuahua ate the demon.

He.

Ate.

The.

Demon.

I watched in fascinated horror as the tiny dog

opened its itty-bitty mouth and slurped that demon in as if it were a bowl full of delicious spaghetti.

When he was finished, he offered a small burp. Then he turned toward me and wagged his tail.

We stared at each other a moment while relief shuddered through me.

"Good dog!" I cried. He galloped to me, so I squatted down and petted him. "What a good boy! Yes, you are. Yes, you are. Who's the badass? That's right. You are."

He licked me right on the mouth, and I could taste the sulfur. *Yech.* Well, hell. I couldn't deny the demon-eating Chihuahua a few kisses after he'd saved me.

"Scrymgeour!" Connor's voice! He was out there in the freaking abyss. "Here, lad."

The Chihuahua flipped around and ran into the shadows.

Sheesh. I'd been worried about Connor. I was ashamed at how much relief I actually felt. Because I couldn't rectify my own feelings, I handily blamed the mating bond.

"Connor?"

"Lass! What're you doin' down here?"

"Your sister . . . um, zapped me."

"I'll send you back. You need to rest."

"I know what you did," I blurted. "I'm not going back without you."

Tap. Tap. Tap.

Tiptiptiptip.

Scrymgeour arrived first. Then Connor ap-

peared at the edge of the shadowy domain I was—
let's be honest—afraid to even approach. He held
a long, gnarled staff, using it to test the ground in
front of him.

A strip of stained cloth covered his eyes.

"Oh, Connor!" I couldn't keep the horror out
of my tone.

He grimaced, but said nothing, continuing his
slow progress toward the wall at my backside. His
clothes were just as grimy as mine, his hair lanky,
and his cheek sported Lilith's deep scratches,
though they'd begun to heal.

Worry fluttered inside me. He was blind, I was
weak, and all we had to help us was the Chihuahua. How many demons could he eat? His diges-
tive system was, like, four inches long.

"Dinnae worry, Phoebe." He knelt down, holding on to the staff, and put out his hand. "Did you
watch over our lady, Scrymgeour?"

The Chihuahua yipped and rubbed his back
under Connor's outstretched palm.

"He slurped down a demon like it was a milk
shake," I said, still astonished by the feat.

"Scrymgeour's a hellhound. He eats demons
for breakfast. Don't you?" The dog wagged his
tail and barked. Then he got on his belly and
crawled toward Connor. He yipped, then whined.
"Oh, now, lad. Dinnae worry. I'm sorry I left you
so long, but I willna do it again." The Chihuahua
popped up and jumped onto Connor's knee. "Go
do a perimeter check, you little rat."

Scrymgeour barked, then sped off to do Connor's bidding.

"You have a Chihuahua hellhound for a pet?"

"Hellhounds choose their forms and their masters. I dinnae know why he settled for a Chihuahua or for me, but I'm glad to have him." He reached out and touched the wall, then settled himself against it. "I imagine you're starvin'."

"No donors," I lamented. I sat next to Connor. I couldn't keep my gaze from the ratty bandage covering his injured eyes.

"Your sister said something about others waiting for us. You gonna tell me what's going on?"

"I'll tell you about it," he said, "after you eat." He tapped his neck.

"Uh, no."

His brows rose, which looked weird with the strip of cloth around his eyes. I reached out, though I wasn't sure if I really wanted to take off the bandage or not.

"No, lass. Dinnae." Connor unerringly caught my wrist. "I'm the only meal around. If you insist on staying here while I heal, then it's me or nothing."

"Uh, no."

"Then how about a kiss?"

"Now? Because I need some Crest, dude. Bad." I crinkled my nose. "And no offense, but so do you."

He laughed. "I'd kiss you anytime, anywhere, Phoebe."

I realized I was supposed to be mad at him, only I wasn't. Just because my anger had taken a back-seat to the obvious problem of Lilith did not mean I wanted to stay hitched to a hottie half-demon.

"C'mon, lass." He tilted his neck. "Dinnae be stubborn."

Hunger scrabbled in my belly. A vampire appetite wasn't assuaged as easily as, say, a human skipping lunch and honking down a midafternoon cheeseburger to stop her belly growls. This kind of craving had an edge of need so sharp, it cut at your morals. Sliced away inhibitions. A pint was enough to keep a vampire going, but it offered minimal satisfaction.

I straddled him and he sucked in a sharp breath. It was the easiest position for me to feed in (yeah, and it so wasn't because I wanted to sit on his awesome lap). His eyes might be injured, but nothing else about the man was experiencing malfunction. Whew, baby.

I pressed my fingers against the strong pulse of his carotid artery. Somehow, I knew he was thinking about my mouth, and I tingled with the need to lay one on him. Because of the bond. Because of the memory of when he kissed me BB (Before Betrayal). He had such wonderful lips, their contours fitting against mine so sweetly.

Oh, dear Lord. I did not just think about . . .

I swallowed hard. A phantom blush heated my cheeks and I was glad he couldn't see me. I didn't want him to guess what I'd been thinking.

"Phoebe." Connor's voice was strained.

His hands lightly gripped my waist. My fangs emerged. Survival meant blood, and I had no problem taking sustenance.

I sank my fangs into his flesh. You'd think getting bitten would be traumatic: teeth piercing skin, tongue pressing wetly, mouth sucking out life . . . but it's not.

Connor's blood flooded my mouth. Though it tasted slightly metallic, his essence was rich and succulent. None of my human donors tasted this delicious. Fire raced through my veins. Real? Imagined? I didn't know. Didn't care.

I couldn't stop the moan. It vibrated against his skin. And still I drank.

"Phoebe," he muttered hoarsely. I wiggled closer. His cock twitched against my woo-woo.

Pleasure rocketed.

Oh, this was such a bad idea.

I realized vaguely that I'd reached the pint level, but I needed just . . . a . . . little . . . more. He was so delicious. And I wasn't just talking about the blood, either.

"Phoebe. God. Lass, please . . ."

The rough tone of his voice, filled with such raw longing, filtered through my ecstasy and I knew I was hurting him. Not with my bite. With my lust.

I had to stop. Before we both drowned.

I wrenched my fangs free.

He gasped, and as penance, I licked his twin

wounds. Vampire saliva had healing properties. The skin was already stitching closed. Demons were good healers anyway. They weren't just immortal; they couldn't be killed. It appeared, however, that Lilith's scratches were slower to heal. Maybe she'd poisoned him, too.

I felt much stronger. I pulled back and looked at him. He was breathing hard, his fingers digging into my skin.

I could almost feel the whisper of his lips on mine. I think we were waiting to see who'd give in first. I might've . . . Okay, I would have, but Connor acted a second before me.

He cupped the back of my head and captured my mouth. Being blind didn't affect his aim at all. He didn't care about that whole hygiene thing, and at this moment, I didn't, either.

He split the seam of my lips with his tongue, and I welcomed that tender invasion. Had I ever thought he couldn't break my heart? Bittersweet emotion tainted my desire.

Connor brought me closer, almost as if he could feel my sorrow, and he deepened his possession of my mouth, of *me*, until doubts were swept away, and all I knew was him. He filled the emptiness I hadn't known I still carried.

He was warm, so warm. That heat burned through me, and with it the aching need I'd known the first time he'd kissed me. Then, too, I had the knowledge of what his mouth could do. And his hands . . . oh, how his hands could touch me. I knew where they'd stroke, what they'd dare.

"Connor." I pulled free and pressed my forehead to his. He was breathing hard, hard enough for both of us, since I no longer had the option. He licked his lips as if trying to keep the taste of me in his mouth.

"If we're stoppin'," he said carefully, "then perhaps you should sit elsewhere."

I scooted off his lap. My girly bits throbbed, and my body demanded satisfaction. I wasn't gonna do the mattress mambo with Connor. I wouldn't strengthen our binding, even though I suspected my feelings had already taken root.

I curled up a few inches away from him, not wanting to be too far from the only safe thing in this place. I glanced at him again. Who was I kidding? He was the most dangerous. At least to me.

Lord above, we'd burn each other up.

And I might just die from the wanting.

Chapter 9

"Why did she take your eyes?" I asked, my voice unsteady.

He didn't answer right away. I wondered about the bargain he'd made, more than one, to this Nera. Demons were bound by the conditions of their bargains. However, bartering with a demon was the worst idea ever. Most people were so worried about getting what they desperately wanted that they didn't worry about little things—like what the friggin' demons demanded in return. Souls. Blood. Appendages. Firstborns.

"'Twas the price she asked for the antitoxin."

"I know," I said. I touched the cloth, and once again, Connor drew my hand away. "I meant, why does she need them?"

"Demon eyes are required ingredients for divination spells. She'll use 'em to bargain with another demon, or maybe a witch who practices black magic."

"Oh, my God." I pressed my face into my hands. He'd given up his beautiful amber gaze so that I would live. I thought he'd donated a little blood to the soup, but now I realized he'd done that only so the demon saliva would go down easier.

Here was a man who'd plotted for a month to get me into bed. To mate with me. It had something to do with the talisman—an object that inspired people to act all kinds of crazy. I wanted to think he was a selfish jerk who'd taken advantage of me, but when he did shit like give up freaking body parts, it was hard to cast him in the role of a pure villain. Immortal or not, getting your eyeballs removed had to hurt like hell. I couldn't begin to fathom how terrible it had been for him to let Nera carve them out of his head.

My stomach squeezed. Oh, God.

I really wished I could take a cleansing breath, but I'd have to settle for pretending. Not nearly as satisfying, though. *Dear Anger: I am not a victim. And I'm not gonna act like one anymore, either. So shut up. Thanks.*

Recriminations were over.

Like it or not, I was in this thing with Connor all the way to the finish line. I could only hope that it would end well. I wanted to be with my son again and to be able to raise him. I couldn't imagine a world without Danny in it, and I'd do whatever it took to make sure we'd be together.

Now all I needed was a plan. I'd take one step

at a time. I'd deal with the marital-bonding thing later.

"Phoebe?" Connor put his hand on my arm. "My eyes will grow back. I'm a demon, remember? Immortal with magical healin'."

"Jennifer told me." And I might've remembered that little fact once the horror of it all had worn off. When a guy tells you that he gave up his eyes for you, it sorta makes it hard to think beyond that statement.

"Grievous wounds take longer to heal, especially when it's complete regeneration," he said, his tone reassuring. "I'll be all right in a day or so."

"Can we afford a day or so?" My question seemed callous, so I kept my voice soft. "I mean, Lilith is on the rampage. What if she gets the other half of the talisman before we do?"

"She won't." He sounded confident.

"You already have it?"

"Yes," he said. "But it's complicated. Everything will be explained. But better to tell you all of it when we meet with the others."

"Who are these others?"

"Astria Vedere and her guardians, Anise and Ren. There's also Larsa. She's a vampire."

He leaned his head against the wall and blew out a shuddering breath. He was pale, and I knew he was in pain. I let him rest while I thought about what he'd told me.

Everyone knew the Vedere females were powerful human psychics. Their prophecies always came true. I wondered who Larsa was, and why she'd help a half-demon steal a valuable magical object. It appeared I was part of the insane quest whether I wanted to be or not.

How much would Connor share with me if I just offered him some trust? Maybe he wouldn't take me at face value. And why should he? He knew my agenda was to get free of this entire mess. However, my freedom was dependent upon helping Connor accomplish his goals.

I felt good as new after feeding. If we could get clean and find some decent clothes, we could move on to phase one of Find the Talisman. Well, and get Connor healed up.

I missed Danny. I wondered what he and Jackson were doing today. Riding the teacups? Watching a show? Eating ice cream? I imagined my son holding his father's hand, the sunshine gleaming on his brown hair, his smile as he saw Mickey Mouse.

What had the Consortium told Jackson? I had no doubt that Jackson would call the backup numbers. He knew I would never miss a nightly phone call. Not on purpose.

I needed to check in with Broken Heart. No doubt someone had figured out I'd disappeared.

Would the demon hunters be blamed? I doubted it. No way they could've popped into town without anyone knowing. The Invisi-shield kept everyone out. There was a process for getting into

Broken Heart—a flawed one, because Connor had managed to get approval for citizenship and live there for a whole month.

It was likely the hunters had gotten into town with Queen Patsy's permission, though I found it hard to believe she would tell them to go to my house and pick up Connor. If she'd known Connor was a demon in disguise, she would've added a team of Broken Heart security. Patsy was not fond of demons, not since she'd nearly been killed by one several years before.

I glanced at Connor, flinching at that terrible covering over his eyes. Had Nera never heard of gauze? Maybe some antibiotic?

"Connor, is there a way to make your eyes heal faster?"

Hey, if Nera could heal me with some spit, then she could probably do something about Connor's eyes—especially seeing as how she took 'em. If not her, then some other demon. I wasn't sure what I would bargain with. Giving up my body parts squicked me out, but Connor had done it. So could I. Vampires regenerated, too.

Connor nodded. "I dinnae think you're gonna like it."

I loved it when his accent got all thick and sexy. A little shiver went through me. *Focus, Pheebs.*

"No good deed goes unpunished," muttered Connor, crossing his arms. His jaw clenched. "Like all creatures created by the gods, demon-kind have a purpose. It's not a nice one, mind you." He sighed. "Unlike most demons, I have a soul and a conscience. I dinnae often assuage my demon side."

"Oh, Connor." I put my hand on his thigh, feeling sorry for him. He hadn't chosen what he was; he could only decide what kind of man, or demon, he wanted to be. I was still figuring it all out, but one conclusion I had was that everything was not black and white. I was dancing in the shadows of gray.

He lightly squeezed my hand. "The more a full demon fulfills his purpose, the stronger he gets. Violence, fighting, rage . . . these are doorways to evil. Despite what you believe about me, I try not to open them."

"Is there an EpiPen for evil?" I asked.

Connor looked down at me, which was sorta useless because he couldn't see me. His lips quirked. How I wished I could see the humor sparkling in that amber gaze, could know he was whole and that he wasn't suffering anymore because of me.

"It seems like being nice is an allergy." I chewed my lower lip. "If you're mean, will your eyes regenerate faster?"

"Aye. My demon side likes a bit o' the naughty. But I am not ruled by my genetics, Phoebe. I determine my own actions."

I felt small and vulnerable. Did I really think I could help Connor? God. This whole thing was so wrong. Right up there with diet soda, fat-free

Ding Dongs, and redoing the original *Star Wars* films.

"I have to be careful," said Connor, as though I were still questioning his moral fortitude. "Evil's attractive, you know. Dresses up a like a whore in expensive jewelry."

"Nice imagery."

He snorted. "Evil whispers things like, 'There is no right or wrong; there's only power,' and you believe it. You use every justification to wipe out conscience and humanity. You forget about love and sacrifice."

"You didn't," I said softly.

"I did," he argued. "Look at what I did to you."

"A lesser evil to prevent a bigger one," I said. Or so I assumed. And I was doing a lot of assuming. *Oh, Phoebe. You a sucka.*

His eyebrows went up, a half expression of surprise.

"You told Lilith you wouldn't release her from her hell-bond. She's stuck in the Pit and she wants to get out."

"She must never get out." He sighed. "But she is not just trying to free herself. She's trying to prevent Astria's prophecy from coming true."

"Maybe she should have a chat with Koschei, Durga, and Lia," I said, naming the Ancients who'd tried to circumvent another Vedere prophecy—the one that said the Ancients would cease to rule their own kind and that a Turn-blood named Patricia would become queen of vampires and lycanthropes.

Guess who was wearing the crown? And guess who was either banned or dead?

"So this prophecy . . . ?"

"It'd be better if Astria told the tale. 'Tis her prophecy."

"All right." I paused. "I'm from the Family Durga, so I have demon mojo. Does being evil make me stronger, too?"

"No!" He sucked in a breath. "No, Phoebe. Your aura is pure."

"You can see my aura?" I knew some of the Wiccans could see auras, and so could my friend Libby, but as I've said before, she was half dragon and one of their abilities was seeing auras.

"Most demons can, even a half-breed. You are innocent, Phoebe."

He thought I was innocent? When did the sins start to show up? I chewed on my bottom lip. "How bad do you have to be to get an icky aura?"

"Very, very bad," assured Connor.

I felt a little better about myself. Just a little, though. I was feeling impatient, restless. My options were to wait for Connor to get well, which would take forever and cause him agony every minute of the day or two it would take to heal. Or . . . or I could do something to speed up the process.

Connor sat with his head bowed. He was

breathing erratically, and his skin was slick with sweat. I knew he couldn't die, but he could suffer. I wondered how bad it would get before his eyes started to grow back. And when they did, would he be able to see right away?

"Take me to Nera," I said. "I'll bargain with her. Maybe we can get your eyes back or get some new ones."

"I willna let ye bargain with that demon bitch!" He ripped his hand away from mine and slammed his fist against the rock-strewn floor. "Ye've been harmed enough in my schemes. Just leave me be, lass!"

Wow. Overreact much?

"Oh, sure. I'll just sit here and be quiet." I punched him in the shoulder and he grunted. "Jerk."

"I willna harm you, Phoebe."

"I didn't tell you to—" Wait. He said acts of evil made him stronger, would help him heal faster. Acts against innocents would probably be like an über-dose or something.

An idea formed. Before I lost my nerve, I sat on his lap, my legs on either side of his. The move surprised him. For all of two seconds. His hands cupped my hips and he pulled me forward, settling me against his crotch. Blind as a drunk mole, still he unerringly touched me as if he'd done it a thousand times. Instead of just a night's worth. I hated the way I wanted him. How I would make love to him . . . if I were desperate and stupid and gullible.

"I dinnae believe havin' sex will heal me." He sighed dramatically. "But o' course, I'm willin' to try."

His brogue had gotten heavier with each word. That accent was oh-baby sexy. I steeled my resolve and glared at him. (Not effective on a blind man, but it made me feel better.)

"Connor, would having sex with me be an act of evil?"

"Aye," he whispered. "Especially if I lied so that I could mate with you, and if I chained you to a man you dinnae want." His hand drifted up and his calloused fingers drifted across my jaw. "I'd do it again, too." His hand dove into my hair and he gripped it until my scalp tingled with pain. His lips curved into a cruel smile. "It gives me pleasure to break your heart, Phoebe."

I stared at him, hurt churning in my stomach. I felt like I swallowed jagged bits of glass and they were slicing me from the inside out. Was this the evil part? I figured it would take a little more than a few barbed taunts to help Connor grow back eyeballs. I lifted my hand to peek under the bandage, and Connor slapped it away.

"Stop!" he said, exasperated. "I dinnae want you lookin' at my sockets."

Ew.

"It's not working, is it?" I asked. Oh. *Lightbulb.* I leaned forward and whispered in his ear, "It's not working because you don't mean it."

He didn't bother to utter a denial. Instead, his

lips brushed my neck and a shiver of pleasure danced down my spine.

"So, then, no sex?" he asked.

"No sex."

"Ouch." He flinched. "Now, that's evil."

"You big baby."

He grinned. I didn't know who sucked worse: Connor at being a demon or me at being a victim. What had he said about the doorways to evil? *Violence, fighting, rage.*

"I have a better idea," I said. No more messing around. I was ready to implement my plan. Sorta.

"I canna wait to hear this."

I ignored his sarcasm, straightened up, and stuck out my jaw. "Hit me."

Chapter 10

"I can take it. I'm a vampire. Go on. Do some violence."

Connor snickered.

"What's wrong?" I asked. "Afraid?"

"Immensely."

Well, poo. I hadn't expected him to answer honestly. Where was the big male ego that could be drop-kicked with a few choice insults?

It wasn't like I didn't understand the concept of penance. I always felt as though I'd never pay enough for failing my mother. I knew her suicide wasn't my fault, but lurking guilt often flayed me. What if I'd stayed with her in Broken Heart? Would she still be alive? I would regret always that I could never look her in the eyes and tell her that I believed her. *Demons are real, Momma. You were right.* What might've happened if someone had just had some faith in her?

As much I wished I could change it, I couldn't

help Momma. But I could help Connor. If he'd let me.

"You have to punch me in the face," I said. "C'mon, you . . . you goat fucker! Hit me!"

Rusty chuckles escaped.

"What?" I asked, trying to pitch my voice into the meanest tone ever. "You like fucking goats?"

His laughter spilled out, sounding like the un-oiled hinges of an old gate. He pressed a palm against his stomach. "Stop, lass. It hurts."

"I'm not trying to be funny, stupidhead!"

He laughed harder.

"You suck."

I considered my next course of action. More anxiety scrambled through me as I realized what I had to do. I gathered my courage, raised my hand, and . . . *smack!*

His neck cracked and his cheek welted. Lilith's scratches hadn't healed entirely, and now I'd wounded the other side. I was a terrible, terrible person.

Connor rubbed his cheek. "Ow."

"Argh! How am I supposed to help you?" I stared at his battered face, my heart hurting for him. I hated to see him like this. Stubborn demon. "Are you really going to try to find the talisman without eyeballs? You kinda need them."

"Just let me heal."

"And what am I supposed to do while you're regrowing eyeballs, huh?"

"Go to Jennifer's and wait. She's verra entertaining."

"You know, Connor, your sister scares me a little."

He laughed. "I'd tell you she's not dangerous, but she's a demon. She doesn't always mean to cause destruction, though. She's trying to learn how to be good."

"Oh? How's that working out?"

"She's stopped imploding people who anger her," he said.

"Well," I said, "that is progress."

He laughed again. I offered a weak smile he couldn't see, but I was thinking, *Implode people? Holy shit! Note to self: Never piss off Jennifer.*

"Why don't we both go to your sister's?"

"I can't heal properly there."

"But you can heal *here*?"

"No more than I deserve, lass. I dinnae need comfort. Just time."

We sat in gloomy silence while I tried to think of another tactic. I gnawed on my lower lip. I didn't want to go back to Jennifer's by myself, but I didn't want to stay here, either. It was creepy, dark, and smelled like ass. I knew Connor wouldn't zap me to Broken Heart. I had nowhere else to go and no way to get there.

I figured my only viable option was to get the man healed already.

"You sure you don't want to hit me?"

He turned his head toward me. The sight of

his grimy bandage ate away at me like the poison he'd saved me from. "Mayhap there is a way I might do as you ask."

"Really?" I perked up. "What?"

He hesitated. "I think I might be able to overcome my aversion to hittin' you if I . . . spank you."

"What?"

"I knew it was a bad idea."

"No," I said, putting my hands on his shoulders. "Let's try it."

Connor shook his head. "I canna ask you to shimmy off your shorts and let me paddle you."

A spanking would be loads better than getting punched in the face. And if it would—

"Take off my shorts?"

"We must take this endeavor to its meanest levels," he said gravely. "Flesh to flesh. Unless you think we can find a flail or a mace?"

I gauged his words. "I guess we could find a tree branch or something."

His lips twitched. I knew it! He was messing with me.

"You asshole!" I shoved myself off his lap and started pacing.

"I'm only tryin' to help you help me," he said in such an earnest tone I kicked him in the ankle. He yelped. "You're not verra nice to a blind man."

I blew him a raspberry.

Well, he might've made the suggestion to be asinine, but it still wasn't a bad idea. I marched over to him and knelt, then lay flat against his muscular thighs. *Ha. Take that, Connor.*

He said nothing for a long moment.

"You . . . um, really want me to . . . er, spank you?" He sounded choked.

"Would you rather give me a right hook?"

"Fine," he said in an unenthusiastic voice. "I'll give you a swat."

"Swear you'll be evil?"

"I cross my black, cold heart." He made an X over his chest.

Then he tugged my shorts and panties down, exposing my buttocks.

"Hey!"

"I crossed my heart," he said solemnly. "I canna renege on my promise."

His palm coasted down one buttock. The light touch sent oh-happy-day ripples to my girly bits.

"S-stop."

"You dinnae want me to do this?" He streaked his fingers over the other buttock.

"No!"

"Hmmm. 'Tis strange, lass," he said, plumping my buttocks. "But I'm not feelin' any better." His palm skimmed up my back, his fingertips resting on my spine. I wasn't wearing a bra, mostly because I didn't think I'd be yanked out of my own house right after stumbling outta bed. "Mayhap you're enjoyin' this."

I wanted to deny it, but my protest came out as, "Oooh."

He stroked the skin of my back.

I will not enjoy his touch. I will not enjoy his touch. I will not—

"You like it." I heard the grin in his voice. "How can I heal if you won't cooperate? At least try to be offended."

"Hoo-kay," I said as I tried to get up. "This isn't working."

Connor pressed down between my shoulder blades, stalling my effort to rise.

"Hey!" I tried to shake off his hold. In the strength department, demon trumped vampire. He pushed harder, his other hand sliding over my ass. Surprise melded into apprehension. "W-what are you doing?"

"Only what you asked." His voice held an edge as straight and sharp as a blade.

"Connor?"

His palm flattened against my ass.

I swallowed the sudden knot in my throat. If he was trying to scare me, he was doing a decent job. I hadn't thought much past the idea of getting Connor to do something evil. I hadn't considered what might happen if he, you know, actually caved in to my demands.

One hand moved off my ass while the other stayed on my back, pressing harder still.

"You wanted this," he reminded me. I could almost feel the vibration in the air, his hand rising, the whoosh of air as it descended.

I yelped.

It took me a second to realize he hadn't actually smacked me.

"You can get up now, lass," he said, chuckling.

I don't know if I was more mortified by his amusement or by my obvious wimp-out. Even though Connor removed his hands and shifted restlessly underneath me, I didn't move. The hard length of his cock pressed into my hip.

I shot up and straddled him, grabbing him by the shirt. "You . . . you . . . you!"

He was stupid and protective and stubborn and cute and . . . and . . . stupid!

You said that already.

I blinked. That wasn't *my* thought. Argh! I double-punched him again. "Stay out of my head!" Then I stopped. "You can hear my thoughts?" Oh, my God. Telepathy. The mate thing was tightening between us. Like a noose. I gulped.

Connor grimaced.

"How long have you been able to get inside my mind?"

"Now, lass . . ."

"Don't you 'now, lass' me! How long?"

"Since the night we mated."

I rammed my fists against his shoulders again. He seized one wrist and yanked it down between us. I let the other fist fly and landed a hard blow to his stomach. He grabbed my other wrist and manacled it, too.

"Why can't I hear your thoughts?" I demanded.

"Have you tried?"

No, I hadn't. Because I didn't want this. I didn't want him. I wanted my unlife back. It hadn't exactly been exciting. Managing a diner had never been my life's dream, but neither had being a vampire. Sometimes, you just had to roll with the punches. I wanted to be at home with Danny, reading him *Green Eggs and Ham*, like we did almost every night before bedtime.

Connor had stolen that from me. Noble reasons or not, big, bad villainess or not, freaking prophecy or not . . . I'd been robbed.

"Stay out of my head."

He didn't respond.

"Connor?"

"I canna make that promise," he said.

I rose to my feet, surprised to realize I was shaking. My legs felt like wet noodles. My eyes ached; my throat was clogged. Symptoms of tears I couldn't cry.

Gah. I was such a freaking mess.

Scrymgeour's insane barking echoed from the dark.

"That's bad, right?" I asked.

"I dinnae think she would find me here."

"Nera?" I asked stupidly.

"Lilith. She canna access this level."

This level?

Something huge and yellow and smelling like cat piss rumbled out of the darkness and backhanded me. I spun and hit the wall. My cheek scraped along the rough surface, and bells rang in my ears as I slid to the earthen floor.

Pain ricocheted through me.

"Phoebe!"

As I wobbled to my feet, Connor jumped to his and, in that unerring way of his, turned to face the demon. The massive creature looked made of popcorn, its body bulbous and pitted.

Another demon?

Wonderful.

"Left!" I screamed at Connor. He ducked and came up under the demon's arm, shoving it hard. It staggered backward, roaring.

The Chihuahua barked and snarled. He ran around the demon's legs, nipping, but the demon didn't even spare the hellhound a second glance.

"Why isn't Scrymgeour eating it?"

Connor sniffed the air. "This one is from deeper in the Pit. Its essence is too strong."

"Deeper in the Pit?" I yelled. "Where the hell are we?"

"Funny," said Connor.

The yellow bastard went for Connor again, and I flinched when its massive arm connected with his poor, beat-up face.

He staggered, then did a roundhouse kick, which snapped the demon's head back. It responded by sweeping its huge arm into Connor's chest.

He flew backward, into the thick darkness. I heard a crash, a loud snap, and a groan.

Shit.

The demon turned its deformed head toward me. It looked like it had been cleaved in two and had healed wrong; one side was puffier than the other. Two orange horns stuck out over its eyes.

I took a fighting stance.

It opened its mouth and showed off double rows of slimy black teeth.

The demon charged toward me.

Chapter 11

I got one punch in, and even though I added some demonfire to it, the demon absorbed the blow.

He shoved me hard.

I slammed into the craggy wall and fell sideways. Okay. That hurt. A lot. I scrambled to my feet.

The demon laughed. Its screeching chuckles scraped at my pride. What kind of lame-ass fighter was I? I'd been trained by the best in Broken Heart, the lycanthropes and even the Roma, who were cousins to the lycans. They were werewolves, too, but could only change during the full moon. They also were very well-known for being excellent vampire hunters. And look at me now. I couldn't even throw a decent punch or protect myself.

Then again, how many demons had I actually fought? I was the cleanup girl, the one Patsy and crew called when a demon was already weak, with one foot in hell anyway.

I half turned, but the demon was fast (now that he'd finished laughing at my incompetence). He embraced me from behind and pulled me flush against him, his lips in my hair, his arm around my neck.

He squeezed.

I choked, a stupid reaction. I didn't need the air. Even though my lungs didn't operate, it was unnerving to have that intense pressure against my throat. I grabbed at his arm, digging my nails into his pitted flesh.

He was squeezing my windpipe. The idea of him crushing it horrified me. How long would that type of injury need to heal?

He lifted me. I put my feet on his ginormous knees and pushed off. I reared my head, slamming the back of my skull into his face. The blow vibrated all the way down my spine, but I heard a satisfying crunch.

Screeching, he dropped me. I whirled around and danced back, gathering my demon magic. I wanted my weapons, damn it. My Glock with Wiccan-blessed silver bullets would even the score.

His cracked nose dripped with obsidian blood. His orange eyes held fury and payback, and I didn't care.

He lurched forward, talons extended.

I released the ball of demonfire too soon. It

didn't have enough oomph to do much more than make the asshole stagger. His gaze never left mine. I could see how much he wanted to hurt me.

I created a binding coil and tossed it over his neck, but he struggled only a few seconds before the red strands broke.

He leapt forward. Claws slashed.

My stomach burned, but I had no time to assess the wound. Instead, I balled up my fist and punched him in the face.

Maybe my Family powers were wonked out, but I still had the strength of a vampire. He flew backward and slammed into the wall. *Ha!* Stone burst around him and I scrabbled back as jagged pieces flew in my direction.

He shook his head, stunned.

I marched toward him. I dropped down to one knee and struck him as hard as I could in the balls. For good measure, I released demonfire with the punch.

I found it supremely stupid of demons to wander around with their packages on display, but they were like male peacocks—showing off their goods to either impress or terrify.

But, hey, a dude was a dude in any species, and getting his balls busted hurt (and burned). A lot. His eyes went wide, and he cupped his injured genitals, wobbling sideways. I jumped to my feet and did a roundhouse kick to his stomach. He fell, curling into a ball.

"Go to hell," I said. It was a command.

He didn't disappear.

Yeah. That's what I thought. I was so gonna kill Connor . . . you know, if I survived.

He lay there, gasping, his eyes filled with hatred. Then I saw his gaze move behind me.

I felt talons on my neck.

Then I was lifted and tossed away.

I flew backward, rocks stabbing and pummeling me. I had nothing to hold on to, no way to stop. It seemed as though I sailed through the darkness forever.

I smacked against another craggy wall; stone crumbled around me. The sound of my skull cracking echoed in my own ears like the blast of a shotgun.

I lay on my side, covered in rock dust. My head frigging hurt. I reached back and felt my tenderized skull. I came away with bloody fingers.

Terrific.

My stomach burned, the wounds caused by the demon's hideous talons throbbing in a disturbing rhythm with the pain in my skull.

I couldn't see a damned thing, but when I touched my tender abdomen, I could tell that the wound was already healing.

For a nearly indestructible vampire, I was getting the shit knocked out of me.

Where was Connor? Was he okay?

I heard noises: screeches, grunts, and the meaty *thunk-thunk* of fists connecting with flesh.

I stumbled to my feet and weaved my way

toward the sounds. I could feel the back of my head healing, the bone reconnecting, the skin knitting together. It was a weird sensation.

I followed the noise through the unrelenting blackness, grateful to have vampire senses. Finally, I saw the faint edge of red light, and I started to hurry. A few moments later, I skidded into the area where the yellow demon and a smaller, meaner booger-colored one—who'd used me for a Frisbee!—were battling a righteously big white demon. It had huge, glossy wings.

Scrymgeour watched them fight. He yawned, blinked, and then lay down, his head on his paws as he sleepily assessed the demons trying to tear one another apart.

I couldn't help but stare at the glittering white demon. The iridescent scales made it shine like diamonds. It more than held its own with the other two. Fast. Dangerous. It'd punch one, kick the other, and then it swept the legs out from under the green one before slamming the yellow one in the throat.

I scooted back into the edge of the darkness, hiding and watching. Why were they fighting one another?

Then Glitter Boy swung the yellow demon into the green demon and I saw its face.

Its eye sockets were dark and empty, the outer edges crusted with black blood.

Connor.

Bile rose in my throat. I'd seen a lot of creepy shit

since becoming undead, but seeing Connor without his eyes nearly made me toss my cookies.

He had a demon form. I don't know why I was so surprised. Half demon was still a demon. I guess. Most demons could take other forms; easy enough for them to create a personal fiction that would appeal to whomever they were trying to trick.

How could I have even thought I had the wherewithal to help him heal? I felt useless. I couldn't figure out obvious deceptions, I couldn't magically heal others, and a Chihuahua was better at fighting demons than I was.

Feeling like a big loser, I watched Connor. Even without sight he was a formidable foe. Should I get in there, try to help him? What if he was full-on, all-the-way-bad demon? Would he know me? Or try to hurt me, too?

I hated the uncertainty churning through me. I hadn't been in control of my life since I invited Connor to come back to my place. I chewed on the tip of my fingernail, wincing when Booger managed to trip Connor. He went down hard, his wings folding around him.

That was when Tweedle Dee and Tweedle Dum realized that a concerted attack on Connor might be a good idea.

They leaned over him, claws extended and maws opened.

I gathered my magic, created twin orbs of demonfire, and aimed one at each. I let go and the fireballs found their targets. They stumbled backward, roaring in frustration.

Connor popped to his feet, and in the blink of an eye, he had his hands around each of their throats.

He squeezed and squeezed.

The demons gurgled, their eyes going wide and bulbous. They struggled—arms flailed, legs kicked—but it didn't matter. Connor was far more pissed off, and much stronger.

I didn't want to watch, but I couldn't turn away. I reminded myself that demons didn't die. If their solid forms were damaged or dismembered, they returned to the Pit to regenerate. The deeper they went, the longer it took to get the veil where they could crawl back through to the earthly plane.

Booger's head popped off. Its one-horned, slimy skull plopped to the ground and rolled away. Brackish blood spewed from its jagged stump, spraying Connor's neck and chest and the side of the yellow fiend still caught in his fearsome grip.

Scrymgeour leapt off the mattress and scurried to sit by me.

Popcornhead snapped and its skull sagged backward.

Connor dropped the carcasses. I waited for them to disappear, but their corpses lay there like dismembered rag dolls. Popcornhead's foot twitched, but that was it.

That just further confirmed the theory that I was in hell. Literally.

Connor screamed.

Light shot out from his eye sockets and he covered his face. I guess perpetuating violence, and offing two demons (as much as a demon could be "offed") was enough healing mojo.

After the longest moment of my life, Connor stopped wailing.

He turned toward me.

He had his eyes again.

Only they were solid black.

Connor's nostrils flared, his monster gaze on mine. He grinned, and I saw those sharp double rows of teeth. Demon teeth.

The hair rose on the back of my neck. The demon was in control. This was the real Connor, I told myself. The one who'd lied to me and tricked me. He'd killed because his evil nature demanded the sacrifice.

Then guilt wedged into my self-righteousness. Hadn't I tried to tempt him to access that side? I wanted him to heal, but I hadn't been prepared for what it might entail.

I whipped out a binding coil and wound it around him.

Connor laughed, and it was the bad kind of laugh, the one a villain always issued before doing something mean. I shot another coil of magic at him and sealed his mouth.

Terror threatened to rip through my magic. I already felt like a weakling. The creature snared in my trap was demon in body, and worse, demon in mind. What if I couldn't reach the human side of Connor?

"Snap out of it!" I shouted. "We have to go get the talisman. And save the world and stuff. Remember?" What was I talking about? I didn't even get why we needed the damned thing, but mostly I didn't want Lilith to have it. If she wanted it, then nothing good would come of her getting her pedicured mitts on it. Connor and I needed to have a heart-to-heart about its significance. And why I was so important to its success.

He stared at me, and even though the magic covered his mouth, I knew he was grinning.

Scrymgeour had disappeared. I didn't blame him. What was he supposed to do, anyway? Connor was his master; he wasn't gonna slurp him down for me.

I held on to Connor and considered my options. The cave was probably twenty or twenty-five feet across. The ceiling was dome shaped, so far as I could tell with all the red, wormy things pulsing on it.

Nowhere to go.

Apparently bored by playing Demon and the Cowgirl, he shrugged, and *poof* went my magic.

So annoying.

"Crap." I freaked. I turned and ran, putting on the vampire speed. The cavern wasn't a big space, but it was filled with detritus and big-ass rocks. I was afraid to go into the darkness again, so I spun around the small, dimly lit space like a hamster in its exercise wheel.

We played chase as minutes ticked by. Rusty chuckles escaped from the demon, who thought this game was ever so fun. Me? Not so much.

I considered my next course of action. Anxiety scrambled through me as I realized what I had to do.

I stopped running.

And let him catch me.

He caught me up into his arms and grinned. A line from *Where the Wild Things Are* ran through my head: *They roared their terrible roars and gnashed their terrible teeth and rolled their terrible eyes and showed their terrible claws.*

And Connor . . . he was the wildest thing of all.

But I couldn't tame him with a magic trick. Staring into his eyes made me realize that the demon was winning. He crushed me to him and pushed his nose against my neck, inhaling deeply.

"Pretty," he rasped. "So pretty."

I wasn't going to give up on him. And if that made me stupid along with crazy, so be it.

I gnawed on my lower lip.

"Connor," I said. "Please."

He blinked and tilted his head. "Ph-Phoebe?"

"Yes. It's me."

"Mate." Confusion and sadness flashed in his gaze. "Mate," he whispered.

I nodded. "That's right. I'm your w-wife."

Here was the real Connor. The one who'd been warrior and brother and friend and lover. The one who'd challenged Lilith and wanted to keep her locked away in the Pit. That woman would serve no good purpose wandering around the earthly plane.

"Connor." I cupped his scaly white face, ignoring the blood spatter. I tried to discern any glimmer of the human within those dark eyes. "Husband."

He threw me against the wall. The back of my newly healed head crunched. *Ouch.* Connor's hard body crushed mine. It was a good thing I didn't need to breathe. He grabbed my chin roughly and forced me to look at him.

"Shut up," he commanded in a low, mean voice. Damn it. I'd lost the tenuous connection. He pressed closer, his hot breath fanning my cheek. His lips ghosted down my jaw until his mouth hovered near my ear. Dread seeped through my every pore.

His tongue flicked along my throat. "Scream," he rasped. "Scream for me."

Chapter 12

Connor snared my wrists with one hand and lifted them above my head, pinning them to the wall. He used his knees to part my thighs. Then he roughly pushed forward, his unsheathed demon cock pressing against the vee of my thighs.

I held still, or tried. I couldn't stop the involuntary shudders that racked my body.

I was afraid.

He wanted to dominate me. Wanted terror to sweep through me, to ravage my courage.

"Fight me," he demanded. His teeth grazed my earlobe, scraped down my neck. "Fight!"

Was that Connor issuing the command? Or the demon? Did it matter?

His hand coasted down my rib cage.

His fingers dove under the band of my panties, inching toward my labia.

"No!" I struggled in earnest now, my voice thick with tears I couldn't shed. "Stop!"

His fingertips skirted the top of my pubic bone and sent me into a blind panic.

I did something really stupid.

I kissed him.

I won't lie and say it was thrilling, because his lips were leathery, and his tongue was split like a snake's. I wouldn't relinquish the thought that this was Connor. So I poured my fear and hope and desire into that kiss, and all my desperation, and my silent plea: *Come back to me.*

He yanked his mouth from mine. He was breathing hard and quivering.

"Connor?"

His obsidian gaze flickered.

I swore my undead heart thudded in my chest as hope and fear warred within me.

Slowly the inky blackness receded until familiar amber eyes stared at me in confusion, in pain. *Slish. Slish. Slish.* The white scales flicked away until only human flesh remained. Dark brown hair flowed from scalp to shoulders.

"M'aingeal." He dropped his head to my shoulder, his body shuddering against mine.

My knees felt like pudding and my stomach quivered. *Oh, God.* I stood still, my throat working, and tried to stop my own shivering.

Connor lifted his head, regret shimmering in his eyes. I knew then that he had never wanted me to see him in his demon form. His *saying* he was a demon was a far cry from my *seeing* him as one.

"Don't ever fucking do that again," I hissed.

"I'm sorry," he said.

The next thing I knew, the world went dark and shifted sideways, and when it righted itself again, I found myself under a warm spray of water, my back pressed against smooth stone.

Connor had transported us to a natural hot spring. The water sluiced over us, washing away the grime and the blood. I wished it could wash away our problems just as easily.

The same wiggling red glow that lit the previous space appeared at the top of the cave. I almost asked what those things were, because they seemed alive, but I didn't really want to know. Sometimes ignorance really was bliss.

The cave was small; from top to bottom it was black and as smooth as marble. It looked as though someone had carved it out of obsidian and buffed it until it shined.

I looked at Connor, and his gaze held so much darkness, I couldn't decide if I should run or weep.

"Phoebe." His voice broke. He dropped to his knees and pressed his cheek against my belly. "Forgive me."

Connor kissed my stomach's jagged scar, which would soon disappear. Gotta love the healing tendencies of undead flesh. He kissed the spot again, and my abdomen tightened. His lips were soft, and the warm rush of his breath made me tingle.

"Forgive what?" I asked. That he'd mated with me? That he'd lied to me? That he'd turned into a demon and killed two assholes that would've happily ripped me limb from limb?

"Everything," he murmured. His fingers wrapped around my hips, and I felt my insides lurch as he dragged off my shorts. It wasn't exactly easy, given that they'd been soaked by the water.

"C-Connor."

"Ssshhh." He kissed the skin above the line of my panties. He hooked his thumbs under the thin waistband and drew the material down.

Here was the part where I should have told him no, that he shouldn't touch me, or kiss me, or make me feel good. We were partners so long as it took to get the other half of the talisman and figure out how the hell to break the bond between us.

"Why is the talisman so important?" I asked. "Why does everyone want it?"

"I'll tell you later," he said hoarsely. "Promise."

Protests hovered in my mouth like trapped ghosts. They melted into nothingness the second his tongue slid between my folds and flicked my clitoris.

I clutched at his hair, and he moaned. His hands cupped my ass and drew me closer to his ravaging mouth. Tendrils of pleasure wound through me, poking through my doubts, through the protests I wouldn't utter.

It was wrong. Wrong to let him think this was acceptable penance. An orgasm wasn't equivalent to forgiveness. That was man-thinking right there—the idea that sex would resolve the worst of emotional crimes.

My back pressed into the wall, and my knees went soft, and into my mind whispered Connor's, *I'm sorry, I'm sorry, I'm sorry.*

And I couldn't hold on to my anger. Or my fear.

I wanted this moment. Even if it turned into regret later, I wanted it.

I felt that hot rush, and then, yes . . . I was going over, coming into his mouth, pulling at his hair, and calling out his name. And he wouldn't stop, even when my thighs trembled and my knees threatened to buckle, and oh, hell, he made me come again.

Then my legs gave way and Connor stood up, his muscular body aligning against mine.

His cock pressed into the wet vee of my thighs. Water poured over us like a baptism. I couldn't find the words to say yes or no. I wasn't sure my legs would hold me long enough to walk away, if I even had the fortitude to go.

My gaze was held hostage by his. I saw questions there, questions I couldn't answer. I opened my mind to his and sent out a single thought: *We don't have forever.*

We have now, lass.

I nodded, even though it wasn't exactly capitulation. More like stepping off a cliff, embracing that long, joyful moment of freedom and the rush of wind before slamming into the ground.

I kicked off my panties that clung to my ankles like lace shackles. Connor grabbed my shirt where the demon had savaged it, and he ripped it. I shimmied it off my shoulders and it plopped to the ground.

Connor's hands slid under my buttocks and he lifted me. His shaft teased my entrance. I was already slick, swollen, ready. He was the only man who'd ever made me feel as though my body were an extension of his, and joining with him was a reconnection of a whole.

He impaled me with one swift stroke of his cock. I wrapped my legs around his waist and clutched his shoulders. We stayed like that for an endless moment, savoring the connection that we both knew was temporary.

He leaned down and tugged one turgid peak into his mouth and swirled his tongue, teasing the bud as heat sparked. He palmed my other breast, all the while keeping me pinned to the wall with the strength of his thighs.

I clenched around his cock, and he sucked in a harsh breath, so I did it again.

Then he was moving, his hands grabbing my ass and his mouth moving to my throat. I dug my fingernails into his flesh, my distended nipples scraping against his chest, and welcomed every hard thrust.

He took me all the way to the brink, then slowed just enough so that I didn't tip over. His gaze imprisoned me. The look in his eyes made promises he could not keep, promises of forever, and love, and *this*.

We were not mates. Our bodies were bound to each other, but not our hearts.

That was the lie I would tell myself.

Because I couldn't have Connor. Maybe if he had been a vampire. Or even a human. Or a goddamned troll. But he was a demon.

My throat went tight as sorrow trickled into the pleasure of having Connor inside me.

"Don't," he whispered; then he sealed his mouth to mine, his tongue mimicking the motions of his cock. Heat flared.

He plunged deeply, his fingers jabbing into my thighs. He lifted his mouth only long enough to demand: "Come with me, Phoebe."

He swallowed my moan, and he increased his pace, and I knew he was close because our mind link was still open. I could feel his pleasure, his desperation, because they felt like mine.

He felt like mine.

"I am," he muttered. "I am yours."

And then he was gasping, pulsating within me, going over the edge, and I went with him, flying into the conflagration we'd created . . . and we burned together.

After a while, Connor reluctantly withdrew and lowered my shaky legs to the ground. He held me until my feet could hold me, and then stepped away.

"Don't say I shouldna done this," he said, his voice hoarse.

I shook my head because I couldn't figure out what to say. He cupped my cheek, tenderness in his gaze, and I believed it—believed he cared about me even after what he'd done. Maybe he was still lying, but my heart recognized the truth: He'd betray me again, damn it. He'd betray me because of the talisman, because of Lilith, because I wasn't the woman he loved. The one he desired, sure. And the one he had to protect. But love wasn't a factor. It was just another pathetic sign of my own loneliness that I wished it were any different.

I ached for Connor, for both of us.

Connor magicked up soap and washcloths and shampoo, and we separated to scrub ourselves. When we were finished, we moved away from the waterfall. He created big, thick cotton towels, and we dried off.

The silence between us wasn't exactly comfortable. There was so much to do, to worry about, to figure out before we could even begin to unravel the mating issue.

I leaned over to rub the towel over my hair. When I straightened, Connor was fully dressed in a black T-shirt, faded denims, and snakeskin boots. Even his hair was dry and brushed.

"Hey, do I get clothes, too?"

"I like you as you are," he said, grinning. Then he flicked his fingers and red magic spun toward me.

Within seconds I found myself dressed in black jeans, a rust-colored shirt and short-sleeved jacket, and black ankle boots. To my surprise, I was also wearing my holster with my Glock securely tucked inside and hidden under the jacket.

"Your knives are in your boots," he said.

He knew I used to wear the Glock, with its Wiccan-blessed silver bullets, before the Invisi-shield had gone active—I'd told him that. He knew I was pretty good with my throwing knives, too, though how he'd known I kept them tucked into my boots, I didn't know. Maybe he guessed. Or maybe he snooped while I was in my vampire coma. From the guilty expression sliding across his face, I figured it was snooping.

"It's not really your stuff," he said. "I just re-created it."

Connor reached for my hand.

The air went still, the world black and zingy, and then, *pop*, we were back in the first cavern. Scrymgeour, who'd been asleep, jumped to his tiny feet and scurried toward Connor. He leaned down and scooped up his puppy, allowing the hellhound to lick his face.

My gaze landed on the demon bodies that still hadn't dissipated. I studied them as several mental pieces clicked into a very ugly puzzle. The smell. The location. The hellhound. The demons.

One thing I knew about demons was that they had to return to the Pit to heal from grievous injuries. Usually they poofed Downstairs quick-like.

Yeah. No denying it now.

"Connor?" I asked softly. Anger fluttered somewhere beyond the relief that I was alive (sorta) and clean. "Are we in hell?"

Chapter 13

Jennifer had told me, in a fashion. She'd said it wasn't too bad on the first level. I hadn't considered what she meant because the conversation had been so odd. Nope. I just said to send me to where Connor was without asking any more questions.

Scrymgeour jumped out of his master's arms and sat next to Connor, his little bulgy brown eyes on me. His tongue lolled out of his mouth. Aw. He was so cute for a mutt that munched on demons.

"You're angry, aren't you, lass?"

"You think?" I waved my hands around. "Does Jennifer live in hell?"

"Sorta."

"What?"

Connor held up his hands in a gesture of surrender, his expression one of trepidation. He looked at me as though he were trying to figure out how to explain why he'd *taken me to hell* in a way that might not upset me.

Right.

"We're on the uppermost level," he said, as though that were a perk.

"I don't want to be on any level."

"It was the safest place to go."

"You have a really stupid definition of 'safe.' Hell is the opposite of safe." I gestured toward the demon corpses as evidence. *Gah!* I wanted to punch him in the head. I clenched my fists. "Get us out of here now!"

"Okay, lass." He wisely refrained from telling me to calm down.

"I want to talk to my son. I want to hug him and rub my face in his hair and tickle his belly." My voice bordered on the edge of whiny. "And I want some cookies." I looked at him in horror. "I can't eat. Oh, my God. I can't eat human food unless I'm in Broken Heart."

"Are you hungry, then?" he asked. He tapped the side of his neck. "You can have another pint, if you like."

"No! I want to eat my emotions. I need comfort food, damn it."

His brows went up and he opened his mouth.

I raised my hand in a "stop" gesture. "Don't even."

Connor picked up Scrymgeour and stepped toward me, his gaze wary.

"You're taking him with us?"

"I promised him I wouldna leave him again."

"You, making a promise?" I asked.

"I never make a promise I canna keep."

Somehow, I didn't doubt that. And I should have, because he'd already proven he was a highly skilled liar.

"C'mon, lass."

I grasped the hand Connor held out, and then the world fell away.

We appeared, side by side, on a very comfortable black sofa. The dimly lit room smelled sickly sweet, like a rose-filled funeral parlor. Black furniture, and red accent pieces—like that vase with dead black roses in it—filled the place. Scrymgeour leapt out of Connor's lap and started sniffing around. Then he meandered out of the room, through an open door that led to a staircase.

"Kitchen," said Connor.

"Really?"

"It's like a real house. Jenny created it on the first level—sorta in the ether. It's difficult to get to if you don't know how to get here." He tapped his temple. "She's very powerful. Not only can she zap from hell anytime she wants; she can be a portal for other demons."

"Demons like Lilith?"

"It's why I protect her," he said. "Lilith can't get her hands on Jen here."

"And dare I ask why Scrymgeour ventures into the kitchen?"

"Jen keeps scraps down there for him."

"Demon parts?" I asked.

"Oh, aye. We hack 'em up fresh an' everything." He smiled broadly.

I laughed.

Jennifer, in her va-va-voom vixen form, sauntered into the room. "Wow. This place is a real drag. What was I thinking?" She waved one slender arm. The entire room changed. Everything turned white with crystal accents. Behind us, the windows melted into nothing and revealed an ocean view. The sun was setting, casting pink lights on the waves tickling white sand.

"Better," she said. She leaned down and hugged Connor from behind. "You healed fast, brother!"

"Phoebe let me torment her," he said.

Jennifer sent me such a knowing look, I popped off the couch and walked to the marble column that had appeared during the instant makeover. I leaned against it and stared at the undulating water.

Jennifer joined me. Red beams shot out from her and I looked away from the brightness. When I returned my gaze, I scrabbled back and screamed.

"What? You don't like dogs?"

The massive three-headed creature was a Doberman pinscher gone horribly, horribly wrong. I gaped up at the middle head, wishing I could be anywhere but under the ginormous chin of a drooling mutt. The heads on either side of the middle one looked down at me, probably thinking I was a really neat life-sized Phoebe-flavored chew toy.

She barked and the sound vibrated right through me. Vampire hearing wasn't always a bonus. I yelped.

"Jen," called Connor as he joined me. He took my hand, and I let him hold it.

She sighed, and her doggy breath gusted over me. I nearly passed out from the stench. Wow. Jennifer really needed a Greenies.

The dog sat on its haunches and one huge leg came up and scratched behind its pointed ear. "You tell her about the talisman yet?"

"No," I said before Connor could open his mouth. "And I don't know what it has to do with me."

"Everything," said Dog Jennifer.

That was so enlightening. I looked at Connor, and he shrugged. "I tol' you, lass, Astria needs to reveal the prophecy to you. It's not like you trust me, after all."

"You haven't given me much reason to trust you," I said. "Did it occur to you to just tell me what was going on?"

"Oh, he couldn't do that," said Jennifer in her reverberating gruff voice.

Connor quelled all three mutts with a look.

"Why not?"

He ignored my question, but I filed it away for later. He couldn't avoid answering me forever. Probably.

"The talisman is old," said Connor. "Something Durga made."

Surprised, I stared at him. "That's why the hunters had it?"

"Self-appointed guardians of Durga's medallion," he scoffed. "They took it after she was banned and tried to hide it."

"How'd you get it?"

"He was meant to find the talisman," said Jennifer proudly. "Astria said so."

That didn't exactly answer the "how." "Let me guess. You took off with their treasure, then made them think you were other places. Oh, say, about a month ago?"

"Aye."

"And Lilith wants it because . . . ?"

"It's what Durga used to bind her to hell," offered Jennifer. "Which is ironic . . . Isn't that right, Connor?"

One corner of his mouth lifted into a grin. "Definitely, little sister." He rubbed his thumb over my knuckles. "The only way for Lilith to make any trips to the earthly plane was to be called to it by worshipers. Back in the day, all the gods and goddesses had human followers.

"One particular cult grew very strong. Its female followers practiced blood rituals, and the occasional orgy, o' course." Here, he filtered me a smoky look, but I didn't fall for it. Much.

"Of course," I said dryly.

"Lilith rewarded the head priestess by granting her demon powers. Then she gave her a demon slave. But then the temple was ransacked and destroyed, and her priestesses and worshipers were killed. All but the one she'd blessed—if you want to call it that. She would've died, too, but Ruadan the First found her."

The red light burst around the dog (er, dogs) and I closed my eyes. When I opened them, I saw the little girl again. She twirled around, then stopped, her blue eyes snaring mine. "Durga turned from her demon goddess and gave her loyalty to the vampire who'd saved her. Lilith wasn't thrilled, and she . . . Well, Connor says she threw a big temper tantrum."

"A lot of people died in those wars, including many vampires," said Connor.

I could barely imagine what it had been like back in the ancient days of civilization. Throughout history, humans fought all the time for territory. Why not paranormals, too? How many times had we fended off the baddies from Broken Heart? It seemed it was the nature of sentient beings to either conquer or protect.

"Were you there?" I asked Connor.

He nodded toward his sister. "'Twas before we existed."

"I'm only four hundred years old," offered Jennifer.

"Verra young for a demon."

She pouted. "You're only seven hundred years older, Con!"

"The talisman?" I interrupted in order to forgo a sibling argument. Then I thought, *Connor's eleven hundred years old? Holy crap.*

"Durga made the talisman. Actually, all the Ancients helped her create it," said Connor. "They needed powerful magic to make it work. They bound Lilith to hell."

Patsy had sent a demon to hell, the favorite pet of Durga, an asshole named Andharka. Patsy had some powerful juju; the demon would never come back to the earthly plane unless she compelled him personally. So, if Lilith had been bound to the Pit, and apparently with a lot more oomph, why could she leave it?

"She just put on a quite a show for someone who can't get out of hell," I pointed out.

"What she did in Broken Heart required a hefty blood sacrifice." Connor grimaced. "We're not talking goats, either."

"Oh, my God," I said, horror washing through me. "She's killing humans."

Chapter 14

"Her new *worshipers* are making sacrifices to her," Jennifer corrected. She looked at her brother, her Cupid's-bow mouth downturned. "Connor says it's wrong to kill innocents."

"It is," I said. "Very wrong. In fact, you should err on the side of caution and not kill anyone. Or anything. Living, that is."

She blinked up at me, her blue eyes guileless. "You can't kill something that's already dead," she said, "or something that's never been alive."

"Well, then you know exactly what I mean."

She turned her gaze to Connor, who shrugged. I loosed my hand from his grip and went to sit on the couch. Connor followed, sitting next to me—as in two inches away. He rested his arm along the back of the couch behind my shoulders and looked at me, as if he expected me to challenge his closeness. It actually made me feel safer, though I did stop short of snuggling. I had my pride, after all—a sliver, which was enough to prevent more foolishness.

Jennifer took the chair catty-corner to the couch, nearest to where I was sitting. She looked at me expectantly, as though I might give her a treat or offer to read to a story. Her gaze was unnerving.

I looked down at my hands and realized I needed a manicure. I studied my jagged nails and thought about the talisman and Lilith. *Jesus.* Someone had killed a human for Lilith, and that had opened the portal. She'd been in my kitchen long enough to threaten Connor and have her demon maul me, but even so it had been—what?—maybe ten minutes? One human life hadn't given her enough time. I had the awful feeling more blood would be spilled in her name.

I felt sick. How had she found a group of humans willing to do such a thing? What had she promised them?

"What's her connection to Asmodeus?" I asked.

I glanced up in time to see Jennifer and Connor share a look.

"She's mated to Asmodeus," said Connor.

"Lilith is your dad's wife?" I absorbed this information. "And you're the result of an affair with a Scottish fairy. So she hates your guts."

"My father's not a being who denies himself pleasure. He beds a lot of . . . er, people. But it's rare that children come about."

I looked at Jennifer.

"Oh, my mother's Lilith," she said matter-of-factly. "She hates my guts, too."

Connor's expression darkened. I imagined that Jennifer's story was even less kind than his. After all, he had a mother who loved him. At least, I assumed so.

He seemed to follow along with my thoughts. "My mother raised me," he said. "Believe what you like about me, but she's a good woman who loves me."

His tone was terse, inviting no other questions. I guessed Mom was a touchy subject.

"Time holds no meaning for immortals." She uttered this with a sigh, as if bored by the concept of eternity. She waved her hand, her pink nail polish glittering in the overhead light. "Mom's always been . . . cranky. And Durga was her favorite."

"Lilith sent the priestesses after Durga, but they ended up with Amahté's mate," said Connor. "Her name was Shamhat."

"This is so not my favorite part of the story," said a female voice.

I looked up and saw her standing in the doorway that led to the staircase.

The woman who'd spoken had been first through the door. She was otherworldly: pale skinned, with bow-shaped lips as red as candy, and green eyes as soft as moss. She wore a ribbed green T-shirt, tight black pants, thick-soled black boots, and on her waist was a weapons belt. On one side was a Glock and three cartridges, and on the other a series of small silver daggers. Her raven hair hung in ringlets down her back, like those of a medieval princess. "Beautiful" wasn't a decent enough word to describe her. The only visible flaw I could see was the jagged pearlescent scar that wrapped around her throat like an ugly necklace. I sensed that she was a vampire, and realized this must be Larsa.

She noticed the direction of my gaze and quirked an eyebrow. Embarrassed, I looked away, toward the people filing in behind her.

A short, curvy woman—make that young woman, maybe sixteen or seventeen—with bouncy brunette curls and violet eyes offered us a smile. She wore faded denims and a purple top that matched her eyes. On either side of her were two very familiar-looking people. Well, sorta. The tall, lithe creature on the left was a woman with moon white hair and golden eyes, and the bigger, bulkier dude on the right had the same features. His eyes were a little darker, his mouth thinner than . . . um, his sister's. Their clothing was black, too, and struck me as military garb. They were loaded up with all manner of weapons.

Holy. Freaking. Shit.

"I know," said Violet Eyes. I had the insane thought that she would skip toward us à la Shirley Temple and start singing "On the Good Ship Lollipop." "It's like looking into a mirror." She blinked. "Well, if you were Gabriel Marchand. Only, he's not here, right?"

Her accent coated her words lightly, like vinaigrette.

"Astria," said the woman, and she was French. "We talked about your focus, *oui*?"

"Oh, right. Yes. I'm Astria Vedere," she said. "The prophet."

She said it without pride, just rattled it off as though it were an obvious fact, like "the earth is round" or "the sun is hot."

"That's Anise, and he's Ren. Did I mention they are most definitely the brother and sister of Gabriel Marchand?" She blinked at us owlishly. "Probably not." She brightened. "You know now, so that's good."

Words tumbled up from my throat and quivered on my tongue, none of them brave enough to issue forth. Gabriel Marchand, the queen's husband, had thought himself an anomaly. He was only two hundred years old, born from a werewolf mother who'd been attacked by vampires. *Loup de sang.* Bloodsucking werewolves. The only one of his kind.

Or so he thought.

"Triplets." I was surprised that I'd said the word, that I'd said anything. Thoughts twirled and collided until only fragments floated like debris. It wasn't much of a leap to assume that Gabriel was a triplet. After, he was the father of triplets, too.

"Yes!" said Astria clapping. "Only they were given to my great-great- . . . Um, I think there's another great?" She paused. Then she shrugged. ". . . -Grandmother to raise for me."

"It was foretold we would be the guardians for Astria," explained Anise.

"And Gabriel?"

"He was meant for the queen," said Astria. "The challenges we face as we fulfill our destinies create within us the resilience we need to do what must be done."

What?

"Looks like your wife is gonna keel over," said Larsa.

I wanted to say, "I'm not his wife," and, "I'm not either gonna keel over," but neither statement was true. I did feel faint, but it was an emotional thing, not a physical one. I was also married to Connor, like it or not.

The four newcomers joined us. Astria sat next to Connor, Ren took up his station behind him, and Anise settled into the chair nearest Astria. Larsa scooted into the chair occupied by Jennifer, tossing the little girl into her lap.

"You're very pretty," said Astria, leaning over Connor to stare at me.

"Thank you," I said. "So are you."

"Oh, I know." She settled back and stared off into space. No one else thought this was odd, and I chalked it up to her youth or the idea that this was the way prophets behaved.

"Finish the part about Amahté," said Larsa. She had a worldly tone, an accent I couldn't place, as though she'd gathered languages like berries and tossed them into a blender to create a verbal smoothie.

Amahté was the only Ancient I hadn't met. Actually, no one had met him, because he'd gone to ground for the last three millennia. His son, Khenti, had taken his place on the Ancients' Council—although the Ancients had since handed over their ruling power to Patsy. Granted, one Ancient had died and two others had been banned to the World Between Worlds. Only three Ancients were around to offer advice and help these days. Ruadan didn't really come around much anymore, but Velthur and Zela lived in town.

No one elaborated on the role Amahté played with either the talisman or Lilith. Connor arched a brow and looked at Larsa.

She rolled her eyes. "His mate died. Sorta."

"How did she sorta die?" I asked.

"Lilith killed her," said Larsa, ignoring my question. "The Ancients learned a harsh lesson the day Shamhat died. All of her line died when she did. Because of the bonding magic, all of their mates died, too."

I held up my hand. Information swirled in my mind like colliding whirlwinds. "We were told that no one knew what would happen if an Ancient died. Everyone was all about not killing them because they *might* end the line, not because they knew—"

If I had the ability to lose my breath, it would've

whooshed out at that very moment. Jennifer considered me with solemn blue eyes. I realized she hadn't changed forms in a while and wondered vaguely if that whole morph thing was just an entertaining diversion.

"Seven," I managed to whisper. "*Seven* sacred sects. Seven Families." I stared at Larsa. "You said Shamhat's line died with her."

"The Family Shamhat," she acknowledged. "The eighth vampire line."

Chapter 15

"**V**ampires with earth magic," said Larsa, as though she hadn't just dropped the mother of all information bombs. "They're very sensual creatures, in tune with creation. With life."

Connor snorted, and Larsa sent him a dirty look.

"*Life*," she insisted. "Ironic, in a way, since we're undead. But you know how it was. Ruadan sought out others who had supernatural abilities. It's no coincidence that all the Ancients have specific gifts."

"Why?" I asked. My mind was reeling. Eight vampire Families had existed once. *Eight*. And Lilith had effectively wiped out one-eighth of the vampire population by killing its founder.

Holy bejesus.

"Ruadan always had the goal of bettering the world. Even then, magic was dying out, giving way to science and cynics. He wanted to preserve as much as possible, to pass it along to the world when it was needed."

"If Patsy hadn't absorbed all the Family gifts, the Family Hua Mu Lan would've died?" A couple years back, my friend Libby had absorbed half of a dragon soul. The founder of the Family Hua Mu Lan, aka Lia the Bitch, had been one of the Ancients who'd turned against us. Libby accidentally fried her with dragonfire.

Near as we could figure, Patsy had saved the vampire lines because she was the queen of all. And not only of us, but of the wolfies, too. The full-bloods had their own problems. They were dying as a species—females rarely got pregnant, and nearly half of all children who were born didn't make it past their first year.

The thought had been that Patsy's miraculous birth of *loup de sang* triplets would be the saving grace of all werewolves. But so far, the full-bloods were still dying, the Roma were still small in numbers, and . . . well, I had no idea what the future held for them. Hell, I didn't know what my own future held.

"If Patsy dies, do we all die?" I asked.

"Probably," said Larsa.

I thought about the nature of magic. It seemed as volatile as human temperament. Or maybe, because it was crafted and invoked by humans, it held within it the flaws of our characters. Our greed and insecurity and envy.

I mulled over the idea that vampires and demons

had been warring for such a long time. I hadn't bothered to find out much about the last four thousand years of our history. Honestly, I hadn't cared. And yet, here I was, dealing with the aftermath of long-ago decisions that had nothing to do with me or with the Broken Heart Turn-bloods.

"So, forever ago, Lilith started a war with vampires and killed a previously unknown Ancient. And they created this talisman and bound her into hell. Except she can create portals to visit earth, so the magic is what? Fading?"

"In a sense, yes," said Connor. Somehow his arm had fallen across my shoulder, his fingers massaging my arm. "Once we reunite the talisman"—and he gave me an odd look that I couldn't interpret—"we'll have to revive its power."

The thought flickered: Did Patsy and the Broken Heart Council know about Shamhat? The founders of the Consortium had certainly been around during that first thousand years of vampire history. Yet nothing had ever been said. Not even Lorcan, who was the official scribe of vampire lore, had ever mentioned it in his texts.

Unease slid through me. Why would that information be kept secret? I mean, how hard was it to say, "Oh, yeah, we had another Family, but they died out." And no one had ever mentioned Lilith before, either. I mean, maybe the other Turn-bloods didn't need to know, but what about me? I was the freaking demon hunter. Had they known she'd return again to wreak havoc?

Who all knew about Astria's prophecy? At this point, I just didn't want to know it. I thought about Danny, about how everything had changed, not just because Connor mated with me (and lied, let's not forget), but also because there seemed to be a larger destiny for me. I had a role to play in a cosmic drama. I was not thrilled about this, not a bit, but I couldn't walk away from it.

"I missed the connection with Amahté," I said. "And the sorta-dead thing for Shamhat."

"Dude was powerful," said Larsa. "Even before he was Turned. He could leave his body and travel into the Underworld. That ability, and being an Ancient, gave him the power to retrieve Shamhat's soul. But her body needed some serious healage."

"So everyone believed she'd died. And he went to ground with her. To protect her. Isn't three thousand years long enough to heal grievous injuries?"

"Yep," said Larsa.

Larsa's green gaze kept assessing me, and finding me wanting. I got the strange feeling she kept hoping I would measure up and was disappointed that I did not. I couldn't stand it, so I looked at the little girl, aka demon, curled in her lap. Jennifer kept her prim hands folded. In her pink dress, she looked like strawberry frosting dropped onto a white cake. Larsa, however, didn't look sweet or soft.

"Khenti opened a casino resort in Las Vegas

designed to look like an Egyptian temple," said Larsa, who apparently was the boss of everything. (Me? Bitter? Why do you ask?)

"I know," I said impatiently. "Everyone knows. Tourists go there because of the attached museum. It's the biggest display of ancient artifacts in the world. Amahté's sarcophagus is on display there."

"But he's not. Neither is Shamhat."

Like tumblers clicking together in a complex lock, my thoughts snapped together and unlocked information that stunned me all over again.

When the Consortium first rolled into town, there had been talk about an archeological dig in the Sudan. At the time, we'd been told the Consortium was looking for the source of the Taint. The disease had flared up every now and then throughout undead history, but the modern-day version had taken them by surprise.

"They were looking for Amahté," I said weakly. "In the Sudan."

"Nobody knows who moved them, or where they are. And the Consortium isn't the only one looking."

I remembered that, too, because some vampires had died on the dig, staked out in the desert to await the sunrise. I shivered.

Then I considered Connor's words and realized we had a big issue. "Won't all eight vampire lines have to reinstate the magic?"

"Yep," said Larsa.

"The queen has only seven of the powers. How do you propose we get the eighth one? Go find the amazing almost-dead couple that's been missing for three millennia?"

"I'm from the Family Shamhat," said Larsa.

Shocked, I stared at her, my mouth open.

She frowned. "That's rather unattractive."

I snapped my mouth shut. "Are there more of you?"

"No," she said, and she lost her lazy grin. "I was the last. Lilith hacked off my mother's head and nearly severed mine." She fingered the scar on her neck, one that had never completely healed because she shouldn't have survived it. I wasn't sure how I felt about Larsa, hadn't decided whether or not I liked her, but she had my respect. "When Amahté pulled back her soul and returned her life, however feeble, it revived me. But none of the others. At least, none that I've ever been able to find." She shrugged. "It took a long time to heal. By the time I was recovered enough to dig out from my grave, more than a hundred years had passed. Everyone believed me dead, and I let them think so."

And the info bombs kept dropping. Shamhat had been Larsa's mother. All of the Ancients, as in the original founding vampires of all the lines, had turned at least one of their biological children.

"Yes," said Larsa. "I am the last of my Family line. We have that in common, Phoebe."

"What?"

Surprise flared in her gaze and she looked at Connor. I didn't like his expression. "Connor?"

"We must go," said Astria, her pleasant voice sounding strange—as if she were shouting into a canyon and having the echo returned tenfold.

I glanced at her and reared back. Her eyes were white, her hands in the air, fingers plucking at strings of light. It was as if she were making a pattern, determining information from a yarn experiment gone wrong.

"Lilith's followers have stolen a charmed one. Ella Freeman is important to this world, and she must live."

Her hands stopped manipulating the sparkling gold strands, and they faded into nothingness. Her arms drifted down to her thighs and she blinked.

Her violet gaze went around the room. She got up, and I noticed she was shaking. Anise handed her a Milky Way and Astria nibbled on it. Anise looked up. "She needs the sugar after an experience."

I imagined she needed a therapist, too, but what did I know?

"What's a charmed one?" I asked Connor.

"Humans with latent magic. Usually starts manifestin' when they hit puberty," he said.

"Ella is thirteen," said Astria. "It appears she is a telekinetic."

I blinked. "A what?"

"She can move things with her mind," said

Larsa impatiently. "Lilith's trying to come through again. Let's go stop that bitch."

Everyone else started getting up.

"What about the talisman?" I asked as Connor helped me to my feet. "Don't we have to find the other half and go to Broken Heart and get the woogy-woo done?"

"Woogy-woo?" he asked, his eyebrows going up.

"You know what I mean!"

"Stay here, then," said Larsa. She plopped a kiss on top of Jennifer's head. Then she looked at me scornfully. "It's not as if you need to go. And we don't need someone around who's so worried about herself she can't focus on rescuing the girl."

No one defended me against her vitriol, not even me. Because she was right: I wanted to be finished with this little adventure; I wanted to be free of this destiny crap. Maybe I'd thought I'd see it through, but . . . damn it, I *was* acting cowardly. I was not a coward, but I was definitely being whiny. Still, I was getting tired of the machinations of men and immortals. Why did they have to make everything so freaking complicated?

I caught Astria staring at me. She smiled. "You were dragged into a situation created not because you chose it, but because of what you are," she said. "Believe me when I say that I know what that's like. Unfortunately, destiny sometimes takes precedence over personal choice."

"No shit," I said, but without any rancor. She smiled again and drifted away.

Connor touched my arm and asked, "Do you want to stay?"

"Can I shoot her?" I asked, jerking a thumb over my shoulder at Larsa.

He grinned. "No, lass."

"I guess I'll go anyway."

He kissed me then, and the brush of his lips sent ripples of pleasure right through me.

I got the feeling he was going to be difficult to give up.

"Where are we going?" I asked.

"She's at the Knights Inn in Tulsa," said Astria.

"That place is abandoned and way creepy. We'll meet on Peoria at the diner," said Larsa, "go over a plan there. We got time?"

"It's a dawn ceremony," said Astria.

Larsa nodded. "Let's go."

Everyone moved away from the furniture in preparation for transporting.

Jennifer tugged on my hand. "No one who worships Lilith is innocent," she said. I didn't know if she meant to comfort me or warn me. "She appeals to the darkness that already splinters a wounded soul."

The red lights popped and spun. This time, Jennifer manifested as a young black woman dressed in a pink jogging suit and Nikes. Her hair was an explosion of corkscrew curls, some neon orange.

She put a hand on her cocked hip. "Good luck, baby cakes."

"Thanks." I went with Connor and stood among the others. "Your sister?"

"Has to stay here," he said softly. "She's . . . unpredictable around humans."

"I like her," I said.

He grinned. "Me, too. An' she's worth savin'."

Damn straight. Just like Lilith was worth sending so deep into the Pit she'd never crawl out again. I couldn't comprehend anyone paying tributes to Lilith, much less gutting someone in her name. I'd seen plenty of death and destruction since becoming a vampire. I envied humans who remained unaware of the paranormal world. But even without knowing about werewolves or vampires, humans could create their own kind of despair and ruin. What kind of dark hearts had Lilith culled from the human population? How long had it taken her to make them spill blood for her?

"C'mon, Scry," said Connor. The Chihuahua had appeared from the kitchen, and maybe it was just me, but he looked a little fatter. The dog ran and jumped, and Connor scooped him up and put an arm around me.

"Ready?" Larsa was alone, and Anise and Ren had their arms around Astria. I wondered who among those three had the ability to transport.

Everyone nodded.

The world fell away. I think I was actually getting used to the pitching sensation, the soft implosion of my flesh. Then I felt a shift, a breaking apart of our energies, and I spun away from Connor's connection.

Aw, crap.

Chapter 16

I spiraled into a soft, endless blackness. Panic screeched through me.

Then the darkness peeled back and my atoms slammed together, and *boom!* I landed on a pile of squishy objects, my boot clanging against a hard metallic surface.

The stench was so bad my eyes started watering. It was dark as a cave where I was lying, although above me, I could see a buzzing light attached to a brick wall.

"Phoebe!" Connor peered over the green edge of the container, and that was when I realized I was in a Dumpster. I heard Scrymgeour yipping, his tiny claws scratching on the other side.

"Son of a bitch," I muttered. I tried to lever myself up, but my hand dove into something cold and slimy. "Oh, gross!"

Connor leaned over and held out a hand. "What happened?" he asked.

"I don't know!" I levered up on my elbow and slapped my defiled hand against Connor's. He grimaced, but didn't say anything. He pulled me to my feet and kept his hold firm while I ungracefully extracted myself from the garbage.

"You let go durin' transportation," he accused me. "That's dangerous."

"I did not," I said. "Maybe you let go of me."

His eyebrows rose, his gaze suspicious. "Dinnae do it again," he said. "Or you might end up in a wall."

"I didn't let go, Connor."

"Neither did I."

"Whatever!"

"Maybe someone broke the bond," he said. "Someone trying to snatch you."

"Like Lilith?"

He nodded, looking both worried and frustrated. Great—the Queen of Evil was trying to demon-snatch me. Or not. We couldn't be sure.

I looked around. We were in the back parking lot of a restaurant. The greasy smells that I could discern beyond the stink of the garbage suggested an all-night diner that served anything fried and slathered in butter. This must be the diner Larsa had mentioned. I wondered why she called it "the diner," and realized they'd been hanging around for a while. Maybe waiting for Connor to fulfill his mission. She'd said Peoria, which was the street that ran through Brookside in Tulsa. And I recognized the Knights Inn reference, too.

"How long have your friends been skulking around Tulsa?"

"For as long as I was skulkin' around Broken Heart," he said.

I ignored the frostiness of his tone.

Not many cars were in the lot, and those that were probably belonged to the people who worked the late shift. My vampire senses told me sunrise was three hours away, maybe less.

I brushed off my pants and straightened my clothes. When I went to rub my backside, I touched the edge of something thick and crusted.

"Ew!" I peeled it off and it glopped onto the concrete. I turned and looked at the remnants of a pizza. I looked over my shoulder at Connor, who was looking at my ass—and not in an "oh, sexy" kind of way. "Well?" I demanded.

"It's a mess," he said. "There's sauce . . . and stuff."

"*Stuff?*"

"You don't want to know."

I faced him. "Work your mojo," I said, trying not to get hysterical about whatever was still clinging to my jeans. "New clothes. Hurry!"

He shook his head. "I'm a demon."

"I'm aware," I said. "Make with the magic."

"My power is my own in hell, but it's bound on the earthly plane."

Remnants of Demon 101 floated in my mind. Demons were powerful creatures, very much so, but their nature was to destroy. In their own realm, it didn't matter how they used their magic, but earth was the realm of the gods, and the majority of Pit dwellers' magic worked best if bargains were made. Transport spells were different. Demons could pop anywhere they wanted.

The reminder was as painful as falling into a pit of rusty spikes: The whole time Connor had been with me in Broken Heart, he'd been dishonest, but had not used his powers. Unless I counted seduction (which I did). Yet this time, when I thought about what he'd done, I felt sadness more than fury, though I still had wisps of that, too.

"How long have you known about the prophecy? About my part in it? About your part in it?"

"When my mother told me," he said. "A couple of weeks before I moved to Broken Heart to . . . see you. She took me to Astria."

"And you just believed that girl?"

"I believed my mother. And yes, Astria, too."

I strode to him. His nostrils flared, because I smelled like old food and rotting meat. Even though I knew I stank as if I'd just rolled out of a Dumpster, his reaction hurt my feelings. Embarrassment flooded my cheeks with phantom heat.

"It's not fair," I said, "to be dragged into a situation fraught with deceptions. You should've come to me and told me the deal. I would've helped you."

Connor gave me a disbelieving look, and I felt cut by it. Then I wondered, *Would I have helped?* I didn't like the idea that some whim of the universe had given me a role to play without my permission. I valued having choices, and mine had been taken from me.

"Lilith would've killed you without my protection. My father made her a sealed bargain that she would never harm me or mine."

"Yeah. I get why, I do, but that doesn't mean it was a forgivable act."

He flinched, and because I was petty and mean, I thought, *Good.*

He looked away from me, a muscle ticking in his jaw. I heard a whisper in my mind: *Do I mean nothing to her? Was Astria wrong?*

"What else did Astria tell you?"

"It dinnae matter," he said, his lips thinning. His resentful gaze burned through me. "Ye're so uneducated about your gifts, Phoebe. It's a wonder ye've survived as long as ye hae."

For a second, his barb hit a nerve, and I reeled from the pain of it. Then I realized his accent had gone thick, which was an indication of high emotion, even when everything else about the man suggested he was as cold inside as an Oklahoma winter.

I put away my hurt and narrowed my gaze. "Don't change the subject." I didn't care about the fury whipping through Connor's gaze or the way his hands fisted. "Well?"

"She said you would love me," he said bitterly. "When none could. I'm half demon, Phoebe. What heart could love mine?"

For a moment, my throat was so dry, I couldn't respond. Then I reached out, but he looked at me with such disgust that I dropped my hand.

"The others are waitin'. We have a girl to rescue."

"We should call the police."

"You really dinnae understand how this works, do you? Astria says we must do it. If we try to circumvent her vision, it goes badly for all of us. Most especially for Ella."

"I don't understand. Everyone's always going on about how she's never wrong."

"She's the strongest Vedere psychic ever born," he said. His gaze drilled holes into me. "And she's never wrong. If we dinnae rescue Ella, she will die in the dawn ceremony. Would you do any less for Danny?"

His question stopped me cold. I would do anything for my child, especially when it came to his well-being. And if it were my child, I'd do the exact same thing. But Danny was safe with his father in Florida, far away from the danger here. It occurred to me right then, in the suck-ass way that so many aha realizations so often did, that Danny would always be in danger because of what I was. Not just vampire, but demon hunter. With burdens that were mine alone to carry. Raising Danny in Broken Heart had been selfish. He was my baby boy, and I loved him more than I loved anything else on this earth.

"He'd have a normal life," I whispered, "with

Jackson." Human parents. A life lived in the sunlight. Why had it taken me so long to realize that Danny would be better off with Jackson? How many lies had I told—had Broken Heart told—to keep our secrets? It suddenly made perfect sense: Danny should live with Jackson. Wasn't he dating a kindergarten teacher? Maybe they'd marry, and then Danny would have a human mother, too. He was only four years old; his memories of me would fade.

I knew it was the right thing to do. When this was over, when it was all over, I'd give my son to his father. I'd walk away so Danny could have the life he deserved. Not living in the dark, not being raised by a vampire, not growing up with a warped sense of reality. Pain cobwebbed inside me, trapping me with silky tendrils of truth.

I looked at Connor, because I couldn't stand to look inside myself anymore.

Connor's gaze flickered, and I realized he was in my head with me. Even after I couldn't give him the one thing Astria had promised. And oh, God, my heart ached with the idea that he'd done everything because he thought I would love him.

Love makes us do really stupid things, Phoebe. My mother liked to brush my hair at night and talk to me in whispers, sharing secrets. I was fifteen and my father had been dead a year. It was before Momma had gotten bad, waking up with nightmares, screaming at shadows. I was getting impatient with this ritual because I was, after all, growing up.

I'd told her I couldn't wait to fall in love. And she smiled so sadly. "Love is a wonderful thing," she said. "It makes you feel like you can fly, like you can conquer the whole world. It can give you everything, and take it all, too."

Momma understood deeply the sacrifice love often asked for to honor its name, its cause. She'd been wounded by it in a way I never had, because I'd never fallen in love. Yes, I loved my child, but he was mine. I'd never had to take another, never had to conquer a heart and claim it.

And was that what Connor had done for me?

Love. And sacrifice.

"It's not the time to make decisions about Danny," he said softly. He cocked an eyebrow at me and crossed his arms. "You makin' a bargain or not?"

"For what?" I asked dully. Then I blinked. "What?"

"I can't just give the clothes to you. My powers are bound. Unless we make a bargain, I canna provide anything for you."

I considered my clothing and the cloying stench. Bargain for clothes? Really? Still, I was mired in thoughts about Danny. I couldn't help it. *He's better off,* whispered my oh-so-helpful conscience; *let him have the life he deserves.* I wanted to wail. I loved him more than anything.

I'd been so selfish. I realized that now. I thought

about the other children in Broken Heart. Most of them had both parents living in town. Or they were paranormal themselves. Patsy's ex-husband, Sean, had passed away from liver cancer. Her son, Wilson, was twenty now, and training with Rand and Ralph to be a dragon handler.

But Danny was young, so young. He had a choice. One I had nearly taken from him because I didn't want to give up being a mommy. He'd be the only child I'd ever have.

"Phoebe." Connor pulled out a phone from his pocket. "Call your boy. Hear his voice. And stop worryin' about whether or not you get to keep him. Love is not always about sacrifice."

"Stay out of my head." It was an automatic demand, and I didn't think that I really meant it anymore. "It's what? Three a.m.? I can't call Jackson and ask to talk to my kid. If I did, he'd think something was wrong. Or that I was drunk."

Connor sighed and put away the phone. "Then you call him before you go to sleep."

"Yeah, okay. They're early risers."

I trembled inside, feeling as though my innards were cracking and flaking away. If I weren't careful, I would crumble. I needed to be strong to get through the next couple of days.

"In exchange for my services, I want . . ." Connor paused.

"What?"

"Sex."

Startled, I snapped my gaze to Connor's.

Scrymgeour was behind me, gnawing on the icky pizza, making growling sounds as if he were trying to kill it first.

"Excuse me?" I pretended to clean out my ears. "I thought you said you wanted sex."

He grinned. "Just seein' if you were payin' attention. A kiss, fair Phoebe, for a set of clean clothes."

"Fine," I said.

He cupped my face and gently brushed his lips across mine. It was such a kind gesture, one I didn't deserve when I'd been nothing but cruel. *This is love*, said my mother's voice, *because love never turns away.*

Chapter 17

Connor looked at me with a terrible longing, and I felt a similar yearning unfurl within me. Oh, no. I'd hit the edge of the precipice, and if I wasn't careful, I'd tip over. And fall. And fly.

Connor stepped back and aimed his fingers at me. Red magic weaved around me, and soon I was wearing another pair of clean black jeans. My top had changed to black as well, and my short-waisted jacket now had silver accents. My weapons were still well hidden.

"If the world were simple, lass," said Connor softly, "and I had choices still, all I would want is you. No denyin' that the prophecy is why I sought you, an' I'm glad for it. I'm glad for you."

The horror of what he said was that I knew it was true. It rang clear in his words, in his expression, and in my own fickle heart.

It broke me.

I turned blindly and strode away. He didn't

follow me, and I was relieved. I liked having my nervous breakdowns alone.

I didn't want Connor to have an honest emotion, because then I would have to admit my own feelings, which weren't all anger and loss and lust. There was tenderness, and understanding, and want, and . . . argh!

I thought of Danny, and of Connor. One I loved because he was my child, and the other . . . Oh, I couldn't profess to love Connor. I wanted him. He made me ache in a way no other man ever had.

I didn't know why my feelings were so intertwined, so confused. My father was long dead, and my mother had taken her life. Even Aunt Alice had passed away last spring, even though we hadn't done much more than exchange Christmas cards since my mother died. Briefly, Jackson had been mine, and then finally I had a forever person, or so I had thought when my son was born.

I'd clung to him because he was mine. The one thing I would never have to give up or lose.

Had I been wrong, or what?

I walked down the sidewalk, past the diner with its tired green sign and sooty yellow building. I stopped at the end of the sidewalk, considering which way to cross. I leaned against the telephone pole, my gaze falling onto a crisp "Missing" poster. The girl in the photo was thirteen and had gone missing yesterday. She had long brown hair and thickly lashed blue eyes. She wore a billowy gold shirt in a style that seemed too old for her, and a sparkly butterfly barrette that seemed too young. In this photo, she was forever caught between what she'd been and what she would become.

It should've been no surprise that this was the face of Ella Marian Freeman. She'd last been seen outside her middle school. Somewhere between leaving school and the bus line, she'd disappeared.

Nowhere was safe.

Except maybe Disney World.

"Lass."

I turned around, not exactly startled, since I knew Connor wouldn't let me go far. "You're like a demonic GPS."

Connor stood behind me, hands in his pockets, his expression inscrutable. Scrymgeour sniffed the telephone pole, then lifted his leg and peed on it.

"Would it make a difference if I said to stay out of my head?"

"Not really," he said. "You have a strong mind."

"Or you have a weak will." The moment I said the words I wanted to call them back. There wasn't a weak thing about Connor, not his will, his body, or his attitude.

He surprised me by nodding. "I'm weak," he admitted. "Especially around you."

"Gee, thanks."

He brushed his knuckles across my cheek. I

couldn't stand the gentleness of the gesture or the look in his eyes, like he'd just suffered a terrible loss.

I knew that kind of grief. And I couldn't be party to his. I stepped back, and regretted it the instant I saw the hurt flicker in his gaze. Then he, too, backed up and looked at the empty street.

Our earlier conversation floated through my mind. If it were possible, I would gladly reclaim my humanity so that I could step into the world of light again with my son. But obviously, that wasn't going to happen. Did I really want to turn my back on my new destiny? I wouldn't let my selfishness lead to failing those I loved. Not again. Momma had slit her wrists. I refused to inflict suffering on others because I couldn't handle what life had thrown at me. As Queen Patsy so often said: *Put on your big girl panties and deal with it.*

Connor was too damned stubborn to turn away from the path he'd chosen. Come hell or high water, he'd march along to the beat of Astria's drum. A believer in fate, a follower of love. I didn't have any faith, and he did.

"What the fuck are you guys doing?" Larsa marched up to us. "We don't have time for a lovers' quarrel. Astria says we gotta steal some ring thing from the Philbrook Museum of Art and give it to Ella. Goddamned prophets!"

For once, I felt a kinship with Larsa. Connor took my hand, as if it were the most natural thing in the world to do, and we followed the irritated vampire into the diner.

As bossy as Larsa was, everyone deferred to Astria. She didn't really take this for granted—not in an arrogant way, at least. She seemed to understand her purpose and spoke in a practical, this-is-just-the-way-it-is tone. Astria had no choice about her destiny, either, but she'd accepted that she was "the prophet." I argued with myself that she'd been born and raised as a psychic, not yanked from a previous existence and told, "Hey, this is what the gods want, so just shut up and do it."

I had been a single mother living and working in a small town. I'd also been killed and turned into the undead. But I was still single, still a mother, and still working in a small town. And I did demon cleanup whenever it was needed. I'd learned to fight, but not, apparently, in a way that would be entirely effective against demons, and hadn't learned to use all my Family gifts. I hadn't delved very far into them for no other reason than that I didn't think I needed to. Maybe even this was a small rebellion against the life that had been chosen for me. I felt ashamed that I hadn't bothered to learn more, to do more. The other hunters knew a lot more than I did, and that really chapped my hide.

I wondered why the hunters hadn't found us again. Maybe they would.

"So which one of you stays with Astria?" asked Larsa.

I noticed that she was looking at Astria's pile of chili fries with the same kind of longing that I was.

"If we were in Broken Heart, we could so eat that," I muttered.

Larsa slid a look at me. "That's true? About the pixie wish letting the undead eat again?"

"Oh, yeah."

We both looked at the chili fries again.

"Anise stays," said Astria, popping another fry into her mouth.

"Fine. Ren and I will go to the museum and pick up the ring," said Larsa. "We're on Fifty-first and Peoria. It's down a few miles. The Knights Inn is closer. Connor, you and Phoebe go get Ella." She tossed a look at me. "Think you can handle that, cupcake?"

"Sure, butter nips," I said. "How about you?"

She wasn't offended. In fact, a smile darted across her lips. "Some people don't think you have the skills, is all."

"Well, some people think you don't have the ability to shut up," I said. "We all have our little flaws."

Larsa grinned.

I'd never been in the Knights Inn before. It had been shut down for years. However, as a human, I'd gone to the Philbrook Museum of Art many times. It had once been one of my favorite places to visit, but never as a vampire with breaking and entering on her mind. Astria had said the ring was important to Ella, but didn't really explain why.

I had also suggested that we contact Queen Patsy or even just Damian to bring in some help from Broken Heart. Everyone was against it, mostly because they didn't know anyone there, or their intentions (my opinion didn't count). Connor pointed out that the hunters had learned our location because they seemed to be in collusion with the council. I didn't agree, but I didn't have proof, either. Astria ended the debate by saying, "It is not time." Everyone accepted this vague comment, and I had no choice but to do the same.

Astria also didn't tell us why we had to get the ring tonight. I'd already asked about getting it later and making sure the girl got it after she was safe, but Astria was adamant. Also, I was the only one arguing with her.

"The less magic we use, the better," said Larsa. "We don't want the hunters showing up. Those guys are too uptight, especially Nicor. And they're still pissed off we took their half of the talisman."

"The inn's a brisk walk for us," said Connor.

"I'll appropriate a car for me and Ren," said Larsa. She looked delighted at the prospect of committing grand theft auto.

I idly wondered if that was a skill I should acquire as well. Hmm. I found myself wanting to learn more. I wanted to work on increasing my powers, my knowledge, and my fighting abilities.

I knew how to use my Glock, how to do hand-to-hand fighting, how to throw my knives. I wasn't a total pussy. Still, in this company, I felt like the weakest link.

I flicked a glance at Astria. "Do you know how to fight?"

Her eyes widened. "Not really."

"She doesn't need to know how to fight," said Anise.

"Why not?" I asked. "Afraid she'll ruin her manicure?"

Larsa muttered, "Nice one." And Astria giggled.

"We are her guardians." Her tone said, *End of discussion.*

I don't know why I couldn't drop the subject. Maybe because learning to fight was an opportunity for Astria to actually make a choice for herself. I was totally sympathetic to exercising some free will here. And Astria was looking at me as if I were somehow her champion. I wondered how often anyone ever asked her what she wanted. *Really* wanted.

"I think she should learn to fight," I said. "If you and Ren die, what happens to her?"

"We won't," said Anise. I noticed that Ren was giving me the evil eye. Did the guy never talk?

"They won't," echoed Astria. "I have foreseen it."

"Do *you* want to learn to fight?"

Astria used a fry to make a pattern in the chili

sauce. Then she lifted her chin. "Yes," she said, "I do."

"Okay. Connor's gonna train me," I said. "You can join us." I looked at Connor. "Right?"

"'Twould be my honor."

Anise and Ren shot twin (*ha*) looks of annoyance at me.

"We will discuss this at another time," said Anise.

Astria looked disappointed, and I figured it was because Anise's words sounded more like, *You will learn to fight over my dead body.*

"Definitely," I said. "We'll discuss when and where the lessons will begin."

"Thank you," said Astria. She smiled at me, almost shyly. "It is time. Go forth, Phoebe, and win another battle."

Chapter 18

We left Anise and Astria in the diner. Larsa and Ren took off toward the parking lot.

"Don't you find it weird that we're off to rescue the victim of Lilith's cult and some Sumerian ring? I can't help but feel anxious about the talisman. Where is it?"

"Safe."

"Connor, I'm getting really tired of nonanswers."

Scrymgeour, who'd been waiting outside for us, whined pitifully. I squatted down to scratch his ears. I felt like a bitch for thinking of Ella as a roadblock to fixing my own problems instead of a scared little girl at the mercy of crazy demon worshipers. I felt as if I were trapped in an episode of *Unsolved Mysteries*.

I straightened, and Scrymgeour tilted his head, giving me a wounded look.

"All right," I said. "Let's go get Ella."

We headed toward the I-44 freeway. I was glad

to be stretching my legs even though vampires didn't require exercise. Besides, I really didn't want to have to deal with Nicor and his bunch; especially if everyone was right about the hunters being able to track magic signatures. Just on the other side of the freeway I saw the large neon sign of a castle. THE KNIGHTS INN gleamed red underneath it.

We didn't talk much on the way there. Scrymgeour followed us. Every so often the Chihuahua would dart away, chasing things I couldn't see, and return looking satisfied. I didn't sense any demon activity, so he could've been eating bugs and rats for all I knew. Blech.

When we arrived at the edge of the rusted fencing, I peered at the scraggly grass poking up through the cracked blacktop. The building was shaped like a castle, its paint made to look like stonework. It was obvious it had been empty for a while. And it definitely had that hollow feeling of something forgotten.

"Why do they leave the sign on?" I asked.

"Who knows," said Connor. "We can get in through the underground garage."

"How do you know about that?" I asked suspiciously.

"I'm psychic."

"Har-de-har."

He laughed, then pointed at the side of the building. Above a dark tunnel was a rusted sign: EMPLOYEE PARKING.

Connor scooped up Scrymgeour and wrapped an arm around my waist. Then, with one powerful push of his legs, we rose into the air and went over the fence. He landed with ease, letting me go as soon as my feet hit the ground.

"I could do that myself, you know," I said.

"Yeah, but I'll take any excuse I can get to put my arm around you."

"Smooth talker."

It didn't take long to make the journey across the weed-filled, cracked outside parking lot.

Our footsteps echoed in the tunnel that led to the underground parking. Even with my vampire vision, I couldn't make out much, although it smelled dank and dusty. When we were far enough inside, Connor touched my elbow. I paused. "What?"

"*Solas*," whispered Connor. Red orbs burst from his palm and floated above us, lighting our way.

"You can do fairy lights?" I asked, amazed. I'd seen other Sidhe create them. They were so pretty.

"It's not difficult magic. I'm half Ghillie Dhu, remember?"

A Scottish fairy, a protector of trees, a cavorter in nature. I couldn't reconcile Connor with such images. But imagining him as a demon was easy. I didn't know if that reflected something about Connor—or about me.

The tunnel ended and we entered the parking structure. The red orbs danced around us. We stepped onto a sidewalk, and I studied a metal door that probably led up into the hotel.

"Are we going back to Jennifer's?" I asked.

"No," he said. "And we canna risk Broken Heart, either. You thinkin' this might be a good place to sleep?"

I was, sorta. Then again, I wasn't sure hanging out in the same place where a bunch of kidnapping murderers had occupied the space was necessarily a good idea. I might not have a choice, though. Dawn was creeping ever closer. I realized that I'd have to trust Connor to watch over me, or stay with me, if I did go toes-up in vampiric rest.

"Definitely sunproof," I said. "But nothing to sleep on." I wondered if the hotel had any sheets or blankets left, and if they did, if they were even worth using as covers. Who knew what crawled among the abandoned relics of this place?

"We must be careful about the magic," he said apologetically.

"I remember," I said. "Asking you to whip up a bed would be like setting off a demon alarm." Then I glanced pointedly at the red lights dancing above his head.

"I told you. That's not demon magic."

How could it not be? It might've been something he learned as a Ghillie Dhu, but wouldn't it still be a beacon to the ones who hunted us?

Connor wouldn't jeopardize us, and I was surprised that I trusted him. At least for now.

"I think we should separate," he said. "You

check the lower floors, and I'll start on the roof and work my way down."

"What?" I couldn't explain my reluctance to be parted from him. Maybe it was the bond solidifying, or maybe it was the flare of foreboding I couldn't shake off.

"Afraid of the bogeyman?"

"You are the bogeyman."

"And you're the one who sucks the bogeyman's blood."

"I don't feel like the late-night-horror-flick villain," I groused.

"Maybe you should practice more."

I laughed.

"If you need me," he said, "use our connection." He tapped his temple.

Connor believed I would love him, but he hadn't yet said a word about loving me. That I had even entertained this idea made me feel like I'd fallen into a dark, cold pool of water. I didn't know what the right thing to do was, not really. How much was my choice? How much was dancing to the tune of a prophecy that Astria still had not revealed to me?

Ella first, I thought. *Then the rest.*

Connor dropped a kiss onto my forehead, which startled me. It smacked of spousal affection. "Scrymgeour will stay with you."

The Chihuahua whined.

"Now, lad, we talked about this. When I'm not here, you'll protect our lady."

That was the second time Connor had called me his lady, and it had an old-fashioned feel that I liked.

Scrymgeour dutifully *tiptiptipped* to me and then sat, his sad eyes on his master.

Connor directed the fairy lights to me. With one last quick smile, he turned and headed toward the exit tunnel. I waited until I couldn't hear the ring of Connor's boots on the concrete before I turned toward the metal door.

"Let's go look around, Scry," I said.

The hellhound yipped at my heels as I pulled open the door and headed up a concrete staircase. The door at the top of the stairs gave way with a hard shove. The lights revealed a hallway with doors open on each side, and another set of stairs at the end.

Two of the doors led to restrooms, one to a break room with empty vending machines and rusted lockers, and the last to an office with listing file cabinets and a black metal desk. It smelled even mustier here, the sense of abandonment so strong I wanted to leave. It was almost like stumbling into a forgotten cemetery.

Still, without Connor to stand with me, or at least tease me until I forgot to be scared, I hesitated on the second set of stairs.

Scrymgeour, however, had no problem bounding up the steps. He got to the top and barked.

"You are so bossy," I said as I climbed up to join

him. I opened the door, and we went through, the fairy lights following us.

Scrymgeour went off exploring, his claws scoring the dusty red carpet. We were behind the oversized check-in counter that stretched the length of lobby. The lights revealed scattered papers, blank monitors, and boxes of card keys. I went in the direction of the hellhound, still feeling uneasy about this place.

The place was massive. The lobby led into a bar that still held its pretty display of dusty liquor bottles behind black marble countertops. Tables had been turned over, chairs broken. I didn't doubt the occasional person had broken in here to wreak havoc or do drugs or hide out, but it seemed the Knights Inn had been abandoned for so long, even the troublemakers had gotten bored with the novelty of it.

I found Scry digging in a turned-over trash can near the bank of elevators. The elevator doors were painted to look like wrought iron, the kind you might see in a castle's dungeons. I grinned. I imagined what this place must've been like when it was open; it had the kind of cheesy atmosphere that made people enjoy it.

Even though poking around the musty old place still made the hairs rise on the nape of my neck, I thought I was falling a little in love with it.

I heard a bang, and an, "Oh, shit!" I turned

around and saw two tiny blond women dressed in red robes scuttling behind me. So much for my vampire senses. I'd been so busy nosing about the hotel, I hadn't heard them creep up. One held a long, thin, bejeweled object that might've been a staff except it was too short.

"You are such a fucking klutzoid, Drusilla," said the one holding the glittering pole. She swiped it at me.

I ducked and backed up. Scry rushed to my side and growled.

"Look at the puppy, Mita! Isn't she adorable! C'mere, puppy. C'mere!" Her empty gaze wandered to the lights bobbing around me. "What are those?"

"Who fucking cares!" The one called Mita took another ineffectual swipe at me and I backed away.

"What are you doing?" I asked. I was more annoyed than scared.

"I'm trying to hit you. Duh."

I zipped past her using vampire speed, stopping when I was in the bar, and whirling to face the crazy girls. They both stared at me with open-mouthed astonishment. Why were they wearing such weird clothes? The crushed-velvet robes were bloodred and covered them from neck to feet. They had to be sweating buckets.

Scry bounded past them and sat next to me. He barked, just once, to let them know who was boss.

"How the fuck did you do that?" asked Mita. "Did you fucking see that? Fucking A!"

"Dude." Druscilla nodded.

"You two are such twits!" The irritated female voice came from behind me. I didn't get a chance to turn around, because something heavy whacked me across the base of my skull.

I saw sparkles dance before my eyes, and then I fell straight into a pit of darkness.

Chapter 19

When I woke up, I realized two things: One, I was on my side, bound to something cold and flat. Two, I faced someone else with tearful blue eyes. Her oval face and brown hair were familiar.

Ella.

"Are you okay?" she whispered. Her face was dirty, and tear tracks were evident in the grime. Her lips were crusted and chapped, probably from the way she was currently nibbling on her lower lip.

"I'm really getting tired of people smacking me around," I answered. "Where's my dog?"

"I d-didn't see a dog."

"Everything's gonna be okay," I said. I sounded more grim than reassuring. I could just imagine how much Larsa would enjoy my being trapped by two ditzy girls and whoever whacked me over the head. I felt like a freaking idiot. "What are we strapped down with?"

"Duct tape."

"Classy."

She offered a quivering smile.

"You're Ella, right?"

"How'd you know? Are you here to get me?" Then she blinked, and the hope in her gaze crumbled. "Oh. You didn't get captured 'cause of me, did you?"

"No, honey. Don't you worry, though. We're getting outta here."

"Probably not in the way you plan," said the same irritated female who'd bashed in my head.

She came around the table, or whatever the hell we were taped to (duct tape, really? Talk about your unimaginative abductor) and leaned over Ella to peer at me. She wore her dark hair in a choppy cut that was highlighted with purple streaks. Both of her ears were pierced all the way around. Silver skull earrings dangled from the bottoms of her lobes. Her eyes were kohled, and unfortunately, her gaze held the keen intelligence the two blondies lacked. Her robe was also crushed velvet, but it was black. The leader, then.

"Lilith will be pleased with a double sacrifice," she said.

"S-sacrifice?" echoed Ella.

"Aw. Now I've spoiled the surprise." She patted the girl's apple-blossom cheek. "My mistress needs blood."

"More like a lobotomy," I said.

"You shouldn't say such things about the goddess of the Underworld!" she hissed. "I'll kill you first, nonbeliever!" She bent closer, her robes nearly suffocating poor, sweet Ella. "I've already killed once." Her voice held the kind of relish that suggested supreme job satisfaction. I couldn't think about the victim she'd sliced open and bled out in Lilith's name, only that she wasn't going to do the same to Ella.

"Let us go," I said, keeping my gaze on hers. I added the glamour, lowered my voice. "Cut through the tape like a good little psychotic. Tell the others we're leaving and not to bother us."

Her pupils dilated; then her eyes went dreamy. "Yes," she said. "Of course."

She unsheathed a sharp silver dagger and used it to saw through the tape binding Ella.

"Penelope!" screeched one of the blondes. Mita, maybe. "What are you fucking doing?"

Yeah, definitely Mita.

"Letting them go."

"Are you nuts? We need them for the ritual!" She removed the knife from Penelope's hand and snapped her fingers in front of her face. "Fucking A, dude!"

Penelope blinked, looking at Mita as if she'd never seen her before; then she stared down at Ella's half-severed bonds. Her crafty gaze met mine.

"I know what you are," she said. "Lilith told me about the creatures who walk the night."

"Like your boyfriend?" I asked.

She yanked the knife from Mita's hand and jabbed it deeply into my side. I hissed as pain tore through me, but I pressed my lips together to keep from crying out. Crazy Penelope probably enjoyed it when she heard her victims scream. Ella stared at me with wide eyes. I tried to convey that everything was gonna be okay, but I probably wasn't all that convincing.

"You're a vampire," cried Penelope. "And sunrise is in an hour." She grinned at me, her gaze finally showing the edge of her insanity. "You're gonna fry, bitch."

"Aw. Your mother should be so proud," I said.

Penelope screeched and jabbed the knife into my side again. Agony ripped through me, but I clenched my teeth. I guessed Penelope had mommy issues on top of everything else.

"Quit hacking her up," said Mita. "She'll be fucking dead before we can invoke our queen."

She dragged Penelope away, but not before Miss Crazy sent me a look that said, *I can't wait to carve you like a Christmas ham.*

Yeah, well, she had another think coming. I'd drain her dry before I let her throw me into the sunlight.

"You're b-brave." Ella's lower lip trembled.

"So are you," I said.

My words managed to stall her quivering lip, which she started chewing on again.

"Did it hurt when she stabbed you?"

"Oh, yeah." I grimaced. "But I heal fast."

Ella stared at me and kept gnawing her lip to bits. "Are you really a vampire?"

I'd already decided to glamour Ella. Why let her remember being abducted and talked about like a side of beef? It wouldn't hurt to be honest, since she wasn't going to remember the experience.

"Yeah," I said. "I'm a vampire."

Doubt seeped into her gaze. "I thought vampires were scary. And strong."

"We are." I sounded defensive, and for a second, she looked as though she pitied me. Then she just looked scared, and I realized I needed to get my ass in gear with the whole rescue operation.

It wasn't like they'd bound me in any magical way. Penelope and her cohorts were having a hushed convo near a table filled with food and drinks. I counted thirteen wandering souls. Twelve in red robes. Lucky thirteen. Nice. How much cheesier could this outfit get?

I could escape, but thirteen humans was a lot, even for one pissed-off vampire. And I couldn't be sure I could save Ella before the Lilith worshipers descended on me. My double wounds had begun to heal, but they still throbbed. I owed Penelope for her petty vengeance.

Phoebe!

Connor's shout reverberated in my mind and made me wince. I felt like an idiot for not remembering about the telepathy.

I'm here, I sent out. *With Lilith's cult members. What!?*

Ella's here, too. We're somewhere in the hotel. The leader is a real nut job. And I don't know what happened to Scrymgeour.

He came to get me. Why didn't you use our link, lass?

I just woke up from another head bashing.

The "again?" remained unspoken.

Sunrise's in an hour. Use your magic so I can find ye.

Won't that alert the hunters?

I dinnae care! Use your magic!

His accent had gone syrup-thick even in his thoughts, and I flinched from the mind shouting. *All right! Sheesh!*

"Do you have to go to the bathroom?" asked Ella.

"What?"

"You're making the same face my brother does when he's constipated."

I laughed, and she gave me a watery smile. It was harder to whip up demonfire with my hands bound. I was used to making the appropriate gestures to control the fire I invoked. Still, the ball of black flames appeared above us like a fiery beacon.

Got it, lass, sent Connor.

"Oh, my God!" squealed one of the red robes. "Lilith's here!"

Everyone turned to look at the pulsing demonfire. I let it float toward the group, and they scattered. I looked at Ella. Her gaze latched onto mine. She looked amazed. "You're like a magician."

"That's me, all right." I drew on my glamour and sent it into the girl. Her eyes went wide and then glazed over. "I want you to go to sleep, Ella. Sleep deeply; sleep well. When it's time to wake up, you will remember only that yesterday you missed your bus. You went to walk home, but you fell and hit your head."

Her eyes drifted closed, she took a shuddering breath, and then she was asleep. Safe. She wouldn't remember Penelope, or being taped to a table, or me.

Or the big, white demon that burst through the floor and captured my demonfire like a beach ball. He landed on the floor with a great *whump*, his wings extended for maximum effect. His roar was fierce, and I wasn't sorry at all when he lobbed my demonfire at Penelope and burned her into ash. I didn't have to ask how he knew she was my tormentor. He was embedded in my thoughts, and I found an odd comfort in knowing he was there. Not that I would ever tell him that, of course. Some thoughts were mine and mine alone.

No one else stayed to play. They screamed and stampeded toward the door, nearly trampling one another to get out. I saw now why Lilith had commanded the sacrifices: Her worshipers were too weak to call her forth. They didn't believe in her. They were just cruel, stupid people who bonded over death and destruction.

Connor stomped to the table and ripped the tape off me, yanking me into his arms. I rested my head on his scaly chest. I felt him shudder, his heartbeat frantic.

"We have to go," I said.

Connor gently released the girl from the tape. Connor carried Ella, and we returned to the parking garage. I watched over Ella while Connor returned to his human form and dressed.

"You hear from the others?"

"No," said Connor. He looked concerned.

"What about the ring? I thought it was all-fired important that we get it tonight and give to Ella."

"Mayhap Larsa and Ren ran into some problems," he said. "We dinnae have time to check. It's gettin' too close to dawn."

"Okay," I said. "We'll follow the plan."

I picked up Scry, Connor hefted the girl, and then I held on to him as we buzzed outta there. We'd already decided to go to Saint Francis, because it was the hospital closest to where Ella had disappeared, and it also had a children's hospital.

Connor and Scry waited outside while I brought the girl inside. Nurses immediately whisked her away. Then I spun a tale to the clerk about finding her unconscious behind the azalea bushes in my backyard. I fuzzed the mind of the woman taking my report so much that the words she wrote made no sense at all.

"She looks like Ella Freeman," I said softly. "The missing girl."

"Oh, my gosh!" She picked up the phone, and before she looked up again, I was gone.

I went outside and met Connor near the entrance doors.

"Sunrise's comin'," said Connor, thrusting the cell into my hand. "Call your boy."

While I dialed Jackson's cell phone number, Connor led me past the parking area for the emergency room and weaved through two parked ambulances. He entered a door marked PERSONNEL ONLY, and I followed him into the bowels of the hospital.

I got Jackson's voice mail. Disappointment mixed with longing. What was Danny doing? Was it only two days ago that Jackson had sent a picture of Danny wearing a Mickey Mouse hat and another of him next to Shrek? I wasn't sure what he'd been told by the Consortium, so I left a simple message saying I missed Danny and I would call again in the evening.

When I handed the cell back to Connor, he crushed it and dropped the mangled phone into a garbage can we passed. I had no idea how he knew how to navigate the narrow halls, with their windings and turns, but before I knew it, we were standing in front of a set of double doors.

I looked at the word stenciled on the frosted glass, then turned to glare at him. "The morgue? Seriously?"

"It will be safe."

"We really need to discuss the dictionary definition of 'safe,' Connor. I don't want to get an accidental autopsy because I'm snoozing in a cold storage drawer."

He drew one finger down my neck. "I'd hate to see your pretty skin marred."

"Sunrise," I said. That simple touch shot through me like an electric shock.

"C'mon, then." He pushed through the doors, and I followed because I didn't have a choice. At least there were no windows down here. It had been a hell of a night, starting with a conquered demon and ending with a rescued sacrifice.

I'd have to give Connor one thing: He wasn't boring.

He led me down to another level, which I assumed was another parking structure, but it was just a series of storage rooms.

"I get the feeling you've been here before," I said.

"Once." He led me into a room that had several hospital beds, some with mattresses and others just frames, along with teetering piles of boxes. It smelled like dust and stale cigarette smoke.

As I worked a couple of the beds free and rolled them against a wall, Connor melted the handle of the door. Nobody would be getting in, even with a key. While he and Scry prowled through the other end of the room, I found a set of sheets in an opened cabinet. They'd probably been freshly laundered sometime in the 1980s, but the exhaustion of vampire nighty-night was weakening me, so I didn't much care.

I poked at the plastic-lined mattresses. They smelled like old urine. I tossed the sheets over and tucked them around, then clambered onto mine.

"Guard us well, Scrymgeour," said Connor. The Chihuahua barked, then sat in front of the door and watched it carefully.

My Scottish warrior strode toward me, stripping off his T-shirt. I looked at his scarred, muscled chest, then up at him. "What are you doing?"

"Gettin' naked for my wife."

My heart stuttered, and then I remembered it wasn't supposed to be able to do that anymore. "Connor." His name was longing and reproach.

"Dinnae deny me this," he asked.

I swallowed the knot in my throat. "Just for now, then."

He nodded. He let me lie, to him and to myself. I'd take it. Because I couldn't think about more than that, about the way this whole thing had begun, and how it would end.

He stripped off his jeans and boots, then climbed onto the narrow bed with me. He kissed me tenderly, slowly divesting me of my clothes until I was naked, too.

We lay side by side, and I let Connor seduce me.

He kissed me, and it wasn't a gentle exploration, either. It was hard and possessive and it thrilled me in a dark, needy way.

"Mine," he said as he trailed his lips over my jaw to nibble my ear. "You're mine."

I relished the tiny, hot flicks of his tongue. Regret stole through me as his hand slid under the sheet to cup my breast.

I threaded my fingers into his hair. After a moment, I threw off my sheet and pushed him onto his back. He went easily, his gaze glittering up at me.

I kissed him, stroking down his chest, touching the hard planes, the funnels of scarring, the hair narrowing beguilingly.

I knelt between his legs and touched his hardon. He was big and thick. I squeezed the base, then settled my lips over the bulbous head.

He groaned, his hands fisting in my hair.

I alternated between sucking and flicking my tongue against the sensitive underside. I squeezed the base, stroking up. Soon, Connor was my prisoner.

Until he grabbed my shoulders and hauled me up to kiss me senseless.

Then I was his prisoner.

His hands were all over me, starting fires in my breasts, my belly, my thighs.

"Phoebe," he whispered. "Take me, lass. Make me yours."

I settled myself over him and guided his cock inside me. I didn't look away from his gaze, though I could see so easily that his passion was tempered by sorrow.

Then I was moving, moving, and his hands cupped my ass and helped with the rhythm. Neither of us lasted long. He cried out my name, and I plunged over the edge with him, collapsing onto his chest, filmed with sweat.

"Connor," I said, and my voice broke.

He held me forever, drawing patterns on my back, and whispered sweet nothings.

I fell asleep curled against him, feeling as though I belonged next to him, someone who was mine.

Chapter 20

Connor found an abandoned showering facility down the hall. There wasn't any soap or shampoo, but the warm water felt good. Without speaking, we gave each other space and made the showers quick. Connor managed to scrounge up towels, and after we dried off, we re-dressed. I braided my hair so I wouldn't have to worry about drying it, too.

I paced the room, waiting for Connor to return with another cell phone. We were trying to keep off the grid. Scry had gone off on a perimeter check, and I was alone with my thoughts.

Connor and Scry returned at the same time. He gave me the cell phone and I called Jackson's number again.

I got voice mail.

Was he not picking up because he didn't recognize the number?

"Hey, Jackson. It's Phoebe. Just wanted to check in on Danny. I'll try back later."

I didn't have the hotel number memorized, but the cell Connor had stolen had Web access. I tracked down the number via the hotel's Web site and called on the direct line.

"I'm sorry, miss," said the clerk. "Mr. Tate checked out yesterday."

"What? I thought he had a two-week stay."

"It seems Mr. Tate had a family emergency and had to cancel the rest of his vacation."

"The boy who was with him," I said, suddenly feeling choked. "He's hurt?"

"Oh, no, miss," she chirped. "His little boy was just fine. Seems there was an emergency at home." She paused as she realized she was giving information to a complete stranger. "Who are you, miss?"

I hung up.

"Phoebe?"

"Jackson took Danny; he left the hotel. Probably left Florida." I was trembling so badly, I shoved the phone into my pants pocket before I dropped it. "He would never steal Danny. That's not like him. Something must've happened."

Jackson's parents were among the humans the Consortium had relocated. They'd moved up to Maine to be near his mother's relatives, and they took cruises year-round. They were always sending Danny trinkets from their trips. Maybe something had happened to them. Jackson was an only child, and as far as I knew he wasn't particularly close to his extended family.

Had his schoolteacher girlfriend gotten into trouble?

"Phoebe?" asked Connor.

I shook my head, panic so thick inside me I felt like I might sink into the floor from the weight of it. I grabbed the phone and dialed Jackson over and over and over until he finally picked up.

"*What?*" Jackson yelled.

I was so relieved to hear his voice that I didn't take issue with his attitude. "Jackson! Where the hell are you? Why did you leave Florida?"

"I don't know who you are," he growled, "but I suggest you stop calling me."

His venomous tone stalled my voice. "W-what are you talking about?"

"Goddamn it! Who is this?"

"It's Phoebe." I felt as though I'd swallowed slivers of ice that pricked me with cold all the way to my stomach.

"Try again."

"Jackson . . ."

"I'm reporting you to the police," he said. "And they'll find you, you sick bitch."

"I won't let you take Danny. He's my son, too!"

"No," he said, his voice cracking. "He's Phoebe Allen's son. And she's dead."

Jackson hung up on me.

The cell phone slipped out of my nerveless

fingers as my gaze lifted to Connor. He swept me up, which was good, because I thought I was on my way to collapsing. My knees felt like pudding.

He sat on the bed with me on his lap and asked, "What happened?"

"You . . . you said the Consortium would come up with a story," I said, feeling a little hysterical. "You were right. They told him I'd died. What does that mean?"

"It means they believe you are dead."

I looked at him. "Why would they think that?"

"I dinnae know." He kissed me. "We'll go ask them."

I wanted to go to Broken Heart *right then* and take apart the Consortium headquarters brick by brick.

Anger pulsed through my shock, shoved away the hysteria that threatened. Then I realized this could be it. The moment I gave Danny to Jackson for good. They would believe me dead, and even though it would be tough for a while, it would give them the freedom to create a normal life. I would be a memory, hopefully cherished and remembered as fun, as laughing.

Danny could live in the sun.

"I'm so selfish," I choked out. "I don't want to let him go."

Connor had been there, in my thoughts with me, the strength I needed without even knowing it. He took my hand and kissed my knuckles.

"Danny needs his mother. Never think he'd be better off without you."

"If we survive . . ." I said. I cleared my throat. "No. As soon we save the friggin' day, we're bringing Jackson in on the secret. I won't live without my son."

Unless I had to. If things didn't work out, then it was better that Jackson already believed I was dead. That way he wouldn't have to relive it. He wasn't my lover, but he was my friend. We loved Danny, and that was bond enough.

Connor kissed my temple. "We have company, lass."

I blinked away the cobwebs of my residual shock. "What?" I looked over my shoulder. No one was in the room except Scrymgeour. He was on all fours, his gaze on the door. Outside the frosted glass pane, I saw several restless shadows. "Who?"

"Guess." He sighed. "Bad news. Anise and Ren didn't get the ring."

I rolled my eyes. "The ring Astria said they had to steal and give an abducted girl?"

"Apparently there was some sort of overnight event at the museum, a party to celebrate the last evening of a children's art camp. They couldn't go inside."

"Perfect."

It was decided we would swing by the museum, steal the Sumerian jewelry that Astria insisted Ella needed, and then go to Broken Heart and explain everything. I was so relieved we'd be headed back to town, I didn't question why everyone else seemed acquiescent.

Astria insisted on accompanying us to the Philbrook Museum of Art, and no one could dissuade her. I didn't know why we all had to go. Yesterday it had been okay for a two-person team to retrieve the item. It seemed overkill for all of us to go.

We arrived in the first-floor hallway of the original house. I didn't know how Ren managed to turn off security cameras and alarms, but he assured us we had five minutes to get in and get out.

Oversized paintings hung on the paneled walls. The place had a hushed, you're-not-supposed-to-be-here feeling.

We didn't speak. We hurried down the red carpet until our feet hit the smooth marble floor of the massive room used for the Sumerian artifacts display. Walls of thick security glass housed tools, ivory cylinder seals, spouted jars, cuneiform tablets, and other amazing details from lives already lived.

"Where is it, *ma fleur*?" asked Anise.

Astria crossed the room and went straight to a display overshadowed by a big piece of statuary. She gestured me over and pointed it out.

"It's carnelian," she said. She sounded apprehensive. "I always thought that stone looked like captured sunlight."

"They carved the whole piece out of it," I said. "That must've been work."

She nodded absently. "You are the first person I've ever met who asked me what I wanted."

"That's a shame, Astria."

"I've always been the prophet, but I've never considered my own happiness." She slanted a look at me. "I think, Phoebe, that the prophecy brought you a gift. You can choose to accept it or not."

"Connor?"

"Yes." She sighed. "I think I would've enjoyed making more choices. I wish now that I had realized I had more opportunities. Small decisions all my own—how fun that would've been."

Her tone of finality was starting to freak me out. "Honey, what's wrong?"

"That's just it. I'm never wrong," she said. Her eyes met mine. "Connor stole the talisman fragment because I told him to. He followed my vision to it . . . and to you."

"Astria," hissed Anise. "We must hurry."

We both ignored the annoyed werewolf.

"Tell me what's going on, Astria."

We stood alone at the jewelry display. Connor was closest to me, trying to give us privacy because he sensed Astria wanted it. The other three stood at the threshold of the room, waiting.

Foreboding chilled me. Astria lifted her hand and a gold beam shot out. Connor was knocked backward, off his feet. I heard shouts and running, but I couldn't take my gaze off this heart-broken little girl.

Within moments, a golden bubble surrounded us. There was no sound or movement, but I knew the others were on the other side, trying to get through.

She grinned. "They didn't know I could do that."

"It's impressive."

"The gods give us prophets a little gift," said Astria. "We know when we're going to die. I was afraid." Tears spilled out of her luminous gaze and tracked down her alabaster cheeks. "I'm only seventeen."

"You mean you've already had a vision about your death?"

She nodded. "It would be wrong to try to protect me, Phoebe. If I don't die, then the world suffers. Something shifts or changes, and not for the better."

"The world would not be better without you in it," I said.

She sobbed openly now. "You must protect Ella. She's . . . important."

"And the ring?"

"It's for you," she said. "It'll break your mating to Connor if you want."

"What?"

"It has a wish in it. Just one."

I gathered Astria into my arms and stroked her hair. I didn't think I'd ever met anyone so lonely.

Prophet or not, she should have some kind of life. She could live openly in Broken Heart, among other children with their own gifts, who were used to the paranormal. She needed it; she deserved it.

"Why did you tell the others the ring was for Ella? That we needed it last night?"

"I wanted you and Connor to be alone. I wanted you to love each other. I would've slipped it to you later and told you its purpose."

"Doesn't giving me an instant divorce go against your romantic scheme?"

"You made me realize that no one should be without a choice, no matter how small. I've followed prophecies and visions my whole life without complaint." She looked at me and frowned. "And sometimes, I really wanted to."

I laughed.

"You and Connor really are supposed to be together. I've seen it. How happy you will be. But . . . you should want him for him. Not because some stupid vision told you to marry him."

"That's why he married me."

"Maybe." She sniffled. "But I think he really does love you."

"Oh, Astria." Another thought occurred to me, one that made me go cold. "You knew we had to come here tonight, didn't you?" I pulled away just a little. "Why?"

"Because," she said miserably, "this is where I'm supposed to die."

Chapter 21

"Let's get the ring, and get the hell out of here," I said. I drew my Glock and shot the glass surrounding the jewelry display. You would've thought it was fancy bulletproof plastic or something, but no . . . not so much.

"You can't save me," cried Astria.

"Bullshit. You got a cell phone?"

She nodded and pulled it out of her back jeans pocket. I slipped the ring onto my finger and told her the number to call. I kept my Glock out, ready for anything. I hoped it worked outside the bubble. The gun was for the last resort. Maybe I was freaking out just a little.

I glanced at the four people standing outside the bubble. They had varying expressions of worry and disbelief. I hadn't asked Astria to drop the shield yet, because I wanted to call in the troops and I didn't want to freaking argue about it.

Astria Vedere wasn't gonna die tonight.

The gods could kiss my ass.

"It's ringing," she said.

I gave her the Glock, showed her how to hold it, and said, "Shoot anything that tries to harm you. By the way, do you have any idea how you're supposed to . . . you know?"

"Demons," she said.

Terrific.

Damian finally picked up. *"Ja?"*

"It's Phoebe. I'm at the Philbrook Museum of Art in Tulsa. I need help. Lots of freaking help. Except from the hunters. I really don't like those guys."

"You are not dead," he said, and I heard relief in his voice. "Why did you wait so long to call us, *Liebling*?"

"Long story," I said. "Damian. Please."

"On it." Then he hung up.

"Drop the shield," I said, stepping in front of Astria.

She did, and four pissed-off people rushed toward us. I held out my hand when Anise tried to bypass me.

"She is mine to guard!" she yelled. "You go too far."

"She's supposed to die tonight," I said. "Demons are coming."

It was as if my words called them.

Five black clouds, a cloying stink of sulfur, and then we were facing some ugly, mean bastards. Ren and Larsa went full throttle, and so did Connor. Larsa easily fought two, while her male counterparts fought one each.

The other one . . . Shit. Where'd it go?

I heard Anise cry out. I whirled around and found her sailing across the room. She crashed against a case displaying a jug, and it crashed to the floor with her. She went limp and I knew she'd been knocked out.

The Glock in Astria's pale hands shook, but she fired at its massive chest. *Good girl, Astria.*

It roared with pain as each bullet thunked into it. I whipped out one of my silver knives, jumped onto its back, and sank the dagger hilt-deep into its thick neck.

He swiped out, angry, and his claws raked through Astria's neck. Blurt spurted in a grotesque arc. She dropped the gun and fell, her eyes going wide.

"No!" I leapt off the demon as it sank to its knees. I kicked its head and knocked it to the floor. I scrambled to Astria and scooped her up. "Oh, my God."

"Told. You." She gasped. "Never. Wrong."

"Phoebe." Damian was kneeling beside me. I looked at him, my throat knotted, my eyes aching to cry. "How did you . . ." I looked up as Patrick joined him, and I realized Damian had 'ported here. No doubt he'd tracked the cell phone from which I'd called or maybe just hooked into my vampire mojo. Patrick was practically an Ancient, and half-*sidhe*. Like Connor.

I could hear the buzz of battle, but I couldn't look away from Astria. "Patrick, can you take her to Brigid? Please. She's a Vedere. She's the prophet."

"I will take her." He placed a hand on her bleeding neck, scooped her up, and sparkled away.

"You should go, too, *Liebling*," said Damian.

"Connor," I whispered. And then, *Connor*.

Damian's gaze narrowed. "He abducted you?"

"He married me."

Connor appeared, and without a word he picked me up. I was bloody and terrified for Astria. Brigid was a goddess; she could save her. "The demons are vanquished to the Pit."

"I want to go home," I said. I looked at Damian. "You told Jackson I was dead."

"Because we believed it so."

"They're not safe," I said. "Nobody's safe."

"We will see to their protection."

I pressed my face into Connor's shoulder and closed my eyes. I already felt as though my world had shifted, so I didn't even realize it when we 'ported into my house in Broken Heart.

I didn't know how we made it past the Invisi-shield, either, but I didn't care.

I called Patrick. He said Astria was under the care of his mother, and Brigid was using all of her magic to heal the girl.

Connor undressed me and put me in the shower. I washed off Astria's blood, but not my sorrow. I had to believe she would be all right.

I pulled on a pair of cutoffs and an old T-shirt, then went to the kitchen. Connor had made coffee, and I greedily drank mine. I felt guilty enjoying such a small treat when Astria fought for her life. I was so glad to be home.

"Is everyone else okay?" I asked.

"Aye. Damian promised to bring 'em all here after seein' to the cleanup of the museum. It was right of you to call your friends, Phoebe." He was staring at my ring. "We'll see that Ella gets that. It's what Astria wants."

I nodded, too chicken to tell him it was our get-out-of-marriage card. My reluctance had a lot to do with the way I felt about Connor. He was man who had faith, who had honor, who had within him the capacity for love. I wasn't sure I deserved him.

I wasn't sure about a lot of things.

I missed Danny. And I'd failed Astria. Suddenly, I didn't want to be at home anymore. I couldn't sit here with my guilt and my worry.

"Connor . . ."

"You need time alone," he said. "You want to drive Sally."

I nodded.

"Go on, then, lass." He pulled me from the seat I'd taken at the kitchen table and kissed me tenderly. "I'll wait for you."

I drove around Broken Heart with the windows on my Mustang rolled down. It was hot, but I didn't care. The summer air blowing inside smelled like honeysuckle and road dust. Like home.

I wondered how come everyone thought I was dead, who had taken over the café, what had happened to everyone during the last two days. The thoughts were as meandering as my path, and I didn't need the answers so much as something to think about. Anything to occupy my mind except Astria. And Danny.

Jesus. Had Jackson told Danny I was dead?

Until I got everything settled here, there was no point in clarifying the situation. He was gonna be pissed off, especially when he figured out how long I'd been undead and how many lies he'd been told. In the end, we'd have to do what was best for our son, and I hoped Jackson agreed that living in town with us would be the way to go.

I wasn't looking forward to that conversation, just like I wasn't looking forward to my part in the prophecy and retrieving the talisman. Although I did relish the idea of putting Lilith in her place.

For some reason, I ended up at the park. I pulled into a slot that faced the shiny plastic slides, bridge, tunnels, and sandbox. I missed taking Danny here, and hoped one day I would again.

God. How did everything get so fucked-up?

Jessica pulled up in her minivan. Jessica had been the first of us to get plowed down by the out-of-control beast that had killed all of us. The creature was a very sick Lorcan O'Halloran, who was now all cured. He was also the twin brother of Jess's second husband, Patrick.

Their children, Bryan, Jenny, and Rich Jr., piled out of the car. Rich was Danny's age; Jenny was ten, and Bryan fifteen. Bryan looked less than thrilled to be part of the family outing. He had an iPod in one hand, and a graphic novel in the other. He went to a nearby picnic table and lay on it. I waited at the curb for the rest of the O'Hallorans to join me.

"It's like we asked him to pour acid in his eyes," groused Jessica as she watched her son stake out his spot. She sighed. "I think he might prefer acid in his eyes to family time."

"He's a teenager. It's his nature to be difficult."

"And my parental prerogative is to beat him with my shoe." She turned to me and flashed a smile. "Long time, no see. How ya doin'?"

"Been better."

"I heard." She hugged me, and it made me feel better. "Any word on the girl?"

I shook my head.

We walked toward the plastic contraptions. We reached the edge of the soft flooring that was supposed to protect the kids from owies. Rich Jr. toddled toward the three steps that led to the smallest slide. Jenny went with him, fussing.

"She's the boss of everything," said Jessica, with a mixture of pride and frustration.

Jessica and I sat on a bench that faced the play area.

"Usually Patrick's hovering over the children. Literally." Jessica laughed.

As part of the Family Ruadan, which was part *sidhe*, or fairy, he had the ability to fly.

"He always says he's doing a perimeter check," Jess said drolly. "But really he's just messing around."

"It must be nice to fly."

"You wanna go up? I can take you." Jessica was also of the Family Ruadan. Their ability to fly probably had something to do with the fairy blood of the founder.

"No, thanks," I said hastily. "I'm not a big fan of heights."

"Oh." She shrugged. "It's a lot of fun."

"So's staying on the ground." I realized Astria would probably love to fly around with one of the *sidhe*, and I made a note to tell her. Because I fully expected to see her again, healing up nicely.

Do you hear me, O gods who rule the universe? She's gonna live.

For a quiet moment, we watched the kids. Jenny helped her brother get situated on the slide, and in three seconds, they were down the chute. Then it was another jaunt up the steps, a lecture from Jenny on proper sliding techniques, and woo . . . off he went again.

I looked at Jess and realized something was off. I studied her a moment, and then I figured out what it was. "Where are your swords?"

No matter what Jessica wore, she always

donned her special belt for her gold half swords. She was a killer with 'em; in fact, she had helped me with some of my knife training.

"I learned how to magic them. I can make them appear instantly now. Of course, I look badass with 'em strapped to my thighs." She grinned at me, then looked up at the night sky. You couldn't see the Invisi-shield's bubble unless you tried to get through it. Then it went blue and buzzy.

"So, about your boyfriend . . ." She batted her lashes at me. "Why'd you take off with him?"

I shrugged. Obviously Damian hadn't let the good word spread about my mating to Connor. I didn't much want to explain anything. Besides, ever since Jess found her true love, she'd been trying to do the rest of us a solid. Her first attempt, hooking up our former librarian, Eva, with my former boss, Ralph, did not work out. On the upside, Eva was now Jessica's sis-in-law, because Eva ended up marrying Lorcan. And Ralph found his own true love, my friend Libby, in a cemetery.

No one could ever call Broken Heart boring.

"Why'd everyone think I was dead?"

"Your house was a mess, your locket was on the bedroom floor, and everyone knows you wouldn't go anywhere without it. Then the hunters told us . . . Well, they figured Connor had killed you."

Uneasiness crawled up my spine. "He didn't hurt me. But those hunters . . ."

"Annoy the hell out of Patsy," said Jessica. "She'll want to talk to you soon. Really soon."

"Uh-oh. Are we talking about a meeting?" I groaned.

"That's where Patrick is," she said. "I hate meetings, too. I'm not gonna bug you about what happened, Phoebe. I'm sure you had your reasons. But you'll have to come clean with Patsy."

I probably should've gone straight to Queen Patsy. Just unloaded everything from my mating to Connor to my role with the talisman, which I was still vague on. And the one person who knew what I was supposed to be doing was dying.

No, she was healing.

Brigid wouldn't let me down.

Still, I was throwing a hell of a pity party for myself, and my friends were letting me do it. Had Gabriel met his brother and sister yet? Had Larsa told Patsy she was the last of her line and necessary for renewing the talisman's magic?

Some part of me felt like I should be there, and another part was grateful that I was not. I was caught between becoming something bigger, more important to the world around me, and staying where I had been, managing the café and vanquishing the occasional demon.

"Jess, did you know there was an eighth vampire line?"

She turned to me, her expression shocked. "Huh?"

"Patrick never mentioned it?"

Jessica shook her head. "What are you—"

Bryan's scream made the hairs on the back of my neck stand up.

Both of us leapt up from the bench and whirled around.

Bryan hovered over the picnic table, his arms and legs pulled straight by two demons. The graphic novel had fallen to the ground and the iPod swung off his side, the buds still stuck in his ears.

His eyes were bulging, his skin gray. "Mooom!" Bryan screeched. "Help me!"

Chapter 22

"Oh, my God! Bryan!" Jessica jumped over the bench and raced to her son in the blink of an eye. She flew into the air and grabbed his arm. "Phoebe!"

"Got 'em!" I whirled around and headed for the slide.

Jenny stood at the top, holding the hand of Rich Jr., her eyes wide and her face white with terror.

"It's okay," I said gently, taking the boy from her. I picked him up. "C'mon, Jenny."

We hurried down the two steps. Jenny tugged on my sweater. I stopped and turned. Tears dripped down her cheeks. "They're gonna tear apart Bryan!"

"No," I said firmly. "They're not."

Bryan's screams were choked, his limbs so straight they looked as if they might just pop out of their joints.

Jessica yelled with frustration as she tried to

free her son. But the demons just laughed and pushed her away. I think she was afraid to engage them directly. They were perfectly capable of ripping him in half.

What was I supposed to do now?

Use my connection to Connor. Get help.

Connor?

Lass?

Demons at the park; please come.

I hadn't sensed demons or demon magic, and it killed me to know we'd been surrounded and attacked without any warning. So much for my evil wonder powers. Yeah, yeah, insert *Super Friends* joke here.

"Phoebe!" Connor cried as he appeared next to me.

I nearly jumped out of my own skin. "Jesus H. Christ!" I pushed Rich Jr. into his arms. Most beings who could transport could take only one other person with them. "Take him to the compound; Patrick's there . . . probably in the council chambers. Hurry!"

"Figured you could use your weapons." He kissed me, swift and hard. "I'll be right back."

He disappeared.

Fear hammered at me. At my feet were my weapons boxes, unlocked. I scooped out the Wiccan-blessed knives, which were made of silver and were poisonous to demons. I took the safety off the Glock and tucked it in the back of my jeans; I didn't have time to mess around.

Jenny screamed again, and her clammy hand was yanked from mine. I was shoved and I went ass-first down the stairs, flat against the spongy surface.

Jenny rose into the air. Panic made her eyes roll. Her sobs went silent, tears and snot dripping from her face as she struggled against the two demons holding her hostage.

The shorter one held Jenny's feet and pulled; the larger one floated in the air and held her arms, yanking and laughing.

"Keep your eyes closed, Jenny!" I commanded with my vampire glamour. "You are not afraid."

Her eyelids shut and she seemed to relax.

Using my vampire speed and agility, I shot back up the steps and slit the closest one's throat. Viscous, inky blood flooded his neck and spattered his chest. He flopped down the slide, disappearing in a hiss of atramentous smoke.

I glared at the one who still gripped Jenny's arms.

"You can't stop us," it yelled. "You will die."

I flung the tiny dagger. The blade slammed into its eye. It shrieked and dropped Jenny.

I caught her.

"Sleep," I whispered, adding another touch of glamour.

She went limp. Her mouth opened slightly; she let out a soft snore.

"I will pluck out your heart!" shouted the demon. One hand covered its profusely bleeding eye.

The air thickened with the sulfur scent of demon magic. Billowing clouds formed in the sky. Thunder echoed, and lightning shattered the dark. Wind blasted us.

Then the demon plucked out the knife and looked as though he would send it back to me. I tossed Jenny over my shoulder in a fireman's hold, took out my Glock, and shot the demon three times in the chest.

It howled. Blood and smoke leached from the wounds. Silver bullets ruled. Silver had inherent magical properties, and that was why it could harm most paranormal beings. Demons particularly hated the substance, especially when it had been blessed with white magic.

"Vampire whore!" it gurgled.

The inky smell of ozone grew sharp in the worsening wind.

"That's no way to speak to a lady," said a voice with an English accent. Berith stood next to me, his eyes glowing red. "Are you and the girl all right?"

I nodded, stunned to see him, and, hel-lo, did Berith just ask me a polite question?

He returned his gaze to the badly injured demon. He pointed his left forefinger and that long beam of red light unfurled from his sharp black talon. The whip snapped as he raised his arm, and *snick*, the beam slashed the demon in half.

I watched the demon halves smack the ground and disappear in plumes of stinky black smoke.

Patrick appeared in front of me. "Let me take her," he said. He slipped Jenny out of my arms and disappeared in a shower of gold sparkles.

I glared at Red. "What's going on?"

"War," he said with a little more relish than I thought necessary. He bared his teeth in a fearsome grin. "About damned time, too!"

"Berith!" yelled another man's voice.

We turned around. Near the picnic table, a battle raged. Berith and I hurried toward the melee.

Bryan lay on his side on the ground. Jessica had magicked her swords; she stood in front of her son, defending him from the attacking demons.

"Save some for me," bellowed Berith. His crazy whip whirled above his head as he joined in the fray.

I jumped on the back of the gray demon trying to disembowel Jess, and jabbed a dagger hilt deep into its scaly neck. It howled and tried to shake me off. I wrapped my arm around its throat and punched with my other fist, landing blows where I could. I would've used my Glock, but given the proximity of Jess and Bryan, I couldn't risk a bullet going astray.

Jessica, looking as pissed off as I've ever seen her, pierced the demon's chest and stomach with her half swords. Fairy gold didn't affect demons the way silver did, but it didn't exactly tickle, either.

Its howls went wild as it fell to its knees. I didn't leap off so much as fall onto the damp ground.

Jess twisted the swords, which made icky squishing sounds, and yelled, "*Fulaing!*"

I think it was Gaelic for, "May pain fill your every pore, you wart on the ass of humanity."

Squealing, the demon exploded into a column of smoke. The stench of rotten eggs clogged my nose. *Phew.*

Somehow, the warriors had pushed the other demons away from us and toward the timberline. Jessica knelt next to her son and pushed his hair off his too pale forehead.

"Get him to the car," I said.

Jessica nodded and scooped up her son. Before she got two steps, Patrick appeared and relieved her of the burden. He kissed her and sparkled away.

Within moments he'd returned and wrapped his arm around her. "The hunters will take you to the compound, Phoebe," said Patrick.

"What about Connor?"

He had no answer for me, which worried me more than the way I was being left in the hands of the hunters.

As they sparkled away, Jess looked up, her swords clenched in her fists. Then her eyes widened.

"Phoebe!" Jessica's cry of warning nearly came too late.

I turned and managed to duck under the arms of the demon reaching for me.

Lilith's pet.

Gray scaled, with those horrible black wings, it kept its horrific xanthous gaze on me.

I slashed at it with my knives, putting my fury in every jab, but it was undeterred. The demon grinned, its eyes promising pain and retribution.

It reached for me, its thick yellow claws relentless as it slashed and slashed until I fell in my own blood. I was burning, burning, and it put the tips of its talons to my throat.

Then it was yanked away from me and Berith delivered a blow to the demon's neck that separated it from its body. Both head and body dissipated. Thank goodness they had finished off their own demon baddies.

"Thanks," I said.

"You need a pint," said Nicor. "Take from one of us."

I realized that doing so felt like cheating on Connor. I didn't want to drink from anyone but him. Not even a donor. Now, what did that mean?

I was sure Astria would point it that it was a symptom of love.

"C'mon," said Nicor. He knelt down and offered his neck. Well, better his than Berith's. I sank my fangs into his carotid artery and drank my pint quickly. I felt almost dirty, like I'd completed an adulterous act.

Get a grip, Pheebs.

I also felt better, and my body was beginning to heal. I needed another shower. Man, I was getting tired of being soaked in blood.

"For the record," I said, "I kicked total demon ass." *Take that, Larsa.* "And also, I want to go home."

"Not yet," said Nicor. "We must report to the council."

Oh, God. What now?

Chapter 23

I stood in the official sanctum of the Broken Heart Council, which was a combination of the Oval Office and the Pentagon. The lycanthrope-vampire queen, Patricia Marchand, created the council not long after her triplets were born—about two years ago.

It was never a good thing to be called before the council in their formal meeting chambers.

Especially when you were covered in blood. I'd taken a moment to clean up as much as possible in the bathroom, but I didn't have the magic to replace my clothes.

The council had seven members: three vampires, three lycanthropes, and the queen. The vampires were Patrick O'Halloran, the son of the first vampire, Ruadan, Ivan Taganov, who was also the chairman of the Consortium, and the Ancient Zela, whose Family power was the manipulation of metallic substances. Needless to say, she had the best jewelry.

The lycanthropes were Damian, a full-blood who was head of security (and with whom I trained), the *loup de sang* Gabriel, who was also Queen Patsy's husband, and Helene, a Roma (lycans who changed only during the full moon). She'd settled in Broken Heart with her husband and her son. They were well-known for their skills in hunting rogue vampires.

Representatives of other parakind served as liaisons between their people and the council. None of them was here today. So, this was about me.

My three kitchen-destroying friends were standing about five feet to the left of me. We had an uneasy alliance, to say the least.

Queen Patsy looked regal sitting at the middle seat of the table that faced me. Her blond hair was swept into an updo, and her tailored blue suit perfectly matched her eyes. Hard to believe she used to be the town's only beautician, who lived in a double-wide behind her shop. Now she was the powerful leader of lycanthropes and vampires and the mother of another kind of werewolf (the *loup de sang*, in case you haven't been paying attention). She also had all seven powers of the Ancients. She was not someone you messed with if you valued living.

"What's going on?" I asked her.

"We will begin proceedings in a moment," she said formally. Her eyes looked like cut glass. I wasn't getting any emotion off her, which made me worry more. For all her polish these days, the queen wasn't one to hide her emotions or eschew plain speaking.

I didn't have to wonder long about when the moment would arrive.

Connor was brought in from a side door. His hands were cuffed in front of him. The manacles were made from fairy gold, and bespelled with *sidhe* magic. No one, mortal or immortal, could escape them.

He held his head up, eyes forward, back ramrod straight. His gaze bored into me. Desperation edged the fury burning in his eyes.

Connor?

He didn't respond. He didn't even look at me.

The vampire Faustus stood behind Connor, looking as imposing and warrioresque as he probably had as a Roman centurion. He wore fatigues with military boots; his scarred face was a handsome kind of scary.

"What the hell is going on?" I cried. I pointed to Connor. "Why is he in handcuffs?"

Patsy ignored me.

"Connor Ballard. It has come to my attention that you moved to Broken Heart under false pretenses," said Patsy coolly.

"Just because I didn't make my intentions known doesn't make 'em false," he said.

Wow. That actually made sense. I slid a glance at Connor.

Patsy's eyes narrowed. "You failed to mention you were a demon."

"Is there a rule against demons settlin' in Broken Heart?"

The question obviously flummoxed her. The council members' faces all held various expressions of surprise, because it wasn't a question we'd ever thought would come up. Demons weren't the type of beings to settle down.

"Phoebe," snapped Patsy, "cool your jets."

"What?" My hands felt hot; I looked down and saw the black flames of demonfire licking my fists. I shook out my hands and made a conscious effort to control the magic. "Take him out of the handcuffs." I appealed to Patrick: "He saved your kid. And you put him in prison?"

"I argued against his being taken into custody," said Patrick. "I was overruled."

"Patrick," admonished Patsy.

He didn't look even a little bit sorry he'd spoken, and I was glad Connor had at least one voice on the council.

"Do you know where the talisman is?" asked Patsy.

"Yes."

"Both parts of it?"

He nodded.

"We'll need them," said Patsy. "After all, you've brought Lilith right to our door."

"You know about the talisman?" I asked her.

"The hunters explained its purpose, but that they have only half."

"And did they explain about the missing eighth vampire line?"

"We've met Larsa," said Patsy. Her tone held apprehension. "And I've reamed Ruadan a new asshole, but it does us little good. The talisman, Connor?"

Connor remained silent. Frustration etched Patsy's pale face. She turned toward Gabriel, and I knew they were having a telepathic conversation.

"Phoebe." The queen's icy gaze pinned mine. "You are bound to him?"

"Yes."

"Why don't we stop dancing around?" demanded Berith. "You know our purpose. Just give us Connor and be done with it."

"What about Phoebe?" asked Patsy. "Should she spend an eternity in hell because she made a mistake?"

"They tell you they're takin' me to hell?" Connor laughed, and the rich sound rolled right through me. Hearing him laugh or talk was like breathing in chocolate air. Delicious.

Patsy's gaze examined the hunters. "It was my understanding that demons go to hell. You didn't exactly disabuse us of that notion when you asked to go get him."

"*You* sent him to my house?" I looked at Nicor. "They brought Lilith into Broken Heart the minute they used their magic to track Connor." I waved my hand at Connor. "He doesn't live in hell. He's only half demon. And half Ghillie Dhu. And how dare you judge him on his parentage!"

One blond eyebrow rose as Patsy stared at me.

"We must secure the talisman and . . . dispose of the demon who stole it from us," said Nicor. He sent me an apologetic glance.

"Honey, you're on crack if you think you're taking either him or the talisman outta town," said Patsy.

"Why don't you tell her about Family Durga?" invited Connor. "It's time she knew."

The room went quiet. The tension was so thick, I felt like a wool blanket had been tossed over us. Foreboding trembled in my stomach. I crossed the space and stood next to Connor. Whether or not I decided to use the ring to break our binding, right now we were still mates.

I studied the council, and though they remained stoic, it was apparent that Connor had hit upon a nerve.

"Patsy?" My voice squeaked with tension; I cleared my throat.

The queen sighed. "There's been a resurgence in the Taint. We've actually formulated a viable cure, thanks to Brady giving us some of his über-technology. Doesn't much matter for the new cases, though, because they're some kind of mutated strain."

"I know," I said. "I also know the cause of the Taint is demon poison."

Patsy looked surprised. Then she shared a glance with Patrick. "And you know this how?"

"Connor told me. And I believe him." Horror wormed through me. "Are you saying there's been an outbreak in Broken Heart?"

"The Taint hasn't breached our borders," Patsy assured me. "But the new virus affects only vampires from the Family Durga."

Whoa.

"The Family Durga is not particularly numerous," explained Patrick in his soft Irish voice. "The only sect with smaller numbers is the Family Amahté. Most of the time, only one in ten humans survive a Turning. In the case of Family Durga, the odds are even less. Men have a better chance of making the transition, which is why there are also so few females."

"I didn't know." It was bad enough that I'd been killed and made into a vampire. Now I was being told that the chances of my transition had been almost nil. "How bad is the situation?"

No one spoke, not even Connor. He looked at me with concern. The silence stretched on until Connor ended it.

He turned toward me. His chains rattled. "The first cases started 'bout three months ago. The disease's been aggressive—working faster than any previous cases. Family Durga's bein' decimated. An' what happens to the vampire happens to his mate."

Dread bloomed in my stomach. Even if the

mates of the Family Durga vampires didn't get the disease, they'd still experience the slow slide into insanity or inevitable death.

"What does that have to do with you?" I asked Connor.

"It has to do with you," said Patsy. "There are maybe a couple hundred Family Durga vampires left. And of those . . . well . . ."

The look in her eyes terrified me. It was the look a doctor gave his patient before announcing a terminal illness, or a vet gave a pet owner when the only option was to put her beloved dog to sleep. For a moment, I didn't want to know. I was bound to a demon through my own stupidity. I had jeopardized my son because I'd acted like a hormonal teen. I soooo didn't want to hear more bad news.

When Patsy kept staring at me, and the council looked away, and not even the hunters could meet my gaze, I found myself looking to Connor.

"The Family Durga is dyin' out," he said softly. "And, lass . . . you're the only female left."

Chapter 24

"Which makes what you did all the more reprehensible," said Patsy. She slapped her palm against the black marble table; given her strength, the fact that it only quivered was testament to its solidity.

"And what pretty adjective do you use to describe your own deceptions?" asked Connor. He laughed bitterly. "I'm a demon, Your Highness. What's your excuse?"

Patsy looked like she wanted to fry him with her laser eyes. She didn't really have laser eyes, but she had seven other powers that couldn't necessarily kill him . . . Maiming was a different issue.

"Wait." I wanted to sit down, take a breath (figuratively), and process what I'd just been told. The last female vampire in the Family Durga? Holy shit. Instead, I commanded my legs to stop trembling and gave myself the suck-it-up-princess speech. I wouldn't show weakness now, no matter how much I wanted to crumble.

"Is that why you mated with me?" I asked Connor. "Because I was the last female of the Family Durga?"

"One of the reasons," he admitted. "I need you, lass." He gaze flicked around the room. "We all do."

Oh. Well, that cleared things right up.

"The prophecy?" I asked wearily. Always the prophecy.

"We got word that the most recent victims included the last-known Family Durga women," said Patsy. "It's no coincidence Connor made his move on you. He knew what we did."

Connor didn't turn away from my gaze. I could see his Adam's apple bob as he swallowed, the only sign of emotion he allowed.

"And if I'd said no?" I asked. My voice cracked, and I cleared my throat. I couldn't cry, thank God; otherwise, I might not be able to hold back tears.

That would've been the end of it, the end of everything. The words ghosted through my mind, and I stared at Connor.

More was going on here than anyone was telling me. And it seemed as though the council preferred that I stay as much in the dark as possible. At least Connor had answered my questions.

"You need me to activate the talisman." It had been Durga's medallion. All the vampire magic went into it to seal Lilith in hell, but I was the conduit.

That's right, lass.

I may still be mad at you.

O' course.

If I thought the silence and the tension had been bad before, they were nothing compared to now. It was like someone had suddenly filled the entire room with Jell-O. It felt thick and slimy and unbreathable. (If, you know, I breathed.)

"Your Highness." Impatience tinged Nicor's respectful tone. "It is imperative we take over this situation. You do not understand the danger Lilith represents."

"Nicor, no offense, but we've dealt with a few dangerous situations over the years. Trust me when I say we can handle damn near anything."

"I disagree." He stepped forward and his two companions straightened. I had the distinct impression that the three of them would take Connor, and maybe even me, by force.

Patsy must've thought the same thing. "Why don't you go away and let the grown-ups talk?" She pointed at them and they all three disappeared at once.

Wow. Patsy had learned some new tricks—like how to teleport vampires with a freaking thought and a flick of her finger. I wondered if she sent them to the prison, which was located in the basement of her mansion. There hadn't really been a reason to build a new prison, especially since that one was state-of-the-art and parakind-proof.

"Let's stop messing around," said Patsy.

A door opened at the far end of the chamber. It was the goddess Brigid. She looked pale and haggard; even her swirling tattoos, her healing magic, looked dim. She'd probably zapped herself to the compound.

Patsy shot me a sympathetic look. "We're gonna take a break."

"Astria?" I asked with an ache in my voice.

She nodded.

"Connor is her friend, too." I grabbed his manacles and shook them. "Take these off. He's not gonna flee Broken Heart or take anyone to hell. Damn it, he's my mate."

"Remove them, Faustus," said Patsy. "Then take Phoebe and Connor to the hospital."

When we arrived in the hallway outside of Astria's room, Anise, Ren, and Larsa were already there. I noticed none of them had been put into magical manacles, and I resented it.

"I like your town," said Larsa. "Think I'll stay a while."

I smiled. Then I asked Anise, "How did the family reunion go?"

She was crying, and Ren held her close, his own eyes red rimmed. "It's good," she said. "But this . . ." She gazed at the shut door. "This is not. *Ma fleur.*"

"Stay strong," whispered Ren. "For Astria."

They filed in one by one, and I made sure I was the last. Brigid leaned against the wall, her bright green eyes on mine. "I'm sorry," she said. "But nothing I've done helps. Prolonged her life a little."

"If you tell me the gods mean for her to die, I'll scream," I said.

"It's an unfortunate gift to know when you'll die," she said. "I have no words for you, Phoebe."

I tapped the ring. "I have a wish," I said. "Can I wish her to life? Or give her immortality?"

"Wishes are tricky things," she said. "Maybe she gets another two minutes or another two decades, or maybe she turns into petrified wood—which renders her immortal."

I nodded. "Okay. Can you get me Ruadan?"

"Yes." She straightened from the wall and considered me. "What are you thinking, Phoebe?"

"That Astria has to die," I said. "But that doesn't mean she has to stay dead."

She smiled. "I'll get my son."

When I entered the room, everyone else drew away from the bed. It appeared they had said their good-byes. I was glad to see Anise had held up well, though she still leaned on her brother for support.

I walked to Astria. She looked so pale, as though the blood had given up arterial flow. Maybe it had. I read somewhere once that everyone technically died from heart failure . . . no matter the initial cause of death, the heart stopping was what killed.

And Astria's heart would stop. Her breathing was slow and her eyes glazed over. Soon, she would fall asleep. Snow White ready for her glass coffin.

"I appreciate that you tried," she whispered.

I reached down and took her hand. "The wish would be a problem. But you knew that."

"You must save it," she said.

"Astria, do you want to live?" I asked.

"Yes," she said. "Oh, yes."

"I can Turn you."

"A vampire?" She smiled. "Like you?"

"Yes," I said. "Another will Turn you, Astria. But you would still be mine."

"What is this?" asked Anise. "What do you promise her?"

Ruadan stepped into the room, his silvery gaze going from Astria to me. "You wanted me, Phoebe?"

"Please leave," I said to everyone.

Connor stopped to kiss me. Then he whispered, "You're amazin'. Save our girl now."

Everyone else left, all casting glances at us.

"Please Turn her," I said to Ruadan.

"Never Turned a prophet before," he said. "And she's under the age of consent."

"You're Ruadan the First," I mocked. "Who will dispute your decisions?"

He grinned. "True. All right, then, Phoebe, my love. I'll Turn her."

Chapter 25

Ruadan insisted that I leave. He said the process was complicated and messy, and he'd be able to concentrate better without an audience.

Connor waited for me in the hallway. The others were there, too. "He's Turning her," I said.

"So, she dies as she must," said Anise. "But she comes back!"

"Yep."

She leaned forward and kissed both my cheeks. "*Magnifique*, Phoebe!"

The meeting reconvened in the council chambers, but this time without the hunters, nor with Connor enchained.

Connor admitted that he'd hidden the talisman at Jennifer's, a place no one could randomly find or get to without an invitation. We agreed to retrieve the gold medallion. And since dawn was approaching, the ceremony would not take place until the next evening.

I wish we could've gotten it done right away, because Lilith was certainly skulking around. We'd disbanded her cult, so it was unlikely she'd be able to create a new portal in time to prevent us from doing the binding spell.

Though she could possibly burst through the veil anyway, since its magic had been weakening.

We arrived at Jennifer's. Both she and Scrymgeour were happy to see us. Connor said he'd sent the dog to his sister's place before we went to the museum. Good thing, too.

I took a shower and crawled into the big, fluffy bed naked. I was bone-deep weary. I happily collapsed next to Connor and fell asleep.

I had just finished my pint (à la Connor) when my cell phone rang.

"You get cell reception here?" I asked, amazed. Caller ID said it was Damian.

"The hunters and I were outside the Invisishield," said Damian without preamble, "checking the weak points and reinforcing the new magic."

"Demonproofing it," I said.

"*Ja.* But someone got inside and . . . You must come see, Phoebe."

"Is someone watching over Jackson and Danny?" I asked.

"*Ja, Liebling.* See you in a few."

"Lilith's pulled another trick," I said.

"Let's go, then." Connor kissed me, and I realized I'd gotten used to his affection and his support. I knew I could count on him, which startled the hell out of me.

"You have the talisman?"

He patted his pocket and smiled.

We decided to assess the damage in town and figure out the message Lilith was trying to send—other than the obvious, I-can-torment-you-anytime-I-choose memo. I wanted to pick up my weapons, which I'd stowed at my house, too. Lilith was erratic and crazy, although that didn't seem to affect her ability to plot and torture. Something bigger was going on here, and I couldn't help but feel we were just a small part of it.

I had been considering other issues, too, mainly the fact that Jennifer, as a full demon, didn't have the advantages of her half-breed brother. No real conscience or soul. And yet she was trying to be good. She loved Connor, too. I wanted to help her.

Before we left for Broken Heart, I made one last phone call.

Only Damian and Nicor met us at the edge of town. Pith and Berith had been inside when whatever happened . . . happened. They'd already been inside once, assessing the situation.

"Patsy's house," said Damian.

Nicor took hold of the werewolf, and Connor wrapped his arms around me . . . then, *pop*.

When we appeared in a darkened room, I lurched sideways. Connor steadied me until the dizziness passed. Damian prowled around the area, his gaze trying to penetrate the gloom. It was rather a thick darkness even for us vampires and werewolves.

A light speared the blackness and we turned toward the source. Nicor. He looked at us, his eyebrows winging upward as he wielded a flashlight.

I think I was getting too used to the paranormal world. A flashlight seemed really mundane.

"Wait," said Connor. "What was that?"

"Why is it so damned cold?" I asked. It was like walking into a freezer.

Nicor's light bounced around, hitting walls with their wolf-inspired art, then the marble fireplace, and one of the formal couches. We were definitely in the main living room of the Silverstone mansion.

The beam danced back and then stopped.

Holy. Shit.

"Is that . . ." I trailed off as I watched Damian stride forward, Nicor's flashlight steadily revealing what couldn't be true.

"It's Patsy, all right." He put his hand against one blue-tinged cheek. "And she's made of ice."

Patsy shone bluish white, as though she'd been carved from a glacier. She stood in the main living room, facing the double doors, arms raised as if she were about to use one of her powers. Whatever she'd been about to do, it either didn't happen or didn't work.

"Everyone else in town is like this?" I asked.

Damian nodded.

Connor walked around frozen Patsy and prodded her back. "How did Lilith manage this?" he muttered. He glanced at me. "Only the person who cast the spell can undo it."

Or a wish could undo it.

"It's a lot of magic. How did she—" His eyes went wide. "The Invisi-shield. Clever bitch."

I followed his line of thinking. "She used the shield to distribute the spell."

He nodded. "In theory."

"Theory is all we've got at this point." I looked at Patsy, and felt bad we couldn't help her. "There's nothing we can do here. Let's go to the compound and make some sort of plan."

"Why didn't she kill them?" asked Damian. "Then it's done."

"It's gotta be because she can't. Not enough power, or maybe Patsy's just too strong to off," I said. "I need to get my weapons. Then we'll meet back at the Consortium headquarters."

"I'll take you, lass."

I closed my eyes and my stomach twisted, and then the world spun.

It seemed like forever. Or maybe it was just a nanosecond.

Connor said, "We're here."

I opened my eyes and clutched his hands until I felt steady enough. At least no miasma of darkness coated my house.

The porch light was on, but the rest of the house was dark. After all I'd been through, you'd think going into my own home wouldn't have given me the willies. Apprehension shivered through me, and I felt Connor's arm draw around my shoulder.

"I'll meet you at the Consortium headquarters."

"I dinnae want to leave you."

"I know." I kissed him. "Please, Connor. Just a few minutes to myself. Then we'll go kick Lilith's ass."

"Twenty minutes," he said. "If you're not at the compound then, I'm comin' back for you."

"Deal."

He kissed me again, and I waited until he'd popped out of sight before I hurried into the house.

"Hey," I said as I flipped on the living room light. "You here?"

"Yeah."

I turned and saw the woman enter from the kitchen. She was dressed in tight black pants and pink boots, which matched her pink jacket. Her inky black hair was cut short, spiked on top, and her light gray eyes were the most unusual I'd ever seen. Diamond gaze—that was what she'd called it once.

"Ash," I said.

The soul shifter.

Chapter 26

I changed into more suitable clothes—black jeans, black tank, and my ankle boots. I loaded up my Glock, got extra rounds tucked into my pockets, and hid my knives in my boots and the specially cut jeans.

"It's not a fucking trout," Ash said as she watched me strap on the Glock's holster. "You can't just fillet a soul."

"Unless it's halved for you." I sent her a significant look.

She shrugged.

Ash was the only one of her kind, a creature that could capture supernatural souls and their forms (you know, the ones who'd once owned the souls), and sorta eat them. She could access a soul's powers by "becoming" the soul itself. It was a painful process, nearly as painful as absorbing the souls.

Ash was dangerous, especially since she had to

take a soul every ninety days or die. It was one of the reasons her kind had been hunted to extinction. It was amazing she was even around, because she scared the hell out of nearly everyone.

Including me. But we'd become friends—well, as much as Ash allowed friendship. She often came to the diner during her infrequent visits to town. I got the feeling she was lonely, though I would never accuse her of it.

"Libby told me you can't even access it because you didn't take the form, too."

"She would've never forgiven me if I'd sucked her husband into my well of souls."

I stopped fussing with my Glock. "Will my idea work?"

"I usually imbibe souls whole. You know, like sushi."

"Nice visual." With all my weaponry in place, I took the time to rebraid my hair. "What about the ones you don't want?"

"If the ninety days are up, it doesn't matter." She grimaced. "I've got a few I don't even access. Too skeevy."

"I can't imagine how horrible that must be."

She shrugged. "I was born a soul shifter. I can't change that."

"Still sucks."

She tossed me a careless grin. "I like you, Phoebe."

"You don't like anyone. And you don't do favors."

One eyebrow lifted insolently. "You've been talking to Libby. She likes to think I'm a heartless hard-ass."

"Aren't you?"

"Yeah," she admitted. Then she grinned again. "But at least I'm not soulless."

Without Connor and his insta-'port, I had to drive Sally to the compound. I went to the Consortium headquarters and parked in front of the big white building. I went around the side, to the stairs that led to the underground facility.

Accessing the door meant smearing blood over the lock, and the spell—which would allow only Broken Heart citizens to enter—snicked open. Connor came out of a door down the long hallway, a conference room, if I remembered correctly. He hugged me.

"I'm not even late!"

"I know," he said into my hair. "But it still feels like years."

Connor loved me.

It was as simple, and as complicated, as that.

He led me to the door that he'd exited and I followed, lost in thoughts and feelings that threatened to overwhelm me. I needed to keep a clear head.

We entered the room and I stopped.

Oh, my God.

"Damian and Nicor collected them," said Connor quietly. "They wanted to make sure the children stayed safe."

It was like a museum display: *Broken Heart Children Rendered in Arctic Ice.*

Patsy's son Wilson in motion, hand out as though dribbling a basketball.

Tamara and Durriken, fingers touching as they gazed at each other.

Patsy and Gabriel's triplets tucked into their cribs, crystalline in sleep.

Glory, face looking up, eyes wide, tears forever glittering on gelid cheeks.

I drifted into the room, horrified. Terrible beauty. I'd heard that once, I think from Eva. I thought it was an odd description, but now I understood. Here was terrible beauty.

I sat down heavily in a chair that had been pushed against the wall. "Holy crap."

Danny could've been here, I realized. He could've been an icy statue along with the rest. I wondered if Broken Heart would ever be safe. I thought about Ella, about her being snatched off the street and taped to a table so a crazy woman could sacrifice her.

Nowhere was safe, I reminded myself. Who better to protect the children of Broken Heart than the wolves, the vampires, the fairies, the dragons? The police didn't have anything on us. We were a lot scarier.

Connor strode to me and knelt. He put his hands on my thighs and stared up, pain shining so brightly it turned his eyes the color of champagne. He kissed me oh-so-softly. "We cannae waste any more time."

I let him help me to my feet. We turned toward the door, but it filled with roiling gray mist.

"Hold!"

The feminine voice crackled with power. The mist cleared and a tall, willowy woman stood in its place. She wore a hooded green robe and held within her bejeweled grasp a gnarled, polished wood staff. At its top sat a gleaming silver crow.

"Morrigu," said Connor in a hushed tone.

Brigid was the daughter of Morrigu, and Ruadan was a vampire because he'd imbibed his grandmother's dark blood. In essence, she was the reason vampires existed at all. Morrigu exuded a you-live-at-my-behest energy that instantly cowed me. Still, I didn't look away from her as I stood, and Connor's grip tightened on my hand.

Morrigu pulled back her hood. Her raven hair hung in long, silken ringlets around a pale, unlined face. Here, too, was terrible beauty. A thin silver crown nestled on her head; a single red stone glittered from its middle. Her dark eyes held ancient secrets.

Morrigu studied Connor. Then she turned her enigmatic gaze to mine. "Talisman," she said, inclining her head.

Uh . . . what?

"Lilith has brought harm upon my kin," she said. "I will not tolerate it."

Lilith probably didn't think she'd draw the attention of the goddess of chaos. I think Morrigu scared me more than Lilith, but at least the crow queen was on our side.

I thought.

Connor asked, "Can you undo her spell over the town?"

"It is not my magic." Her eyes were dark and flat as river stones. "Spells are like cloth, woven intricately. It will take much too long to unravel threads. Lilith intends to come through tonight. It is a new moon; the power of your talisman will be at its weakest."

"She won't have a portal. We disbanded her cult," I said.

"Yet her demons roam free. They kill in her name, too."

I shared a look with Connor. He looked just as horrified as I felt.

"Why did she just freeze everybody?" I asked.

"Expediency. Or the demon she sent to do it had limited powers. Or she's a ravin' bitch." Morrigu looked at me with those ancient eyes, and I saw the flames of funeral pyres and the bleached bones of the dead reflected there. She said, "You can fix this."

I twisted the wish ring around on my finger, and I nodded.

"Then go."

"Take me to Main Street," I said to Connor. "That's where the middle of the Invisi-shield is. If Lilith can use it to spread her magic, then so can I."

He frowned as he gathered me into his arms, but I couldn't look at him. I didn't want to explain that I'd been saving the wish to break our mating. Or maybe I'd kept it for another reason. Maybe this one. Astria had said I would need it.

Had she foreseen this very circumstance?

I hoped I would have another opportunity to talk to her. I had to believe she'd survived the Turning, and that I would survive this night.

I snuggled in Connor's arms while he transported me to the middle of Main Street. It turned out that the center of the Invisi-shield was above downtown, almost right over the Old Sass Café. I felt doubly offended that the bitch had cursed everyone practically above the place I worked.

From the street, I could see into the still-lit windows of the café.

"I've spent a lot of time being scared for Danny, for you, for Broken Heart. We've been terrified by Lilith, bullied by her demons, and I'm sick of feeling helpless and afraid." I pointed up. "Let's go."

Connor's face went stony. "I cannae take you unless . . ."

"You go demon? We don't have any Family Ruadan here," I said. "So make with the wings already."

For a moment, I didn't think he would do it. Then he stood back and invoked his demon form. It took only seconds for him to meld from human to demon. He looked like diamonds to me, magic and glitter and beauty.

Connor gripped my arms. "I'll take you up to where the points of the shield converge."

He stroked his fingers down my spine—just a reminder that he was there for me. He had my back. No matter what I did. That was a powerful feeling.

He launched upward, his impressive wings pushing us skyward. We flew up, up, up into the starry sky.

"Here." Connor pointed above his head and then whispered, "*Solas.*"

Red orbs appeared, and their *sidhe* light reflected the otherwise invisible lines of the shield.

"What will you do now?" asked Connor.

"I'll make a wish," I said. I wasn't quite sure how it would all work. Keeping it simple was best. I took off the ring and pressed it against the thin streaming lights of the Invisi-shield. "I wish for everyone in Broken Heart to be free of all spells invoked by demons."

The glow burst from the ring and connected with the shield. For a moment, the entire bubble glowed gold. I felt the tingle of magic, and then it burst, raining gold sparks of magic to the town below.

Connor took me back down to Main Street. We landed softly; then he put some space between us. He shifted to his human form, and then magicked up some clothes for himself. He didn't say anything for a long moment.

"Astria gave the ring to you," he said. "She knew there was a wish trapped in it."

"She thought telling everyone it was for Ella would be enough for us to steal it. Then she planned to find a way to give it to me."

"I don't need to ask why."

"No," I said, my voice catching. "You don't."

"You don't love me," he said. The finality of his tone sliced through me.

"Connor."

"No, lass." He shook his head and smiled. "It's all right."

He took me into his arms, but I sensed his distance—distance I had created by not admitting how I felt about him. My choice had been taken from me; how could I know that what I felt was real? I didn't want some prophecy or destiny telling me what kind of life I should live. I wanted to choose whom to love.

And yet, Connor had embraced it all, and didn't doubt he was mine.

By the time we returned to the Consortium compound, it was buzzing with activity.

Damian beckoned us into a room, where he and his brothers, Drake and Darrius, guarded the door.

Inside were Patsy and Gabriel, Anise, Ren, Larsa . . . and Astria! I hurried over to her and hugged her.

"I have fangs," she said. Then she leaned back and showed them to me. "Drinking blood isn't that bad."

I laughed. "I'm just glad you're still walking around."

"As are we," said Anise softly. "Ruadan and you, Phoebe, will have our loyalty always."

"Thank you," I said, touched by her words. "A good way to repay me is to give the girl some freedom. A few choices of her own."

Anise nodded. "*Oui*. I see the wisdom in such advice."

"Let's get down to business," said Patsy. "We need to transfuse the talisman, and then Phoebe needs to invoke the magic, right?"

"Tell them the prophecy, Astria," said Connor. He sat in a chair next to me, but he might as well have sat across the room. It was as if all the affection, and—*gulp*—love he'd offered had been tucked away. I shouldn't have been hurt by his need to protect himself, to protect his heart, but I was. I knew it wasn't fair to want him, to bask in the warmth of love he'd given to me, and offer nothing of myself.

I felt so ashamed.

"Where's Morrigu?" I asked suddenly, as if it mattered.

"Haranguing Brigid and Ruadan," said Patsy sourly. "That woman is scary as shit."

"The prophecy," said Connor again. His gaze swept the room, but went past me. He wasn't in my thoughts anymore, either. I sensed his withdrawal keenly, and I didn't like it.

"Lilith returns," said Astria. Her words had the cadence of poetry. "'And the world weeps. The talisman weakens, its champions gone. The valiant arise, a demon lord and his bride, O daughter of Durga. Only they possess strength enough to stop the queen of hell. Mated together, they stand as one and defeat evil.'"

Her voice echoed into the room; then she sat down. She smiled at me, but it was sad. I looked down at the table.

"I am the only one left."

"The last female of the Family Durga," agreed Patsy. She sent me an empathetic look. She knew, better than anyone, what it was like to have your life altered due to prophecy. Her relationship with Gabriel and even her rise to queenly power had also been predicted by another Vedere prognostication.

And she seemed happy. A husband who adored her, three adorable toddlers, a grown son, and now two additions to their *loup de sang* family.

"Connor was the only possible demon lord," said Astria. "No other demon has a soul or the will to see Lilith returned to the Pit."

"Tell her the rest," said Connor.

Astria's gaze skidded away from mine. She swallowed; then she turned back to me. "Two halves of the talisman," she said. "One is the medallion infused with the magic of all eight Ancients. And the second . . . is you."

Chapter 27

"I did not see that coming," I said. "It's why I had to live. Because . . ." I trailed off, overwhelmed.

"Because if Lilith had managed to wipe out Family Durga, none would be left to join with the talisman. And the other half must be a female," said Connor.

"Durga was joined to it?" I asked faintly.

"Her daughter," said Larsa. Even she was looking at me with a kind of pity. "She offered to be the vessel for the magic. But the kind of power needed to force Lilith into hell destroyed her. It left the talisman, though, and Durga kept it with her. Until she was banned."

"That's why the gods wanted a demon to mate with the talisman," said Astria. "You'll need Connor's power and strength."

And I had turned him away.

I felt sick to my stomach. How could I draw

from Connor what I needed when he'd taken it away? No, when I'd refused it? If I said I changed my mind now, he would never know if I'd done it out of self-preservation or out of love. Hell, I didn't even know.

Connor took out the circle of gold. Around its edge were eight symbols I didn't recognize.

"The ancient symbols for the Families," said Larsa, her tone respectful.

It turned out that Larsa was unable to give Patsy the power of the Family Shamhat. Apparently Patsy had tried to absorb it, but the transfer didn't happen. She needed to get it directly from the Ancient. I knew now why Larsa believed we had one thing in common: We were both the last. She was the last of all the Family Shamhat. And I was the last female of Family Durga.

It appeared the hunters were the only ones, along with me, to have escaped the deaths of the Family Durga. Only four of us now who could claim the Family line. And only Patsy stood between almost all of us and destruction.

I didn't know how Patsy or Larsa knew what to do. Probably Larsa had given the queen the 411, because she'd been there when the first talisman had been made.

Patsy put her fingers on one side of the talisman, and Larsa did the same on the other. They whispered words, ancient words that I didn't understand.

One color after another lit each symbol. It was like a really freaky Simon electronic game.

When they were through, the talisman glowed in a rainbow of colors.

"It won't work," said Astria. "Not until you unlock its magic, Phoebe. You must add your blood to it."

Ren silently offered his knife, but I had already pulled a thin blade from my boot.

My stomach squeezed, and I looked at Connor. He offered me a smile, but it didn't reach his eyes. I ached to see tenderness, even a sparkle of humor. But there was only distance. I'd hurt him, and I wasn't sure I could undo the mess I'd created. How did you unbreak a heart?

I cut my palm and placed it on top of the medallion.

I felt as though hot fingers reached inside my chest and pulled out something hard and small, something beating softly like the wings of a bird. Then the sensation was gone.

And so was I.

The magic zapped me instantly to . . . well, I had no idea where. I squatted on the rocky ground and slowly stood up. I feared exploring this odd place.

Where was I?

As a vampire, my lack of blood circulation meant that most temperatures, hot or cold, rarely bothered me. But in this place I was cold. It wasn't so much that my outsides were frigid; more like an insidious chill crept through my insides, freezing me slowly. I wondered whether that was what my friends had felt as Lilith turned them into icicles. I really wished that someone could figure out how to make that woman implode.

I was outdoors. I thought. Thick fog boiled above the ground, hiding my feet. It was dark, but not pitch-black. I could make out stubby, dead trees and boulders.

"You honor us, daughter of Durga."

The woman walked toward me, dressed in a diaphanous white gown—a total Greek vibe. Most of the immortal females I knew really liked this look. Or they got a discount at Goddesses R Us.

The darkness parted for her reluctantly. It seemed as though the shadows had fingers clawing toward her, but maybe that was my imagination. This place seriously gave me the creeps. The woman stopped about a foot away, looking at me with solemn eyes.

"Who are you?"

"The gods," said a multitude of voices. "We heard your prayers."

"I didn't pray."

She smiled. "Your . . . exclamations."

"It's nice to know you're listening," I said, caught between anger and fear. "Even if you're not doing anything."

"You mean, even if we are not doing as you think we should." Her tone held both censure and humor. The voices had melded into one, for which I was glad.

"The time for secrets is nearing its end." Her gaze skimmed me. "Do you love Connor?"

"I . . ."

"Confusion is a lie," she said. "We come to a decision, and our hearts say, 'This way.' But it is dark down that path, and fraught with danger. We do not want to go. We look at the other path, the easier one. And we think of all the reasons not to follow our heart. Our thoughts tangle with our intuition and we say, 'We are so confused.'"

"I didn't have a choice."

"You did," countered the goddess. Or the gods. Or whatever. "For example, you used your wish to save your friends. . . . You could've used it to break your binding."

"The needs of the many," I insisted. "I'm not that selfish."

She cocked an eyebrow. I felt guilty because I *had* been selfish, thinking only about how the prophecy had affected me. Connor hadn't struggled nearly so hard. He'd just . . . fallen in love with me.

"Do you love him?" she asked. "It is a simple question."

And it was. I culled through my emotions, my memories. I saw in so many instances where I had made my own choices. I slept with Connor. I gave up the wish. I followed through with the talisman.

"Is it fate?" I asked, my throat thick, my voice unsteady.

"Does it matter? If you love Connor . . . does it matter?"

"No," I said, and I felt released, the burden of my emotions sloughing off. "I love him." I sounded strong and sure, and my heart beat, at least in my mind, for Connor.

"The talisman." Her gaze flickered to mine. "Are you strong enough, daughter of Durga, to be its new protector?"

"Yes."

"For so long as there is a talisman, there will be those who seek it."

I wasn't sure exactly where this was heading, but I thought about Connor, and knew I'd do whatever it took.

"What do I do?"

"Give me your knife. And give me the talisman."

I'd be crazy to hand over the most important object ever made, and a friggin' blade, but I did it. I regretted it immediately, because the bitch stabbed me.

"Ow!"

The woman ignored my reaction, working the blade in and cutting deeply into my chest. It hurt. A lot. But I shut my trap and let her work.

She slipped the talisman into the slit and pressed the wounded flesh over it. I felt a tickling warmth and the talisman burrowed deeper still, and the muscle she'd savaged healed instantly.

"You are the talisman," she said softly.

"I have its powers?"

"Yes. You and only you can wield them."

"I can send Lilith back to hell?"

"More than that. You can create bonds"—she looked at me significantly—"or break them."

"Vampire matings?" I asked.

"Yes. The other talisman, the daughter of Durga, was not strong enough to wield its power. She bound Lilith to hell, but died. She didn't have time to learn the magic or the limits of it, but you do. And you are strong enough."

"Because I have Connor."

"And he has you." She placed her hand on my forehead and muttered some words, and then my atoms exploded and I was racing across the darkness . . . back to the destiny I wanted.

Connor.

I arrived in the room in the Consortium underground facility, where an argument was raging.

My appearance stunned the participants.

"Where have you been?" roared Connor. He'd been leaning against the wall, and he pushed away from it, striding forward and snagging me. "You scared the life outta me."

He seemed to realize he'd shown more emotion than necessary, and he took a step back as he dropped my arm. But I wouldn't let him retreat. I put my arm around his waist and leaned into his shoulder. He stiffened, but didn't pull away. Then he put his arm over my shoulder, a small concession. I still felt the distance between us, but since

I'd been responsible for creating it, I supposed I should be the one to cross it.

"She did what she was supposed to do," said Astria. "Don't be mad, Connor."

"He wasn't angry," I told her. "He was scared." I hugged him and felt him soften more. "So was I."

I looked at the others in the room: Larsa, Patsy, Astria, Anise, and Ren. Damian and Nicor had joined us.

"Danny and Jackson, are they still all right?" I asked Damian.

"Asleep in Jackson's apartment," he confirmed. "And well protected, I promise you, *Leibling*."

"The talisman," said Nicor, "where is it?"

"You're looking at it," I said.

He seemed shocked, then appalled. I got the feeling he wanted to reach inside me and pull it out. *Good luck with that*, I thought.

"I don't want to wait for Lilith to make an appearance," I said. "We need to draw her out."

"How?" asked Damian.

"We'll use one of her tricks."

We sat down and hashed out a plan. And the whole time, I never let Connor go.

Chapter 28

When we arrived on Main Street, downtown was dark and quiet, too reminiscent of the nightmare. I was not alone. Connor stood with me.

Broken Heart would not be destroyed. Lilith would not win.

"Are you sure?" he asked me. I gripped his hand, and he allowed it. He wasn't ready to trust my affection, but I knew he would not leave me alone. I could rely on him; his strength and even his love were mine to call upon.

"Yes," I said. "Call her."

He looked at me one moment more, and then nodded.

"Jennifer," he said. "Come."

In her blond-bombshell form, she wavered into view, a couple of feet to my left.

"Wow," she said. She turned and sauntered toward us. "This is rad!"

"Remember what we talked about, Jennifer?" asked Connor.

She nodded. "No killing innocents. No implosions. No tricks."

The red lights sparkled, and when they dissipated, she was male-CEO Jen, with a nice suit and gray hair. His gaze softened as he looked at me. "I see magic in you, Phoebe. It's pretty."

"Thanks, Jennifer. We need you to get Lilith now."

He frowned. "Are you . . . sure? She's not very nice, and she doesn't like me."

"But you're her daughter," I pointed out. "And you can bring her here."

My heart broke for Jennifer, who'd been abused by Lilith's abandonment, languishing in that nonspace in hell until she was found by her brother. Connor taught her about love, about sacrifice. And she'd somehow retained her innocence. She was not designed to be good, but she'd chosen it. And was not the act of choosing right instead of wrong the sign of inherent goodness?

Red lights pulsed again, and a little girl stood there looking prim in her lacy dress and patent-leather shoes. "I have to go. So long as I stay at my house, I behave."

Her gaze was solemn, and I figured that Jennifer knew her limitations far too well. I sensed her sorrow, along with the eddy and twirl of her increasingly confusing thoughts. Could I sense the crack in her mental state because I was the talisman? It wouldn't have surprised me. At this point, a spaceship could land on Main Street and Elvis could saunter out singing "Love Me Tender," and I wouldn't be surprised.

I knelt and wrapped my arm around the little girl. I hugged her tightly and said, "Call her, Jennifer. And I promise she will never hurt you again."

She nodded, and then closed her eyes. I felt the power of her mental link, and realized that Jennifer was not a weak being. No, she had power beyond measure.

Certainly enough to draw her mother to Broken Heart. Jennifer was a portal that required no bloodletting at all.

Lightning hit the street. The whole area shook as I nearly lost my balance. The air smelled like ozone, and then Lilith appeared, right where the bolt had landed.

She still looked like a teen—innocent and sweet. Her blond hair was pulled back into a ponytail. She wore a concert T-shirt for Paramour, faded denims with holes in the knees, and a pair of zebra-striped flats.

Her favorite pet was behind her, and a few of its friends. We'd expected she'd show up with reinforcements. Her sneer took in the little girl.

"Thanks, daughter. For once you did something right."

"Go with Ash," I said softly as a shadow stepped out from under the eaves of the Old Sass Café. "She has a present for you."

"Did I mention that I haven't done this before?" whispered Ash. "It's dangerous and crazy and stupid."

"Sounds like it'll be fun, then."

She grinned.

"And she's worth it, too."

Ash nodded, and led the little girl away.

I had explained my idea to Connor: Giving Jennifer a soul, a way to temper her demonic tendencies, was the only reason he agreed to call his sister forth from the Pit. He loved her, but he knew her limitations as well as she did.

Lilith lost interest in her offspring the moment Jennifer was out of sight. She didn't seem to care much about the soul shifter, either. She was arrogant. And ruthless.

"You want the talisman or not?" I asked.

"I want it all, baby," she said. Then she grinned, because she thought she was going to win.

"Come and get it."

She narrowed her gaze, her smile going sloppy. "Oh, no, sister," she said. "The talisman is mine. Mine!" She stepped toward me, vibrating with fury. "I will take it from you. I'll rip it right from your bony little fingers."

The demons behind her spread out, maybe ten of them, and their eyes were trained on us.

Lightning flew from Lilith's extended palm.

"No!" roared Connor.

The pain was instantaneous. It threw me backward and I skidded across the pavement, banging up my elbows and arms as every nerve ending throbbed in electric anguish.

Lilith aimed a palmful of lightning at Connor, too.

I'm sure she didn't expect Ash to shoot her. The bullets were more annoyances than anything else, but it gave Connor time to rush toward me.

"Ouch," I said.

"Lass. God, Phoebe." He scooped me into his arms and took off toward a row of parked cars. He ducked behind a silver truck and looked me over.

"Sweet Jesus."

"I'm not gonna pass out," I said, gritting my teeth. Holy crap, I was hurting. "I refuse."

"Good." He lifted me so that my face brushed his neck. "Drink from me. Get your strength."

My fangs elongated and I pierced his flesh. His blood was as delicious as hot chocolate, and as I drank, I healed.

When I was finished, I felt a lot better.

"C'mon. Let's finish this."

Connor stood and helped me to my feet. We crouched behind the truck bed.

Morrigu appeared and pounded her staff against the street. Thunder roared into the sky. "Enough!"

I had to give the goddess some props: She knew how to make an entrance.

If the look in Morrigu's eyes was any indication, she was trying to decide whether to slice and dice or flambé Lilith.

Personally, I was hoping for flambé.

Three demons stepped in front of their mistress, forming a wall of victims. Lilith easily sacrificed her protectors to the dark goddess, who wielded chaos like the rest of us wielded a rake or a spatula.

Clouds roiled above her, fierce wind whipping her dark green robes. She raised her staff and silver bolts issued from the raven. Thunder roared, and Morrigu added her screeches to the booming noise.

Seriously? I almost wet myself.

Lilith watched Morrigu with a small, mean smile. She hadn't figured out that she was making a dumb-ass move. What did she expect? Applause? Instant world domination? A gold star for her weekly evil chart?

I was pretty damned sure she didn't expect Morrigu to aim her staff and send a huge silver jolt downward.

There was no stepping out of the way. That kind of furious puissance sought its target unerringly.

The demons couldn't escape Morrigu's wrath.

Within seconds, they were nothing but smears on the street.

She aimed her staff again, at the demons standing behind Lilith, and seven more flashes of lightning destroyed them all.

Lilith began to realize she was no match for Morrigu. She was maybe a midmorning snack for one such as the crow queen.

The storm died down completely, and the black clouds inspired by Morrigu's ire broke apart and drifted away.

Then black puffs of smoke appeared around Lilith: Nicor, Pith, and Berith materialized. Connor dropped a kiss on my head, and then took my hand.

We joined the hunters.

Magic surged from Connor and the hunters. Four coils cinched her, imprisoning Lilith in pulsing red. Her expression was a mixture of emotions, including desperation and fury.

"I will not go!" she wailed.

The most selfish, tyrannical, asinine creature I'd ever had the displeasure to meet could not forestall the inevitable.

I walked forward, and she tried to move, but she was stuck, bound by the magic of the four men surrounding her. I placed my hands on her cheeks.

"I am the talisman. I bind you to the deepest, darkest part of the Pit, Lilith," I said. "You will never leave hell again."

Her wails echoed into the heavens; the terrible screams threatened to cleave me with their serrated sounds. I wanted to clap my hands over my ears, but I couldn't.

The horrible keening stopped.

Then Lilith started sinking into the ground. She tried to move away, but it didn't matter how many times she moved; it didn't stop her progress. She clawed and screamed and tried to hold on, but in the end, she could do nothing but go to hell.

It felt as though the tilted world had finally righted. Maybe this was the feeling of balance being restored. Well, semirestored.

"Very good, Talisman," said Morrigu. Then she disappeared in a cloud of silvery mist.

I had to wonder why the goddess showed up to smite demons, but left us to stick Lilith into the Pit. I was tired, and frankly, as long everything was okeydoke, I wasn't gonna waste brainpower worrying about the whims of Celtic goddesses.

"Connor?" A girl stumbled out from the café, rubbing her eyes sleepily. She looked as if she was sixteen, maybe seventeen, with sable hair and brown eyes as soft as a doe's. She wore black capris with a blousy pink top and matching flip-flops.

"Jennifer?"

"That's the form she chose. It's hers. She has a soul now," said Ash. She looked a little worse for wear, but she grinned. "That was a bitch, O mighty Talisman. You owe me big." She slung an arm around Jennifer's shoulder. "C'mon, honey. I need a drink."

We returned to my house. Connor was subdued, and I was nervous.

I asked him to come in, and he followed me into the bedroom. I flipped on the light, and he watched me sit on the bed. I tugged off my boots and socks, wiggling my toes.

"I've decided to keep you, Connor."

"Oh, really?"

I looked at him and said, "I'm sorry. You offered me love, and . . . I was a real bitch about it."

"And now?"

"Still a bitch," I said, "but very much one in love. With you."

He looked pleased, a smile curving his lips. Small joys. Tiny, happy slivers. It was all we had. And I'd take it.

"C'mere." I patted the bed.

He shut the door behind him and slid next to me. We lay down together, my cheek pressed against his chest, and I listened to him breathe.

"I'm not sorry you followed the prophecy," I said fiercely. I slid up his muscled frame and cupped his face. "If you hadn't, I would've never met you. And I can't be sorry about everything that's come before, you know?"

"Aye," he said, his gaze tender. "I think, lass, I've waited my whole life for you."

I kissed him. A quick, soft promise. When I pulled back, his eyes had gone hot, and an answering heat thrummed in my belly.

He lit up my world, this demon. I wrapped my arms around his neck. "Do you want to talk about our relationship?"

"God, no." Connor's lips dipped down to my throat and roved over the sensitive flesh.

I angled my neck to give him better access, and he growled (really, he did), and electric pleasure jolted through me.

I moved my hands to the edge of his T-shirt, and he paused long enough to help me tug it off. I remembered this. I remembered him.

I pushed him onto his back, and he let me, his lips cocking into a sexy half grin. I knelt between his legs and explored the planes of his chest, my fingers skimming every muscle, every old wound.

"I know who you are now," I whispered. I leaned down and let my words drift across his skin. "You can't hide from me."

"I dinnae want to," he said. "Not ever again."

My lips paid homage to his sacrifice. For every second of pain, however inadvertently, that I had caused, I showed him my gratitude. With soft scrapes of my lips, and flicks of my tongue, and the touch of my fingers, I said, *Thank you*, and, *I'm sorry*, and *I love you*.

His heart was the frantic beat of an ancient drum, and his flesh quivered beneath my mouth.

His hands dove into my hair, and he tugged until I scooted up and lay flush against him. He took my mouth, plundering . . . no, begging, and I gave him everything. I didn't want him to beg. I wanted him to know he was mine, and I was his, and he never had to worry about my heart.

Because I knew I would never have to worry about his.

I worked off my top and let it fall to the floor. He unsnapped my bra, and dropped it . . . oh, I don't know. Somewhere. I had other things on my mind.

He flipped me onto my back. His cock pressed into the vee of my thighs. The sweet pressure dragged a moan from me. Damn. My panties were already soaked.

His hands trailed up my rib cage, stopping under my breasts. I felt the barest touch of his fingers. His lips found the curve of my neck; he pressed his mouth against the hollow of my throat; then his tongue traced a path to my ear.

I pushed my hand between us and unbuttoned his jeans, pushing them down until I could get my hand inside.

He gasped, and stilled. "I think that's"—he gulped—"verra unwise."

There he went with the brogue. *Hoo, boy.*

"Hmmm." I grasped his cock, lightly stroking. He swallowed, his eyes closing, and then he got me back by sucking a nipple into his mouth, teasing it to hardness.

"Wow," I murmured. I felt electrified. "I feel like there's lightning inside me."

His gaze caught mine. "Is that a demon joke?"

"No." I grinned. "What? Are you saying you're lightning?"

"Oh, yes," he said, his tongue flicking across the top of my breast. "And thunder. And rain. And wind."

He blew on my nipple, and it gusted cold, so cold my flesh crinkled and the peak went tight. Then he did it again, this time with heat. Desire blossomed, petals of heat and light curling. I squirmed.

"You want more, lass?"

"Is that even a question?"

He knelt between my thighs. He shucked my jeans and underwear. Then he knelt down until his face was even with my thighs. He looked up at me from that most intimate spot, his gaze such a mixture of emotions. Wonder. Mischief. Love.

Then his tongue flicked out.

Tiny blue sparks squirmed over my swollen flesh.

The electric sensations were so intense my eyes rolled back into my head. I grasped his hair and pulled. Then, when I could talk again, I said, "Do it again."

And he did.

I might've blacked out.

When the haze of sensation faded just a little, Connor pulled me into his mouth . . . sucking . . . licking . . . kissing. Every so often he offered one of his little zaps, and I arched and grabbed onto the sheets.

Having a demon lover had its perks.

Connor savored me a little too much. He'd bring me to the brink without letting me fall over. He did it until I was freaking mess, so eager for release I could scream.

"Connor," I begged. "Please. Oh, please."

He withdrew from tormenting me, dragging his lips over my stomach, between the valley of my breasts, along my throat.

My hands clawed at his jeans. He looked at me, smiling, and the next instant the pants were gone.

"You mean you could've done that the whole time?"

"Well, now, I dinnae want you to think I was easy."

"You're a fibber!"

He grinned more broadly, completely unrepentent. Well, that's what I get for loving a demon.

I grasped around his buttocks and rubbed against his shaft.

His heartbeat went wild as he slid his cock between my slick folds, expertly rubbing against my clit. I arched against him, offering my breasts. As he scraped my sensitive nipples with his teeth, he slipped inside me.

He paused, sucking in a breath, and I squirmed, both expectant and impatient.

Then he started to move.

I held on to him, my nails scoring his back. Connor whispered words I couldn't understand. Old words that surely meant passion and devotion.

I tipped over the edge, flying into a burst of light, of bliss, and then Connor cried out my name and spasmed.

For a long moment, we did nothing else but

hold each other. Connor tightened his grip and the world went black and off center.

We arrived in the bathroom. As Connor turned on the shower and made sure it was the right temperature, I said, "We could've walked in here."

"What fun is that?" he asked. He put me under the warm spray and then joined me.

I was happy. I could imagine creating a life with Connor. With Danny. And, yes, Jackson. He would always be part of our lives, too. We'd be safe, and mostly content. I wasn't a complete optimist. There would be arguments and tribulations and hurt feelings. But more important, there would be love, always love.

All we really had was now.

I was determined to make the most of it, so I kissed Connor until the water started to steam.

He reciprocated.

Let me tell you, that boy is hell with a bar of soap.

Chapter 29

I knocked on Jackson's apartment door. It was a little past nine. Connor waited in the parking lot below. I had to do this alone, at least for now.

Jackson opened the door, his eyes red rimmed and his features gaunt. He dropped the beer bottle that was in his hand.

"Phoebe?"

"Hi," I said. "I need to talk to you."

And I closed the door behind me.

Chapter 30

When I woke up, I realized two things:

1. The sexy male presence pressed against me was naked.

2. Today we were getting married.

"Connor," I whispered.

"Danny's fine," he murmured as he moved my hair to kiss my neck. "He's with Jackson, remember? They're moving into the same neighborhood as Jessica and those sexy Wiccans."

"Sexy Wiccans?"

"I mean those poor, butt-ugly witches."

I laughed. "They've been a nice addition to the town. Their herbal shampoo is da bomb."

"I dinnae know if I can wait for our vows. . . ." He trailed off because his mouth got busy with my ear, then my throat.

It figured my almost husband knew I'd ask after Danny and had answered the question before I could phrase it. All three of us were paranoid about his safety, but had agreed we couldn't live in fear.

Even now, Dr. Michaels and Brady were consulting with all the paranormals to search for ways to make the Invisi-shield more invulnerable. There was talk about creating sensors for the ground.

If Queen Patsy had her way, a gnat wouldn't be able to squeeze by the perimeter without setting off an alarm.

Then there was, of course, renewed talk about finding Amahté and Shamhat. Larsa was the leader of that cause, and I wouldn't have been surprised if some kind of paranormal search party were launched soon.

Connor lifted up and cupped my face. "You'll make a lovely bride."

"You'll make a handsome groom."

He kissed me, and my undead heart skipped a ghostly beat.

"You know," I said, walking my fingers up his impressive chest, "who's to say we can't have our ceremony now?"

He grinned. "I cannae believe you'd suggest such a thing, lass." His hand dipped underneath and palmed my buttock. "I'm an honorable man."

"I know." I tugged on his shoulders. "I'll totally

take the hit for this, I promise. Besides, we can have two ceremonies if we want."

"You've talked me into it." He rolled on top of me. His muscled form warmed mine instantly. I explored the hard contours of his back, right down to his awesome butt.

I writhed under his touch. His fingers slid between my thighs, one finger stroking my clit and stoking the flames. Pleasure spiked. I moaned and rubbed my slick flesh against his palm.

He trailed soft, slow kisses down the curve of my stomach. I quaked under his tender assault.

He parted my trembling thighs, knelt between my legs, and placed his mouth over my swollen clit. He tugged the sensitized nub between his lips and suckled.

I moaned, my restless hands plundering his hair.

He slid his hands underneath me and pulled me close. He stroked me with his tongue, torturing me with tiny, brief suckles. I moved against his mouth, taking pleasure in every movement.

"This is sinful," I said.

"I'm a demon. 'Tis my nature to sin."

He nipped and the sharpness rocketed, a blend of pleasure-pain that made me gasp. Now, that was a feat, since as I've pointed out, I can't use my lungs.

Connor continued to torment me until I was at the edge of bliss. I grabbed at his shoulders, digging my nails into his flesh.

He growled. That sound vibrated through me, rumbling my core. Now it was time to do the traditional vampire marital rites. I was excited to share these with Connor, to truly become his in body, mind, and soul.

"The claiming," I managed. "First the claiming."

Connor knelt on the bed and helped me to sit up. I put my hand on the back of his neck. "I claim you, Connor Ballard." I frowned.

Heat flared, and my symbol—the heart—imprinted on his skin.

"The word-giving?" he whispered. His eyes were bright. He swept a thumb over my cheek.

"I love you," I said simply. "I want to be with you forever. You are my family."

"And you are mine." He kissed me. "I love you."

"Okay," I said. I flopped to the bed and spread my arms. "Take me."

Connor chuckled as he covered me; then he surprised me. He lifted me and entered me with one swift stroke. He kissed me, his tongue mimicking the movements of his cock.

He was relentless.

I couldn't hold on.

I flew over the edge, and as I soared, Connor shattered with me.

I rode another wave with him, into the bright bliss that was ours.

*   *   *

The ceremony presided over by Queen Patricia was held in the backyard of her massive home. The garden was lush with multicolored flowers and big, leafy trees. At least a hundred or so chairs were set up, and every one was filled. The demon hunters chose to stand like sentinels behind the back row.

With the stars out and the moon shining bright, I married my demon.

It was short and sweet. We'd asked for an abbreviated version, and mimicked our earlier commitment (save the mating ritual, of course).

We wanted to include Danny in our commitment to each other, so he stood close and we held our son in our joint embrace.

After the vows were over, everyone cheered. Jackson picked up Danny, gave me a kiss, and shook Connor's hand. All in all, he'd handled the transition from Tulsa to Broken Heart rather well. Now that I was training with Connor and Larsa, we needed every demon ass-kicker we could get; it only made sense for Jackson to live in town. We would share custody of Danny, and he would watch over him when I had to go deal with demon and/or talisman business. The schoolteacher girlfriend was already history, and Jackson seemed to like living in town, though it had certainly changed since our childhood days.

It meant letting go of managing the café, but Astria and Jennifer were doing trial runs as waitresses, and seemed to really like it. Astria's bodyguards, not so much. Still, Ren seemed to like to cook, and Anise was a hell of a manager. They made a weird team, and an even weirder family, but at least Astria was safe. It seemed that getting Turned had stripped her of her prophetic abilities. I considered that a good thing. Jennifer was living with us, though she was hanging out with Astria for the next couple of days. Connor promised to build a new addition to the house; and he also said he'd redo the kitchen, complete with dishwasher.

Gabriel had been shocked to learn that he had a brother and a sister—there was a lot going on there that no one had revealed to the rest of us. Like why Ren and Anise hadn't tracked him down before now, and what they wanted, and why they'd been protecting a Vedere prophet.

Broken Heart still had its secrets.

I guess we all did.

Damian avoided Anise, who was probably the only female who could kick his ass, and whenever she was mentioned, he would mutter something about insufferable women, and go elsewhere.

My thoughts were interrupted when Connor kissed me until my legs went watery, and I forgot about everything else except him naked in a big, fluffy bed. We hadn't even moved from the altar yet.

"Excuse me," said a soft female voice.

I pulled away from Connor. Before us stood a woman I knew was a donor.

"Leslee, right?"

She looked relieved. "Yes."

Next to her was a vampire who looked vaguely familiar. I'd probably seen him around town or at the café. We'd had a lot of influx of parakind hoping to settle down here.

"This is Avery," she said. "He moved here about a month ago. Um, we understand you can break bindings."

"And goofer you, as soon as I figure out the ingredients for the dust."

She blinked at me.

Then I realized what she'd said. "Oh. You're bound?"

"Things got out of hand," said Avery. He looked uncomfortable. "We . . . you know."

"He's a nice guy," said Leslee quickly. "But I don't want to be a vampire. This is just my summer job."

"Say no more."

I put my hands on each of their shoulders and invoked the magic of the talisman. Heat flowed between us and then I heard the familiar *snick*.

"Done," I said.

"Thank you," gushed Leslee. "Thank you so much."

Avery smiled and nodded. Then they both took off in opposite directions like their pants were on fire.

"You're going to be a popular girl," said Connor.

"Don't remind me."

He drew me into his arms and smiled. "I could remind you of other things, lass." He leaned down and whispered a few into my ear.

"Hmmm." I looked at him coyly. "Actions speak louder than words, husband."

He tugged me close and kissed me; then the wily bastard popped us right out of our own reception.

We arrived in the bedroom of our house.

I stood within the arms of my husband, who had a very lascivious look.

"Let me love you, *m'aingeal*," he whispered.

"Yes," I said. "Yes."

The Eight Ancients
(In order of creation)

Ruadan: (Ireland) He flies and uses fairy magic.

Koschei: (Russia) He is the master of glamour and mind control. He was banned to the World Between Worlds.

Hua Mu Lan: (China) She is a great warrior who creates and controls fire. She was killed during her attack on Queen Patricia.

Durga: (India) She calls forth, controls, and expels demons. She was banned to the World Between Worlds.

Velthur: (Italy) He controls all forms of liquid.

Shamhat: (Babylon) She controls all elements of earth magic, especially as it relates to all living things.

Amahté: (Egypt) He talks to spirits, raises the

dead, creates zombies, and reinserts souls into dead bodies.

Zela: (Nubia) She manipulates all metallic substances.

The Broken Heart Turn-bloods

* **Jessica Matthews:** Widow (first husband, Richard). Mother to fifteen-year-old Bryan and ten-year-old Jenny. Stay-at-home mom. Vampire of Family Ruadan.

Charlene Mason: Mistress of Richard Matthews. Mother to two-year-old Rich, Jr. Receptionist for insurance company. Vampire of Family Ruadan.

Linda Beauchamp: Divorced (first husband, Earl). Mother to nineteen-year-old MaryBeth. Nail technician. Vampire of Family Koschei.

MaryBeth Beauchamp: Single. Waitress at the Old Sass Café. Vampire of Family Ruadan.

* **Evangeline Louise LeRoy:** Single. Mother to sixteen-year-old Tamara LeRoy. Owns and operates the town library. Vampire of Family Koschei.

Patricia "Patsy" Marchand: Divorced (first husband, Sean). Mother to twenty-year-old Wilson.

Beautician who owns and operates Hair Today, Curl Tomorrow. Vampire of Family Amahté.

Ralph Genessa: Widowed (first wife, Teresa). Father to toddler twins Michael and Stephen. Fry cook at the Old Sass Café. Vampire of Family Hua Mu Lan.

Simone Sweet: Widowed (first husband, Jacob). Mother to seven-year-old Glory. Broken Heart's mechanic. Vampire of Family Velthur.

* Phoebe Allen: Single. Mother to four-year-old Daniel. Waitress at the Old Sass Café. Vampire of Family Durga.

* Darlene Clark: Divorced (first husband, Jason). Mother to seven-year-old Marissa. Stay-at-home mother. Operates Internet scrapbooking business. Vampire of Family Durga.

* Elizabeth Bretton née Silverstone: Separated (first husband, Carlton). Mother of seventeen-year-old Venice (who lives with her father in Los Angeles). Socialite. Vampire of Family Zela.

---

* Direct descendants of the first five families to found Broken Heart: the McCrees, the LeRoys, the Silverstones, the Allens, and the Clarks.

Glossary

Ancient: Refers to one of the original eight vampires. The very first vampire was Ruadan, who is the biological father of Patrick and Lorcan. Several centuries ago, Ruadan and his sons took on the last name of O'Halloran, which means "stranger from overseas."

banning: (see: World Between Worlds) Any vampire can be sent into limbo, but the spell must be cast by an Ancient or, in a few cases, an Ancient's offspring. A vampire cannot be released from banning until they feel true remorse for their evil acts. This happens rarely, which means banning is not done lightly.

binding: When vampires have consummation sex (with any living person or creature), they're bound together for a hundred years. This was the Ancients' solution to keep vamps from sexual intercourse while blood-taking. No one's ever broken a binding.*

Consortium: More than five hundred years ago, Patrick and Lorcan O'Halloran created the Consortium to figure out ways that parakind could make the world a better place for all beings. Many sudden leaps in human medicine and technology are because of the Consortium's work.

Convocation: Five neutral, immortal beings given the responsibility of keeping the balance between Light and Dark.

donors: Mortals who serve as sustenance for vampires. The Consortium screens and hires humans to be food sources. Donors are paid well and given living quarters. Not all vampires follow the guidelines created by the Consortium for feeding. A mortal may have been a donor without ever realizing it.

drone: Mortals who do the bidding of their vampire Masters. The most famous was Renfield—drone to Dracula. The Consortium's Code of Ethics forbids the use of drones, but plenty of vampires still use them.

ETAC: The Ethics and Technology Assessment Commission is the public face of this covert government agency. In its program, soldier volunteers

---

*Johnny D'Angelo and Nefertiti's mating was dissolved by a fairy wish. It was the only known instance of a binding being broken.

have undergone surgical procedures to implant nanobyte technology, which enhances strength, intelligence, sensory perception, and healing. Volunteers are trained in use of technological weapons and defense mechanisms so advanced, it's rumored they come from a certain section of Area 51. Their mission is to remove, by any means necessary, targets named as domestic threats.

Family: Every vampire can be traced to one of the eight Ancients. The Ancients are divided into the Eight Sacred Sects, also known as the Families.

gone to ground: When vampires secure places where they can lie undisturbed for centuries, they *go to ground*. Usually they let someone know where they are located, but the resting locations of many vampires are unknown.

Invisi-shield: Using technology stolen from ETAC, the Consortium created a shield that not only makes the town invisible to outsiders, but also creates a force field. No one can get into the town's borders without knowing specific access points, all of which are guarded by armed security details.

loup de sang: Commonly refers to Gabriel Marchand, the only known vampire-werewolf born into the world. He is also known as "the outcast." (See *Vedere prophecy*.)

lycanthropes: Also called *lycans*. They can shift from human into wolf at will. Lycans have been around a long time and originate in Germany. Their numbers are small because they don't have many females, and most children born have a fifty percent chance of living to the age of one.

Master: Most Master vampires are hundreds of years old and have had many successful Turnings. Masters show Turn-bloods how to survive as vampires. A Turn-blood has the protection of the Family (see: *Family*) to which their Master belongs.

PRIS: Paranormal Research and Investigation Services. Cofounded by Theodora and her husband, Elmore Monroe. Its primary mission is to document supernatural phenomena and conduct cryptozoological studies.

Roma: The Roma are cousins to full-blooded lycanthropes. They can change only on the night of a full moon. Just as full-blooded lycanthropes are raised to protect vampires, the Roma are raised to hunt vampires.

soul shifter: A supernatural being with the ability to absorb the souls of any mortal or immortal. The shifter has the ability to assume any of the forms she's absorbed. Only one is known to exist, the woman known as Ash, who works as a "balance keeper" for the Convocation.

Taint: The Black Plague for vampires, which makes vampires insane as their body deteriorates.

Consortium scientists have had limited success in finding a true cure.

Turn-blood: A human who's been recently Turned into a vampire. If you're less than a century old, you're a Turn-blood.

Turning: Vampires perpetuate the species by Turning humans. Unfortunately, only one in about ten humans actually makes the transition.

Vedere prophecy: Astria Vedere predicted that in the twenty-first century a vampire queen would rule both vampires and lycans, and would also end the ruling power of the eight Ancients.

The prophecy reads: "A vampire queen shall come forth from the place of broken hearts. The eight powers of the ancients will be hers to command. She shall bind with the outcast, and with this union, she will save the dual-natured. With her consort, she will rule vampires and lycan-thropes as one."

World Between Worlds: The place between this plane and the next, where there is a void. Some people can slip back and forth between this "veil."

Wraiths: Rogue vampires who banded together to dominate both vampires and humans. Since the defeat of the Ancient Koschei, they are believed to be defunct.

Read on for a sneak peek at the next
book in the Broken Heart series
by Michele Bardsley,
coming soon from Signet Eclipse.

"You wanna make out?" asked the man standing on my welcome mat.

"You're rather young, aren't you?" I asked, fighting a smile.

"And?" He cocked a pierced eyebrow at me and leaned on the doorjamb, tucking his hands into his pockets. The gesture flexed his muscled, tattooed arms and drew attention to the six-pack abs defined by his tight T-shirt.

He was gorgeous and youthful and impetuous.

"Rand, you make me feel old." I caved in to the smile flirting with my lips. "And I'm immortal."

His grin widened. "Aw, Lizzie. You're tops in my book."

"Don't call me Lizzie. It's puerile." I opened the door and gestured for him to come inside. "C'mon. It's ready."

Rand moved to Broken Heart when he was seventeen. Now he was twenty-two, and, for a human, his specialty was a rarity in a town filled with paranormal residents. He was the expert on the care and feeding of dragons.

I was forty-three when Lorcan O'Halloran, or rather the beast he'd become, attacked and killed me and ten other residents of Broken Heart, Oklahoma. He suffered from the Taint, a disease that affects only vampires. Luckily, a cure has since been discovered.

Every vampire has strength, speed, the ability to glamour, and, unless your head is chopped off or sunlight gets you, immortality. There were eight vampire Families, each with its own particular power. I was from the Family Zela, and our ability was to manipulate and control any metallic substance.

As a human, I hadn't been able to conquer my vanity about getting older. Going under the knife, taking the injections, getting the acid peels . . . I did them all. However, becoming undead rid me of crow's feet, stretch marks, cellulite, and forestalled other atrocities of the aging process.

"I'll make tea," I said as he stepped inside and shut the door.

"Earl Grey?" he asked.

"Of course."

Though I enjoyed my solitary lifestyle, I couldn't resist having a cuppa with whomever crossed my threshold. Thanks to an accidental fairy wish, vampires within the borders of Broken Heart could eat and drink again. That is, drink liquids other than blood. I had missed taking tea, and had been pleased to reestablish the routine.

The old Victorian opened into a wide foyer. Straight ahead was the staircase to the upper floor. On the left side, you could enter the formal living room. On the right side was a smaller room, the parlor, which was where I typically entertained visitors.

Rand paused by the antique coat tree. He studied it, then glanced at me. "New?"

"Yes. It's French. Hard-carved oak, circa 1870. See the hooks? They're cherubs." The darkened wood had been polished with beeswax. I'd fallen in love with the piece merely from its picture. EBay was a glorious boon for vampires. "The bench seat opens." I flipped it up and we looked down into the emptiness.

Rand shook his head. "You've got a thing for old stuff."

"So do you." I tweaked his earlobe, and he laughed.

The kitchen was accessed through a narrow door at the back of the parlor. While Rand took a seat at the small table I used for tea service, I went to the kitchen and put on the kettle.

"Hey, I forgot!" Rand called from the parlor. "Patsy gave me something for you. Said they found it in the attic and it belongs to you."

I poked my head into the parlor. "I've told her a hundred times that whatever she finds, she can have or toss out."

He shrugged. "I'll go get it."

While Rand went to get whatever it was, I returned to the kitchen. I cleaned up the mess I'd made earlier during a botched attempt at making scones. I heard the front door open and shut, and then steps in the foyer.

"Elizabeth."

The man's voice seemed to come from right behind me. It vibrated with fury. I could practically feel strong hands try to creep around my neck.

Startled, I whirled around, my hand pressed against my chest. My palm flattened over the spot where my heart no longer beat.

Nobody was there.

The kitchen was small. I'd kept it simple during the renovation, thinking it pointless for me to even have one. The cabinets were whitewashed, the countertops and walls a cheery yellow, and the floor, as was the rest of the house, was polished oak. About the only place for someone to hide was the pantry. I opened the door, but saw only the fully stocked shelves, and in the back, cleaning equipment.

Unnerved, I returned to the stove and opened the cabinet that held my tea stashes. I pulled down the tin and pried off the lid, looking down into the dark, loose leaves. It smelled strong and fragrant, as good tea should.

"Elizabeth." The voice was stronger now, insistent. I had excellent hearing thanks to my vampire ears, but this wasn't someone speaking from a distance. The man calling my name did not like me. I had the uneasy feeling that he wanted to hurt me. Foreboding sat in my belly, as solid and heavy as an iron weight.

"Hey, you need help?"

I yelped, dropping the tin. It bounced and rolled, its contents spilling onto the floor.

"Shit," said Rand. "I didn't mean to scare you." He crossed to the mess and picked up the container. "I don't think there's much left."

"I have another one." I hesitated. "Did you hear anyone just now?"

He frowned. "Who?" He glanced around the kitchen, the same way I had earlier. "You think someone's in the house?"

I shook my head, feeling foolish. "I'm just being silly. Never mind."

"You're a lot of things, Lizzie, but silly isn't one of 'em." He grimaced. "I mean, you know, you're mature." He slapped a hand against his forehead. "I'm not saying you're not fun, just that you're serious."

His face went red. I swallowed my laugh and reached for the second tin of Earl Grey so he wouldn't see my amused expression.

"Maybe you should stop complimenting me," I offered, "and go get the broom."

"Yeah," he said, sounding relieved. "I'll clean up the mess. No prob."

"Where's the all-important thing?" I asked.

"I left it inside the coat tree."

"Why on earth would you do that?"

"So you'd have a surprise to open."

I stared at him, but he shrugged and grinned. Then he went to the pantry, grabbed the broom, and busied himself with cleaning up.

Later, we settled at the table with our tea and conversation. However, I didn't want to torment Rand for too long. He'd come to my home for a singular purpose.

"Here." I slid the velvet the box across the table and Rand accepted it.

His face had a look of wonder and, if I wasn't mistaken, an edge of panic. I suppressed my smile as he flipped open the box. His mouth fell open and his eyes went wide.

It was gratifying to see his reaction to my work.

He plucked the ring from its silk confines and studied it. "I knew you did great work, Lizzie, but . . . wow. This is art."

"Thank you," I said modestly.

Rand had procured silver and gold for me, and a small, rare dragonfire gem that was deep purple in color, passionate in promise. Two dragons—one silver, one gold—stretched in a circle, from joined tails to snouts, pressing against the oval stone.

"It's perfect," he said. He dragged his gaze from the ring to me and smiled broadly. "Now all she has to do is say yes."

Rand was in love with MaryBeth Beauchamp,

a vampire who'd been Turned at the tender age of eighteen. I supposed she would be twenty-three now, if vampires counted years. (And, thank goodness, they didn't!) She was a nice girl who was the official full-time nanny of Queen Patricia's triplets.

When Rand approached me about making an engagement ring for MaryBeth, I asked him about his concept of forever. He was human, after all. Then he explained that as a handler of dragons, he fell within their protection, and one gift given was immortality. He said he'd probably stop aging around thirty human years, which was the same as dragon shifters.

So he and MaryBeth would truly have forever. Part of the vampire curse, if you want to call it that, was that sex equaled an instant hundred-year commitment to your bedmate. Needless to say, most of us were very careful. In my case, I avoided dating altogether, although I sometimes yearned for the emotional and physical intimacy of a relationship.

Ah, well. Love was for the young, and all that.

I stood on the porch steps and waved good-bye. Rand drove a white Ford truck, a rather mundane vehicle for a man with such a wild nature. Soon he would give MaryBeth the ring, and his love. And I hoped she returned the favor. It was a difficult thing to do, to entrust one's heart to someone else.

Or so I suspected.

I had never really been in love.

I married Henry Bretton when I was twenty-two, in the fall after I graduated from the University of Tulsa. Not for love, though I certainly enjoyed his company and found him an amiable companion. No, I married the man my parents picked for me because I understood the limitations of my own life, and certainly the figurative dangling scissors they held over the line to my trust fund.

In my late twenties, I discussed with my husband the possibility of having children. I wanted a baby, maybe even two or three.

Henry had no choice but to admit that he'd had a vasectomy, and then he confessed why.

The month before Henry married me, he'd had a one-night sexual romp with a Las Vegas showgirl named Trinie. Nine months and one DNA test later, he was the reluctant father of a baby girl. His solution to this problem was to throw money: at Trinie, at the baby girl she named Venice, at whomever promised to help with such a delicate situation.

I was aware my husband enjoyed extramarital activities, but he'd always been discreet. It was a terrible blow to learn he had a child, one he'd kept hidden not only from me, but from the world.

I was the one who insisted he publicly claim her.

After that, Henry and I kept separate bedrooms, and though he continued having affairs, I never took a lover. I kept busy with planning parties, chairing committees, heading charities, and mixing martinis. According to my mother, a dry martini and a good cry could fix damn near anything.

It's understandable that Venice grew up with a skewed sense of self-esteem and a damaged moral compass. She was embarrassed to have a showgirl mother and desperate for the attention of the wealthy father who'd emotionally abandoned her.

The drama started in her early teens. Kicked out of boarding schools. Arrested for underage drinking. Photographed with a lifted skirt—and no panties.

Henry was mortified by his daughter's behavior. He shipped Trinie and Venice off to Europe. Anytime Venice ended up in the tabloids, he'd pack them off to another country.

When Venice was seventeen, her mother died in a car accident in France. Henry had no choice but to bring the girl into our home.

Venice never realized she didn't have to compete with me for her father's affection. I wanted so much to be a good stepmother. Every time I reached out to her, she ignored me, and worse, she viciously rejected any show of kindness.

Venice became a fashionable club girl. Famous only for being famous. With her father's money, she started a perfume line, and then a clothing line. She acted a few bit parts in low-grade horror movies. Henry financed her return to France, and she left without so much as a good-bye.

Not long after my forty-third birthday, Henry died of heart failure. I left New York after the funeral. I dropped every obligation, abandoned every project. I spent the next couple of months at my parents' home, completely out of sorts. They took an anniversary trip to Europe, and asked me to inventory the old Silverstone estate in Broken Heart. It was busywork, but I didn't care. I needed to do something productive.

The Silverstones had long since moved away from the town they'd helped found—everyone but my grandfather's brother. He was a greedy man, somewhat lecherous, too, and he liked his privacy.

Then Great Uncle Josiah just . . . left. He never told a soul why he abandoned the manse. He went off to the Alaska wilderness, where he later died. In his will, he stated that the house could not be occupied by, or sold to, any member of the Silverstone family.

On my first evening in town, Lorcan found me outside Broken Heart's one and only motel (now demolished). I'd been trying to coax a can of Sprite from the uncooperative soda machine. The beleaguered beast threw me against the wall and sucked me dry.

I woke up undead—courtesy of the Consortium, an organization created by vampires who wanted to better the world. It moved into Broken Heart, ousted most of the human residents, and created a parakind community.

I donated the Silverstone mansion to the town. Officially. It had already been abandoned by my family, and my parents couldn't have cared less what I actually did with it. Now it belonged to the vampire queen, her lycanthrope husband, and their three darling four-year-old triplets.

My parents were surprised when I told them I wanted to stay in Broken Heart, but they didn't question my choice. They certainly didn't know that I was a vampire. I found a lovely old Victorian that I renovated to suit me and settled down into the life of a well-to-do bloodsucker.

I very much wanted to be a mother, and I will always regret never knowing the experience, the joys, or the sorrows. I think, maybe somewhere deep inside, I had hoped to have a little piece of it with Venice. No matter how small the slice of motherhood she might've allowed me, I would've been so much the happier for it.

Alas, motherhood was no longer an option for me.

I was not holding out for romantic love, either, and certainly not the giddy, passionate, moon-eyed kind that seemed to afflict so many of Broken Heart's residents.

What was that saying? Oh, yes. We were the sum total of our experiences. Sometimes I felt more subtracted from than added to.

I shook off my pensive mood. Sunrise was in less than two hours. Like everything about my un-life, I embraced the sudden sleep that affected all vampires. I usually prepared for bed earlier than necessary and read until I passed out.

My guilty pleasures were romance novels. Though I didn't even dream of finding that kind of love in my own life, I very much enjoyed reading about it. Every happily-ever-after gave me such a thrill of satisfaction. Each novel was like a Godiva truffle. I enjoyed every one, and when finished savoring, I was eager for the next.

I heard thunder crack. Startled, I looked up into the cloud-swirled sky. It was nearing mid-September, and still warm by Oklahoma standards. The suddenness of the storm shouldn't have concerned me. The attitude of Oklahoma weather could be summed up thusly: *I'll do whatever I damn well like.* Come to think of it, that was also the attitude of the state's residents. Especially the ones in Broken Heart.

The rain began in earnest, and, suddenly chilled, I went inside.

I paused by the coat tree. Thinking about the silliness of Rand's hiding whatever family heirloom Patsy had discovered, I looked inside.

Foreboding shot through me like a poisoned arrow. I knelt down and picked up the silver box. Uneasiness quelled my admiration for its simplistic beauty. As strange as it sounds, I felt as if I was touching something evil. Something wrong.

I removed the lid.

Empty.

Though it was only a four-inch square, its dark blue silk lining pegged it as a jewelry container. It might be big enough for a couple of bracelets or a few rings. It was an odd size.

Then I saw my name was engraved on the lid. Mine and another: Lucas.

It made me shiver.

Elizabeth was a family name passed down through generations. It was likely that this item belonged to my great-great-great-grandmother, who was married to Jeremiah Silverstone. She'd died not long after their second child had been born.

I was fuzzy on family history, though curious enough now that I might call Eva, our resident expert on the town, and chat about it.

The box was tarnished, obviously old. I stared at the lid and frowned. If the Elizabeth on the lid referred to my ancestor, to the *wife* of Jeremiah . . . then who the hell was Lucas?

The storm raged with a ferocity that made me distinctly uncomfortable. I lay among my pillows with the covers pulled up to my chin, like a child frightened of closet monsters. I tried to focus on my novel, but my gaze kept wandering to the flickering light of my bedside lamp.

We vampires didn't do coffins, but crypts were another matter. I had created my bedroom in the basement of the house as a precaution against sunlight. I added a full bathroom down there as well, with a jet tub and glass shower. Everything was luxurious, from the rich green, gold, and bronze colors of my decor to the Egyptian cotton sheets and towels.

Beautiful interior design and lavish materials, however, did not offer the kind of comfort I currently needed. I was too much a woman alone in her creaky old house—a horror-movie heroine stalked by an ax-wielding maniac.

I gulped.

I couldn't shake off my trepidation. No amount of self-lectures about my maturity, my vampire traits (as Jessica would say, I totally kicked ass), or security reminders (werewolves, Invisi-shield, neighbors) helped. Granted, my neighbors weren't exactly close. I lived on three acres, two acres of which were woods. I had blazed my own trails numerous times hiking through them, but now the closeness of the forest merely represented optimal hiding places for the nefarious.

I badly wanted to hear another person's voice, but I would feel utterly ridiculous if I gave in to such an urge. How would I explain such a phone call to my friends?

It was still an hour away from sunrise.

I decided to make some jasmine tea to calm my nerves. I gave in to cowardice and used vampire speed to zip from my bed to the staircase, which led directly into the kitchen.

The rain pounded like a hundred fists against the windows. The storm was unsettling me. I set the water to boil and wandered around downstairs, flipping on all the lights.

I stopped in the parlor, my gaze falling on the little silver box. I'd left it on the table where Rand and I had enjoyed our tea.

"Elizabeth."

I whirled around, but the man's angry voice had no owner. I reached out with my vampire senses and felt no one, nothing. My own powers didn't include communing with the *dead* dead. The very idea of a spirit roaming my house gave me the willies.

I snatched up the box, thinking I should just toss it into the trash. I was disturbed by its presence, and equally disturbed by my irrational fear.

"Elizabeth!" The scream pummeled my ears. "You betrayed me!"

"Who are you?" I cried.

Then I felt a pair of big male hands encircle my throat and squeeze.

I'm the Vampire, That's Why

by **Michele Bardsley**

Does drinking blood make me a bad mother?

I'm not just a single mother trying to make ends meet in this crazy world....I'm also a vampire. One minute I was taking out the garbage; the next I awoke sucking on the thigh of superhot vampire Patrick O'Halloran, who'd generously offered his femoral artery to save me.

But though my stretch marks have disappeared and my vision has improved, I can't rest until the thing that did this to me is caught. My kids' future is at stake—figuratively and literally. As is my sex life. Although I wouldn't mind finding myself attached to Patrick's juicy thigh again, I learned that once a vampire does the dirty deed, it hitches her to the object of her affection for at least one hundred years. I just don't know if I'm ready for that kind of commitment...

"A fabulous combination of vampire lore, parental angst, romance, and mystery."
—Jackie Kessler, author of *Hell's Belles*

Don't Talk Back to Your Vampire
by **Michele Bardsley**

Sometimes it's hard to take your own advice—
or pulse.

Ever since a master vampire became possessed and bit a
bunch of parents, the town of Broken Heart, Oklahoma,
has catered to those of us who don't rise until sunset—
even if that means PTA meetings at midnight.

As for me, Eva LeRoy, town librarian and single
mother to a teenage daughter, I'm pretty much used to
being "vampified." You can't beat the great side effects:
no crow's-feet or cellulite! But books still make my
undead heart beat—and, strangely enough, so does Lorcán
the Loner. My mama always told me everyone deserves a
second chance. Still, it's one thing to deal with the usual
undead hassles: rival vamps, rambunctious kids adjusting
to night school, and my daughter's new boyfriend, who's a
vampire hunter, for heaven's sake. And it's quite another
to fall for the vampire who killed you….

"The paranormal romance of the year."
—MaryJanice Davidson

"Hot, hilarious, one helluva ride."
—L.A. Banks

Available wherever books are sold or at
penguin.com

Because Your Vampire Said So
by Michele Bardsley

When you're immortal, being a mom won't kill you—it will only make you stronger.

Not just anyone can visit Broken Heart, Oklahoma, especially since all the single moms—like me, Patsy Donahue—have been turned into vampires. I'm forever forty, but looking younger than my years, thanks to my new (un)lifestyle.And even though most of my customers have skipped town, I still manage to keep my hair salon up and running because of the lycanthropes prowling around. They know how important good grooming is—especially a certain rogue shape-shifter who is as sexy as he is deadly. Now, if only I could put a leash on my wild teenage son. He's up to his neck in danger. The stress would kill me if I wasn't already dead. But my maternal instincts are still alive and kicking, so no one better mess with my flesh and blood.

"Lively, sexy, out of this world—as well as in it—fun! Michele Bardsley's vampire stories rock!"
—*New York Times* bestselling author Carly Phillips

Wait Till Your Vampire Gets Home
by Michele Bardsley

Undead fathers really do know best...

To prove her journalistic chops, Libby Monroe ends up in Broken Heart, Oklahoma, chasing down bizarre rumors of strange goings-on—and finding vampires, lycanthropes, and zombies. She never expects to fall in lust with one of them, but vampire/single dad Ralph Genessa is too irresistible. Only the town is being torn in two by a war between the undead—and Libby may be the only thing that can hold Broken Heart together.

"Has action aplenty and a free-spirited, wittily sarcastic heroine who will delight [Michele Bardsley's] fans."
—*Booklist*

Available wherever books are sold or at
penguin.com

Over My Dead Body
by Michele Bardsley

Hot enough to wake the undead...

Moving into Broken Heart seemed like the perfect transition for Simone Sweet and her young daughter, Glory. With her ex-husband gone after attempting to murder Simone, and Glory being mute since the incident, it is one place where she can feel safe, and almost forget she's a ravenous vampire.

No one is without secrets, but Simone's are big. She'd hate to have them interfere with what's developing with local hunk Braddock Hayes. When not turning her legs to jelly, he's building an Invisi-shield around Broken Heart and helping Glory speak again. But when Simone's past resurfaces, it threatens to ruin her second chance...

"Bardsley's romantic series is a roller-coaster ride filled with humor and action, and sure to entertain."

—*Booklist*

Available wherever books are sold or at
penguin.com